7-11		
10-23		
12.28.10		
7 mocard 22:11		
3.26.12		

THE
JASMINE MOON
MURDER

Tea Shop Mysteries by Laura Childs

DEATH BY DARJEELING
GUNPOWDER GREEN
SHADES OF EARL GREY
THE ENGLISH BREAKFAST MURDER
THE JASMINE MOON MURDER

Scrapbooking Mysteries by Laura Childs

KEEPSAKE CRIMES
PHOTO FINISHED

THE
JASMINE MOON
MURDER

Tea Shop Mystery #5

LAURA CHILDS

BERKLEY PRIME CRIME, NEW YORK

A Berkley Prime Crime Book
Published by The Berkley Publishing Group
A division of Penguin Group (USA) Inc.
375 Hudson Street
New York, New York 10014

This book is an original publication of The Berkley Publishing Group.

Copyright © 2004 by Gerry Schmitt.
Cover design by Lesley Worrell.
Cover illustrations by Stephanie Henderson.

ISBN-13: 978-0-425-19813-1

ACKNOWLEDGMENTS

My heartfelt thanks to some very special people: Gary, who lent me an office at Mill City Marketing/Survey Value; Lillian in North Charleston, for all her wonderful news clippings; my agent, Sam Pinkus; my editor, Kim: all the very talented folks at Berkley Prime Crime—publicists, artists, designers, line editors; my mother, who still loves everything I write; my sister, Jennie; my husband, Bob, who always believes in me; all the wonderful and very hard-working tea shop owners who recommend and retail my books; all the writers, reviewers, and columnists who have written such kind words; and all the tea-drinkers and mystery-lovers who have sent me their personal messages and good wishes. Thanks to you all!

This book is dedicated to Maximillian.
I miss you so much, dear flower dog.

1

Theodosia Browning rested her steaming cup of tea atop a marble gravestone and gazed at the ghostly tableau unfolding before her. Tendrils of fog swirled across dry, brittle ground. Lights flickered and dimmed from towering monuments and obelisks. Shimmering figures in Civil War-era costumes slid silently out from behind ancient tombstones that tipped and canted in all directions.

It was all quite shivery and atmospheric, Theodosia decided, this first-ever Ghost Crawl in Charleston's famed Jasmine Cemetery. Of course, the fog was man-made, the klieg lights powered by sputtering generators, and the ethereal-looking "ghosts" were actually amateur actors and good-natured volunteers lit with pale blue lights.

Theodosia grinned as Drayton Conneley, posturing grandly and looking rather gallant as General P. G. T. Beauregard, recited his lines in a scene that was meant to commemorate the Battle of Fort Wagner. It seemed a far cry from his role as genial host and master tea blender at the Indigo Tea Shop. There, Drayton was arbiter of all things tea, conducting tea tastings, creating new blends, and hobnobbing with customers. Theodosia, on the other hand, was the shop's owner and sole proprietor. Which meant she had the pure joy of fretting over payroll, negotiating leases, promoting her shop, and worrying about on-time deliveries and Internet tea orders. Plus she did her fair share of waiting on tables, planning menus and events for their catering accounts, and devising new tea blends with Drayton.

Glancing at her watch, Theodosia noted that the hour was getting late and the one-act play was about ready to conclude. She also knew that once this tableau was over, the good-sized crowd that had come here tonight for an enjoyable dash of history and an October evening's ramble would soon descend upon her tea table en masse.

With fair English skin inherited from her mother's side of the family and her father's curly auburn hair, Theodosia looked like she should be one of the actors in the play. Her blue eyes sparkled with barely contained energy, her face, with its high cheekbones and full mouth, was highly expressive. Theodosia wasn't a woman who kept a tight rein on her feelings. Her passion, her drive, and any discontent she might feel were generally out there for everyone to see.

"Haley," whispered Theodosia as she approached the large folding table they'd set up among the gravestones, "How are the pumpkin muffins holding out?"

Haley Parker gave a quick smile and touched her thumb to her forefinger, giving the OK sign. There were four different tableaus being performed by four different sets of actors in Jasmine Cemetery tonight. And Theodosia's tea table was located at the third stop. The *only* stop where refreshments were being served.

And even though the costumed guides had been working valiantly all night to lead their audiences on to the fourth and final tableau, many of the folks who'd turned out seemed to want to hang around *here*. Nibbling at Haley's baked goods, sipping cups of steaming jasmine tea, talking excitedly about their trip through Jasmine Cemetery, where costumed guides carrying flickering lanterns had given them a fascinating overview of the historic old cemetery and some of its more famous residents.

In order to amass enough baked goods for tonight, Haley had virtually barricaded herself in the Indigo Tea Shop's tiny, aromatic kitchen for the past two days, whipping up countless batches of pumpkin muffins and apple fritters, as well as the shortbread cookies they'd playfully dubbed ghostly shortbread.

Served up in red and white cardboard containers, like those often used for french fries at county fairs, Haley's baked goods were the perfect walk-around treat.

Except, Theodosia had noted with a certain degree of consternation, people *still* weren't eager to move on to the next tableau. They seemed to prefer hanging around here. Helping themselves to even *more* tea and muffins.

Theodosia slid behind the table next to Haley just as a burst of applause erupted from the audience.

"Oh boy, here comes the next wave," murmured Haley. "Better brace yourself."

Theodosia grabbed for a teapot and began pouring tea into indigo blue paper cups. She didn't really mind that the crowd was heading for her table like a herd of stampeding elephants. Because the Ghost Crawl, sponsored by Charleston's Medical Triad, was an extremely worthwhile cause. In fact, all the money collected from ticket sales tonight would be donated to various charities.

Likewise, Theodosia was happy to donate her tea and baked goods as well as her time. She was a big believer in volunteering and also welcomed the opportunity to showcase the tastes and talents of the Indigo Tea Shop. Maybe even turn a few more people on to tea. And, praise the lord, tea drinking seemed to be gaining a stronger foothold with every passing day!

It hadn't taken Theodosia long to realize that, when she

left her job in marketing and signed the lease on a dusty, long-abandoned tea shop in Charleston's historic district, she had also found herself swept along by a veritable tsunami wave of tea. Women, and men, too, were rediscovering and embracing the gentle art of tea. And they were doing it in droves and with a single-minded passion. Seemingly overnight, a silent majority of tea drinkers had become enthusiastic and highly verbal tea connoisseurs. The lowly teapot that had been stashed in kitchen cupboards for so long was rediscovered, and people were flocking to tea specialty stores for thermometers, tea infusers, tea cozies, and tea warmers. Boxes of orange pekoe were being replaced with tins of fresh Darjeeling, robust oolong, malty Assam, toasty Japanese green tea, and everything in between.

Now, hardly a week passed that Theodosia didn't receive a request to cater an engagement tea, garden tea, luncheon tea, high tea, or cream tea. And women were once again sporting elegant broad-brimmed hats and even wearing gloves when they attended these special event teas.

"As usual, your baked goods are a major hit," Theodosia told Haley as she continued to pass out cups of tea to the eager Ghost Crawl visitors who crowded their table.

"Proof's in the pudding," declared Haley, happily placing muffins onto little paper trays and pressing them into outstretched hands.

Haley Parker was twenty-three years old and Theodosia's baker extraordinaire at the Indigo Tea Shop. You could lock Haley in a room with nothing more than butter, eggs, flour, and sugar and she'd emerge with an amazing repertoire of scones, muffins, tea breads, and desserts that would literally bring tears to your eyes. Drayton had once accused Haley of being a kitchen alchemist, and he hadn't been far off in his playful assessment. Haley was a remarkably gifted baker with a flair for creating scrumptious pastries and desserts that truly rivaled the offerings in some of the great Parisian patisseries.

"Were you able to get a quick peek at the play?" Drayton

asked Theodosia as he came up behind her, looking very ripped-from-the-pages-of-history in his gray and gold-fringed costume.

Theodosia's eyes danced with amusement as she pushed a voluminous pouf of auburn hair behind one ear. "Of course, Drayton. And you were absolutely wonderful." Her broad, intelligent face with its cheery smile seemed to echo her sentiment.

"Extremely professional," responded Haley.

Drayton, who was in his mid-sixties and beginning to look slightly gray and grizzled, pulled himself to his full height of six feet and looked pleased. "Our little one-act really *is* first rate, isn't it?" he said.

"I keep telling you," said Theodosia. "You missed your calling. You're a natural on stage." Her elbow touched Haley with a gentle nudge.

"Sir Drayton Conneley," chimed in Haley. "Star of stage, screen, and Jasmine Cemetery."

"All right, you two." Drayton slid the plumed cap off his head and ran a hand through his thinning hair. "I guess I know when *my* leg is being pulled."

"More like getting yanked," muttered Haley as she ducked down under the table to grab yet another picnic hamper stuffed with muffins and shortbread. "Hey there, Drayton, oh great one," she said. "Pitch in and give us a hand, will you?"

"But of course," said Drayton in his slightly over-the-top theatrical manner. "Why should *this* be any different from medieval times when the poor actors had to charge from village to village doing absolutely *everything*. Huckstering folks in for shows, selling tickets, and setting up the stage. Only *then* could they perform their magnificent comedies and tragedies for the enjoyment of their audience. So of course, once the curtain fell, the poor, overworked actors had to pack everything up and do it all over again the next day."

"Packing up?" said Haley. "That's when we're especially going to need your help. For sure."

So many people had crowded their makeshift tea table that it was a good ten minutes before Theodosia, Drayton, and Haley had a moment to breathe. But by then, most of the Ghost Crawl audience had been served and was being co-axed along by guides to the final tableau that was set up just over the hill.

"Have Jory and his uncle stopped by yet?" Drayton asked Theodosia.

Theodosia straightened up and gazed about. "Not yet. Although I'm expecting them any minute." Jory Davis, the man Theodosia had been dating for the past year and a half, had asked her to cater this event as a favor to his Uncle Jasper. Uncle Jasper Davis was a medical doctor who was also vice president in charge of research and development at Cardiotech, a medical products company in Charleston. Theodosia liked Jory's Uncle Jasper immensely and was glad to help him out. She and Jory had stayed at his condo over on Kiawah Island this past summer and had played golf with him on several occasions. Since then, however, she hadn't seen him as often as she'd have liked. Uncle Jasper was one of the developers of a device known as the Novalaser and had been secreted in the laboratories at Cardiotech for the past few months.

The Novalaser was an intercoronary device that utilized a nonthermal laser beam. Transmitted through fiber optics, the Novalaser would allow surgeons to perform a new, less invasive type of angioplasty. The doctors and scientists at Cardiotech had high hopes that the Novalaser would some-day replace traditional balloon angioplasties altogether. The device had already gone through preliminary laboratory trials, and Cardiotech had put the Novalaser into the hands of surgeons at various universities and teaching hospitals in the area, allowing them to use it experimentally.

"Isn't this a lovely evening," declared Drayton. He was still ebullient from his play-acting and eager to perform one more time for the final group of visitors who'd be ankling by in another five or ten minutes.

Indeed, the evening was dry and relatively cool, with a big fat yellow moon rising overhead like a giant wheel of cheddar.

"Look at that moon," Drayton rhapsodized. "I believe that, according to the *Farmer's Almanac,* this is technically called the hunter's moon. But my dear old mother always referred to it as a jasmine moon."

Haley cocked her head inquisitively at Drayton. "That's very poetic. But why a jasmine moon?"

A smile played at the corner of Drayton's mouth as he answered. "I suppose because it's so buttery yellow. Like the fragrant jasmine blossoms that are so often blended with Chinese black or green tea." He gazed up at the moon again. "And, of course, it's very dreamy looking."

"Let's get a picture," said Theodosia as she pulled her camera from the pocket of her suede jacket.

Drayton and Haley immediately threw their arms around each other and smiled widely.

Theodosia aimed, tilted up a notch to hopefully catch the moon, then snapped the picture. "For our Indigo Tea Shop scrapbook," she told them.

"Say now," said Drayton, blinking from the flash and peering at her quizzically. "Is that the camera you told me I could use?"

"Yes, it is," said Theodosia, turning the compact device over to him.

Drayton fumbled in his pocket, pulled out a pair of tortoiseshell half glasses, and put them on. They promptly slid down his aquiline nose, giving him a slightly owlish look. He studied the camera for a few seconds, obviously liking its small size and sleek design. Then he tapped at the viewfinder. "Just look through here and push . . . what?"

"That tiny silver button," said Theodosia, pointing. "See it? Easy as pie."

Drayton studied the camera for another few moments, reassured that he had the exact button he wanted. "I really want to get a picture of Tom Wigley in his brigadier general costume," he told Theodosia gleefully. "The old fellow looks like he just stepped out of one of the oil paintings at the Heritage Society." Drayton was a big gun with Charleston's Heritage Society and served on the board of directors as parliamentarian. Over the past couple of years he had also smoothed the way for Theodosia and Timothy Neville, the octogenarian president of the Heritage Society, to become friends. In fact, Theodosia was house-sitting for Timothy Neville right now. Instead of residing in her cozy apartment above the Indigo Tea Shop, she and her dog, Earl Grey, were living in grand style in Timothy's magnificent Italianate mansion on Archdale Street just a stone's throw from Charleston's historic Battery.

Haley watched Drayton hurry off, Theodosia's camera in hand. "He's using your camera," she said. A doubtful look creased her young face and she tossed her head, shrugging her stick-straight, long blonde hair back behind her shoulders.

Theodosia nodded agreeably. "Sure. No problem."

"You're too much," said Haley, waggling a finger at Theodosia. "You just gave Drayton your digital camera to use. And you *know* Drayton detests anything that smacks remotely of technology." Haley was really warming up now. "We're talking about a man who doesn't believe in cable TV. A man who still plays vinyl records on an old-fashioned stereo." Now Haley was positively chortling. "Drayton's probably the *only* person in Charleston who still calibrates his turntable and buys phonograph needles."

"I hear you," responded Theodosia with a grin. "Which is why I didn't complicate matters by telling him it was a digital camera."

Haley widened her eyes in mock surprise. "You *lied* to Drayton?"

Theodosia considered the question. "Not exactly. I just told Drayton it was a point-and-click camera. Which it is. Technically."

Haley, who loved a harmless prank or joke, especially

when it was at Drayton's expense, cackled in agreement. "I don't see any great moral dilemma either."

"For sure," said Theodosia as she pried open another tin of shortbread cookies.

"Oh, Theodosia dear!" called a lilting, slightly demanding voice. "Hello there!"

Clearly recognizing the owner of that voice, Haley rolled her eyes in an elaborate gesture. "Delaine," she said with an air of resignation.

Delaine Dish, owner of Cotton Duck Clothing Shop, was not on Haley's top ten list of favorite people. Delaine projected an air of entitlement and a superior attitude that could often be quite maddening. And, of course, Delaine was also a ferocious gossip. If you didn't want everyone from North Charleston to the Isle of Palms gabbing about something you'd said or even *thought* about saying, then it would behoove you not to confide in Ms. Delaine Dish.

On the other hand, Delaine was a whirling dervish when it came to volunteering and raising funds for the likes of the Heritage Society, the Garden Club, and the Lamplighter Tour. If you needed someone to sell overpriced raffle tickets, wheedle a donation from a well-heeled curmudgeon, or browbeat a flock of volunteers into working a few extra hours, Delaine was your woman. She might look like a sweet-talking Southern belle, but beneath that frothy exterior beat the heart of a pit bull.

Delaine chugged up to the table, looking adorable as always, with her heart-shaped face perfectly made up and her dark hair pulled into a low knot at the back of her head. Wearing a cornflower yellow cashmere twinset and elegant taupe silk slacks, Delaine radiated casual confidence. She also looked slightly preppy, like she was about to dash off to the country club. Theodosia noted that Delaine's hobo bag, slung so casually over one shoulder, perfectly matched the burnished leather Tod's loafers she wore. Gold, real uptown, eighteen-karat yellow gold, shone at her ears, her wrists, and on several fingers. In her khaki slacks and wheat-colored suede jacket, Theodosia suddenly felt slightly wrenish and underdressed.

"Looking good there, Delaine," said Haley, who still dressed student-style and tonight was turned out in a short nubby sweater, long paisley skirt, and low boots.

"Hello, dear," said Delaine, barely entertaining a glance toward Haley. "Theodosia," she cooed, "could there be a more lovely evening for this little soiree?" Delaine surveyed the entire area with the aplomb of a grand duchess, noting the clutch of costumed actors in their leathers, boots and spurs, velvet coats, and shimmering silk gowns, who seemed to be regrouping for their final tableau.

"It's a perfect evening," agreed Theodosia.

"And such a clever idea, this Ghost Crawl," said Delaine. "A simply marvelous way to highlight the historical significance of our glorious Jasmine Cemetery." She paused, looking toward the actors, the stage area, and the waiting folding chairs. "A fund-raiser couched in a lovely social event. That's what I'd call a definite home run." Delaine suddenly looked a trifle wistful. As though, with all her prodigious fund-raising and ticket-selling skills, she *still* hadn't been able to pull off a coup as grand as this.

"The Medical Triad came up with a real winner of an idea," agreed Theodosia. "Especially the fund-raising part. Most of the proceeds will be going to clinics that serve at-risk children." Theodosia was a big believer in giving back to the community. She herself had raised and trained a service dog, a mixed-breed dog she'd dubbed a Dalbrador. In fact, from the moment she had found Earl Grey huddled in the alley behind her tea shop, shivering in the rain, she had vowed to nurse him, love him, and turn the little stray into a service dog. And she had. Responding eagerly to Theodosia's loving care, Earl Grey had grown and flourished. He'd sailed through obedience training, won his Canine Good Citizen award, and passed the therapy dog test to gain accreditation with Therapy Dog International. Now, when Earl Grey donned his bright blue nylon vest with his TDI service dog patch, he was an officially approved visitor, welcome in children's hospitals, as well as senior citizen homes.

Glancing about, studying the clutches of people that seemed to ebb and flow under colored spotlights, Delaine gave a tiny shudder, then finally met Theodosia's eyes. "I declare, there are so many good-looking *doctors* here tonight!" she said in her best Southern drawl.

"Cardiologists, actually," said Theodosia. Many of the companies that were members of Charleston's Medical Triad produced cardiology-related pharmaceuticals and medical products. And a high percentage of their top executives were, logically enough, cardiologists.

Delaine's eyes suddenly shone with a predatory gleam. "Cardiologists," she repeated. "Even better."

"You're not dating Cooper Hobcaw anymore?" Haley asked, a mischievous smile playing at her mouth.

Delaine arched one of her perfectly waxed brows and gave a delicate yet slightly disdainful wave. "That fellow is ancient history." She turned to Theodosia. "But you're still dating the oh-so-available Jory Davis . . . ?"

"Are you kidding?" laughed Theodosia, fumbling to unwrap a tall stack of indigo blue paper cups. "He's the one who roped me into this thing."

"I hear Jory's uncle is rather famous," said Delaine. "Or will be soon."

"Dr. Jasper Davis does seem to have emerged as a rather prominent member in the field of angioplasty," said Theodosia, handing the cups to Haley.

"And I understand he's also in the throes of a divorce," said Delaine, smiling sweetly. "A rather *public* divorce."

Theodosia spread her hands, as though to disavow any knowledge of Dr. Jasper Davis's personal life. "So I understand," she said slowly. "But I really haven't been privy to any details."

"Details?" tittered Delaine. "Details aren't all *that* important now, are they, dearie? In my book, a fellow is either available or he's not. There's no in-between."

"That's one way to look at it," noted Haley. "The old flat-earth-society view of things."

Delaine glanced over at her. "What did you say, dear? I'm afraid my mind was elsewhere."

"Nothing," said Haley with a touch of smugness.

"My goodness," said Delaine, narrowing her eyes and peering about. "I do believe that's Vance Tuttle over there. Chatting with Drayton."

"Hmm," said Theodosia as she peeled plastic wrap off another stack of indigo blue paper cups.

"I think it's *marvelous* that the executive director of the Charleston Repertory Company isn't a bit self conscious about consorting with a passel of amateur actors," said Delaine. "I've just *got* to run over and ask dear Mr. Tuttle how his new production is coming along." And off she dashed.

"Delaine said the word *amateurs* like she was talking about manure," said Haley to Theodosia. "That's not a very charitable attitude. Amateurs participate because they *love* it. They're really just volunteers. Like us."

Theodosia patted Haley's hand. "Don't let Delaine get to you, Haley. She means well, but she does have a slightly stilted way of phrasing things."

"No kidding," said Haley, still shaking her head.

"Say now," said Theodosia, "here's our Jory. And I do believe he has a couple of esteemed doctors in tow."

"Cardiologists?" asked Haley, managing to mimic Delaine's slow drawl perfectly. "Even better."

"Shhhh," said Theodosia, giggling as she put a finger to her lips. "Delaine will be back here in a flash if she hears you."

"Theodosia!" Jory Davis greeted her. "I've got a couple fellows here who want to thank you." He grinned widely. "You know my uncle, of course," he said as Dr. Jasper Davis gave Theodosia a warm hug. "And this is Dr. Rex Haggard, president of Cardiotech."

"Dr. Haggard, so nice to meet you," said Theodosia, shaking hands with him.

"Good to meet you," replied Rex Haggard.

"This was such a lovely idea," Theodosia said, turning to Jasper Davis. "And your idea of donating the proceeds makes it even better." She smiled warmly at Jory's uncle. He was an attractive older gentleman with bright blue eyes, silver hair, and a ruddy complexion. Just like Jory, Jasper Davis looked like he genuinely enjoyed spending time outdoors, playing tennis or golf or sailing the intercoastal waterway. *Sporting blood definitely runs in the family*, Theodosia mused to herself.

But Dr. Jasper Davis was quick to deflect her praise. "No, no, it's not me you want to thank. Talk to Dr. Haggard here. He sits on the board of the Medical Triad. They're the folks who were anxious to create a fund-raiser that would also showcase the historical aspects of our fine cemetery. Some people might think it's a little morbid . . ." Dr. Jasper Davis looked around happily at the costumed actors, the makeshift stage, and the rows of empty folding chairs awaiting their next audience. "But I think it's a fitting tribute to those who have gone before us."

Dr. Rex Haggard nodded sagely at Theodosia and Jory. He was tall and long jawed, with a shock of ginger-colored hair and flat brown eyes. He looked intelligent, thoughtful, and prudent, all the things you'd want in a doctor. "Actually," said Rex Haggard, "our PR people were the ones who put the final spin on things. A fellow by the name of Ben Atherton and his assistant, Emily Guthro, really spearheaded the whole idea."

"You know them?" Jory Davis asked Theodosia.

"Ben owns Vantage PR?" said Rex Haggard helpfully.

"I've heard of them," Theodosia replied. "In fact, their company has a very fine reputation. They usually take home a couple awards every year from the Charleston Ad Show." A little more than two years ago, Theodosia had been an account executive at an advertising agency, helping to develop cutting-edge marketing strategies for high tech accounts. She'd loved her work and the wacky creative people she'd worked with, but the hustle-bustle, 24/7 lifestyle always seemed to leave her a little frazzled. That's when she'd made the conscious decision to chuck the corporate lifestyle and begin life anew as a female entrepreneur and opened the Indigo Tea Shop. Thankfully, she'd never looked back.

"This Ghost Crawl fund-raiser hits a happy medium," piped up Jory's Uncle Jasper. "Especially since Cardiotech has scaled back its funding of community activities."

"There's a lot of that going around," said Theodosia. "Even the Heritage Society is struggling to make ends meet. And in the past, they were a real powerhouse when it came to raising money and garnering major donations."

Rex Haggard gave a solemn nod. "They're a fine outfit. We used to fund them, too." He smiled sadly at Theodosia, Jory, and Jasper Davis. "Unfortunately, the medical products industry, being what it is today, has forced us to make some very tough decisions. And many of those decisions have proven rather unpopular." His long face suddenly brightened. "On the plus side, once our Novalaser is in widespread use in the medical marketplace, Cardiotech will soon be turning red ink into black. A feat our shareholders will no doubt heartily applaud."

Theodosia and Jory nodded appreciatively. There had been numerous articles in the Business Section of the *Charleston Post & Courier* about Cardiotech's Novalaser. In them Dr. Rex Haggard had been quoted as saying the Novalaser would revolutionize the angioplasty market. He had been photographed posing in one of Cardiotech's labs, looking knowledgeable and confident.

He still looked confident tonight. Only Dr. Jasper Davis looked thoughtful.

"We're still a good ways . . ." began Jasper Davis, but Rex Haggard cut him off.

"Cardiotech is *extremely* optimistic about the Novalaser," said Rex Haggard. "And looking forward to an aggressive market launch."

*   *   *

"*What was that* all about?" Theodosia asked Jory once the two of them were alone. Rex Haggard had obviously interrupted Jory's uncle quite deliberately.

Jory shrugged. "I'm not completely sure, but if I had to hazard a guess, I'd say internal politics just reared its ugly head. You know, the new-product-touting, investor-appeasing CEO running up against the more conservative, safety-minded clinician."

"In other words, your Uncle Jasper is butting heads with Dr. Rex Haggard."

Jory looked glum. "It did seem that way, didn't it?"

"With all his glowing talk of turning red ink into black," said Theodosia, "I'd say Dr. Rex Haggard is fairly chomping at the bit to release the Novalaser." Theodosia knew Rex Haggard wasn't unusual. In several of the high tech companies she'd worked with, she'd seen CEOs and CFOs push hard to release new products as fast as possible. It was usually the research and development guys who spun a more cautionary tale. They wanted to make sure their products were perfect before they went spilling out into the marketplace. If there was the least little problem, it would come galloping back a few months later and bite them squarely in the butt. Unfortunately, once a new product was highly touted in the media, it often became a roaring freight train, impossible to stop.

Theodosia caught one of Jory's hands in hers. "Let's go talk to your Uncle Jasper again."

Jory pulled her toward him and encircled her with both arms. "You're so nice. Always worrying about people's feelings."

"He's family," she said.

Jory brushed his lips across the top of Theodosia's forehead and smiled knowingly. In the South, family was everything. Even second, third, and fourth cousins were considered kinfolk. And, when you took a long, hard view of things and saw the fragmented, buckshot-scattered lives that many people lived these days, the extended family point of view wasn't a bad way of looking at things.

Theodosia and Jory were weaving their way between a stand of oleander and an enormous marble monument adorned with Greek columns when Theodosia suddenly said: "Uh oh."

Vance Tuttle, the outspoken director of the Charleston Repertory Company, had cornered Jory's Uncle Jasper. Wearing a crimson velvet jacket and a face to match, Vance Tuttle appeared to be giving Jasper Davis a piece of his mind. His arms waved, his eyes bulged, his voice shrilled. In fact, Vance Tuttle seemed to be doing everything but gnash his teeth. Ectomorphically thin, taller than Jory's uncle by a good six inches, and with a hawk-nose and shock of curly gray hair, Vance Tuttle railed on with fierce intensity.

Theodosia and Jory stopped in their tracks, unsure what to do, reluctant to put themselves in the middle of this strange one-sided tirade.

But from where they stood, they could catch snatches of conversation.

"Do you know how difficult . . ." Vance Tuttle raved.

Jory's uncle slowly nodded in agreement, looking sober and more than a little embarrassed.

But Vance Tuttle was not to be appeased. ". . . has literally dried up," he shrilled. Fragments of his words drifted across to Theodosia and Jory like a faulty recording.

"Ouch," said Jory under his breath. "I think this is about one of those unpopular decisions Rex Haggard alluded to."

"A funding cut," said Theodosia.

"Yup," said Jory.

"But corporations *do* have bad years," said Theodosia. "And nonprofit organizations shouldn't completely depend on them for financial support. Companies like Cardiotech give what they can to the community, *when* they can."

"That's a nice rational argument," said Jory. "But *he* sure isn't buying it."

Vance threw his hands in the air with great disdain. "We're talking *culture,* man," he thundered, his voice rising above the general hum of activity. "We're talking about a tradition of live theater that stretches all the way back to 1736, for heaven's sake!"

"Yipes," said Theodosia, as all about them, volunteers suddenly stopped worrying about spotlights and costumes, sound effects and props, and turned to stare at the two men who had suddenly taken center stage by virtue of their loud, heated argument.

Suddenly, like a deus ex machina in a Greek play, Drayton hustled over to join the two men. He spoke quietly but intensely for a moment, placing a hand on Vance Tuttle's shoulder in an obvious effort to calm him. The conversation downshifted to a whisper, then Drayton led Vance Tuttle away, his hand still firmly gripping the man's shoulder.

"The voice of reason," said Jory. "Thank goodness for Drayton."

Theodosia nodded, breathing her own sigh of relief as volunteers lost interest and slowly returned to the tasks at hand.

"Let's go speak to him," began Jory. He was obviously worried about his Uncle Jasper.

"Why don't we give your uncle a couple minutes," said Theodosia tactfully. "That little scene was embarrassing enough for him."

"Good point," agreed Jory. "He doesn't need us gallumping up and making him feel like he has to explain things." Jory looked grim. "Not that he has to explain *anything*. Not to me anyway."

"Don't worry," said Theodosia. "It's done with." She glanced over her shoulder. "And it's time to for us to get cracking. Looks like the Ghost Crawl guides just led in our last group of visitors."

Now Jory turned to look as approximately fifty people began filing into the rows of folding chairs. "Good grief, you're right," he said. "I guess this means you have to get back and do your tea and crumpet thing."

Theodosia wrinkled her nose. "Tea and *crumpets?* I can't say the Indigo Tea Shop has ever actually served crumpets. Not that it's a bad idea."

Jory stared at her and a slow smile spread across his face. "Well, it sounds like something Sherlock Holmes and his sidekick Watson would enjoy after a rousing chase across the moors. Which, for some strange reason, reminds me of you." Jory paused. "So, my dear, what does a *modern* Sherlock serve?"

"Pumpkin muffins, apple fritters, hot spiced jasmine tea, and ghostly shortbread," Theodosia told him.

Jory grinned. "Sounds fabulous, especially to a lawyer who skipped dinner because he had to stay late at the office and finish writing a brief. But what the heck is ghostly shortbread?"

"Come and find out," said Theodosia playfully. "Drayton's going to be busy acting up a storm, so Haley and I would welcome an extra hand."

"Then you've got it, ma'am," said Jory happily. "But I'd kind of like to keep one eye on this tableau thing, too. Drayton mentioned they were going to showcase some antique guns."

Jory was as good as his word. He dutifully laid out paper napkins and stacked pumpkin muffins on the large cut-glass platters Theodosia had brought along.

"Not too high," Haley cautioned him. "I can never resist tossing in a few extra eggs and sticks of butter when I whip up my batter. Makes the muffins sinfully rich but a little crumbly, too," she admitted.

"Now we know your tricks of the trade," joked Jory. "Better watch out!"

"You want a piece of me?" Haley laughed. She gestured at Jory. "Come on. We'll have a bake-off. My muffins against your . . . your *anything!*"

"No way," laughed Jory. "You'd clobber me!"

"You bet I would," laughed Haley.

"Shhh," said Theodosia as the overhead lights dimmed

and the prerecorded music track began. "This is where Drayton makes his grand entrance as General Beauregard."

The three of them stared at the makeshift stage, where a giant wine-colored plush velvet curtain hung from a wire stretched between two live oaks. The fog machine began to crank out its steady stream of ground fog and a single blue spotlight glowed against the curtain.

The music, a fanciful flute and harmonica Civil War ditty, segued to a more symphonic, mournful orchestral piece. A hush fell over the audience and they straightened in their seats. Just as live theater was supposed to, the visual and audio cues told the crowd something exciting was about to happen.

Then, the plush curtains parted halfway and a man staggered out.

Theodosia stared at the hunched figure that stood in front of the curtain and frowned.

Are my eyes suddenly playing tricks on me? she wondered. *Because that doesn't look like Drayton. And this sure isn't the way this play began last time . . .*

Slipping out from behind the table, Theodosia took a few hesitant steps toward the stage. Now she was even with the audience just to her left. As the music swelled, Theodosia stared harder, wishing the stage wasn't in such darkness and suddenly getting an awful feeling something wasn't quite right. Because the actor . . . and she was pretty sure it wasn't Drayton . . . seemed positively ill.

Taking another step forward, Theodosia's eyes widened in recognition. She whirled about, searching frantically for Jory's familiar face. "Jory," she gasped.

Jory Davis rushed to her side, knowing something must have gone awry, then gazed at the man bathed in ghostly blue light who stood so hesitantly in front of the dark velvet curtain.

Panic flooded across Jory's face. Disbelieving, he took a half-step forward.

That's when Jory's Uncle Jasper staggered toward the audience, uttered a low gasp, and collapsed in a heap.

Screams erupted from the audience.

"Sit down," growled one man. "It's part of the show! It's got to be part of the show!"

But Theodosia knew this was definitely not scripted. This was a real medical emergency.

Rushing forward, Theodosia threw herself on the dry grass next to Jory's Uncle Jasper. Gasping for breath, the man was beyond pale and starting to turn blue. His fine, white hair fluttered in the light breeze as his clenched hands beat the ground futiley.

If she could just turn Uncle Jasper onto his side, maybe he'd be able to catch a breath. Or if she loosened his shirt and tie. Theodosia's hands fumbled clumsily at the buttons.

"Help! We need a doctor!" cried Jory, who was crouched alongside her now.

"What can I do?" asked Drayton, suddenly hovering above them.

Theodosia dug in her jacket pocket and pulled out her cell phone. She handed it to Drayton. "Quick! Call 911!"

Drayton grabbed the phone and fumbled frantically with the high tech apparatus. "I don't know how!"

Grabbing the phone from Drayton's trembling hand, Jory hammered in the numbers.

Then Dr. Rex Haggard was down on the ground beside Theodosia, his voice urgent yet calming. "Let me," he said. Relieved, Theodosia moved out of the way and watched as his practiced fingers checked Jasper Davis's airway and respiration. Then, clasping his hands together, Dr. Rex Haggard, raised them high above his head and drove down hard on Jasper Davis's chest. A sharp *whack* resounded as Dr. Haggard began cardiac compressions.

Figuring Jory's uncle was in extremely capable hands, Theodosia scrambled to her feet, exhaled slowly, and took a single step backward.

A faint *crunch* sounded under her shoe. Startled, Theodosia glanced down and scanned the grass, even as she kept an eye on Dr. Rex Haggard laboring over Jory's uncle. In her panic, she noticed that Jasper Davis's fingernails had turned blue. And it wasn't just a reflection from the blue lights.

What does that mean? she wondered, as the word *cyanotic* streaked through her head.

Cyanotic. That means oxygen isn't getting to Uncle Jasper's brain. And that . . . what? He's near death?

Shuddering, Theodosia cast her eyes downward again and caught the glint of something shiny in the blue glare of the klieg lights. She bent over and searched the grass, even as she heard Dr. Rex Haggard's voice saying *It's no good.*

No good? You mean Jasper Davis is dead? Oh no! He can't be!

The *whoop whoop* of an ambulance siren suddenly sounded nearby. Red and blue lights flashed at the bottom of the hill, then bounced erratically as the ambulance veered onto the grass and slalomed its way up the hill toward them, dodging and weaving between gravestones.

Two paramedics piled out, creating a sudden bustle of activity as they unfolded a clanking gurney and hustled an oxygen apparatus and a portable defibrillator to the scene.

"We've got to get him to County Medical," said one of the paramedics.

They worked on Jory's Uncle Jasper for no more than thirty seconds, then loaded the man's still form onto a gurney.

"You'd better take this along," called out Theodosia. The stunned crowd was talking in low murmurs and her voice, shaky and just on the verge of being shrill, rose above it.

The paramedic who'd spoken glanced quickly toward her, eyebrows raised, a puzzled expression on his face. "Take what along?" he asked.

Theodosia held up a syringe just as someone aimed a light directly at her. The audience, still seated in their chairs and watching the scene unfold before them like some bizarre improvisational play, let loose with a collective *ooohhh.* Theodosia put up a hand to shield her eyes, fervently wishing that blue spotlight wasn't focused so squarely on her.

Seeing the syringe in Theodosia's outstretched palm, Jory buried his face in his hands. "Dear God," he moaned.

2

Teakettles whistled and chirped as Drayton carefully measured four rounded teaspoons of oolong into a teapot, then poured boiling water over the leaves.

"Is that pot ready yet?" called Haley. It was a few minutes past nine and she was bustling about the tearoom, laying out linen napkins and popping sprigs of daisies into tall crystal vases, trying to make everything in the Indigo Tea Shop absolutely perfect. A pair of early birds, tourists who were staying at the nearby Candlelight Inn B&B, had come in a few moments ago and were seated at the table nearest the cozy stone fireplace, gazing about the picturesque tea shop appreciatively and eagerly awaiting their pot of tea and basket of scones.

"Hold your horses," Drayton muttered under his breath. "This tea's still busy infusing." It was a general rule of thumb that the smaller the pieces of tea leaves, the quicker the tea will brew. That said, this was a Formosan oolong, with lovely big leaves and silver tips of the bud. So this tea would take a trifle longer to brew, but the rich body and fragrant aroma would make it well worth the wait.

"You're using the Primrose Chintz," said Haley, sidling up next to Drayton. Indeed, the Indigo Tea Shop's master blender had selected one of the prettiest pots from their vast collection of teapots. Blue forget-me-nots and pale yellow primroses danced across the pleasingly plump body of the bone china pot. The handle and spout were a lovely pale pink.

"Cheers me up," said Drayton, although he looked morose and sounded far from cheery.

"I know," said Haley, commiserating. "I feel terrible about last night, too."

"Imagine how Jory feels," said Drayton somewhat irritably. "Seeing his poor uncle stagger out and collapse in front of everyone."

"And then get hauled to the hospital and be pronounced dead on arrival," said Haley. "Tragic."

"Tragic," echoed Drayton.

Haley nibbled at a fingertip, thinking. "What do you suppose *really* happened? You know, with the syringe? Was Jory's uncle a diabetic or something?" She lowered her voice. "Or was he using some sort of drug? I heard that a lot of doctors seem to get hooked on drugs just because they have such easy access to them."

Drayton pursed his lips and shook his head. "I haven't the faintest idea," he murmured. "I never even met the man before last night. And I'm not entirely sure that interceding in the argument he was embroiled in with Vance Tuttle remotely qualifies as *meeting* him." Drayton lifted the Primrose Chintz teapot onto Haley's tray and nestled it alongside a plate of lemon raisin scones and a pretty little glass slipper brimming with generous white poufs of Devonshire cream. "There you go," he told her, glancing at his watch. "Twenty seconds more. By the time you pour this tea, it will be perfectly steeped."

Haley gazed back at the celadon green velvet curtains

that separated the front of the tea shop from the kitchen and Theodosia's small office. "She's still on the phone," Haley said.

"I would imagine so," said Drayton.

"Jory's taking it awfully hard," said Haley.

"As well he should. But, of course, his mourning also affects our Theo," Drayton sighed. The bell above the door jingled and four ladies sporting casual clothing and jogging shoes entered the Indigo Tea Shop. Another group of tourists, smiling tentatively, yet clearly eager for a steaming cup of tea and a fresh-baked scone.

"Well, well," said Drayton. He slipped a long white apron over his head and tied it in back. In his starched white shirt and dark gray slacks, he suddenly looked all the world like a Parisian waiter. "Somehow these old bones tell me we might be in for a busy morning." He carefully adjusted his trademark bow tie. "Better look sharp."

In her back office, Theodosia slid the phone into its cradle and stared at the wall across from her perpetually cluttered desk. It was her scrapbook wall, filled with precious photos and mementos. Pictures of her parents, now deceased, hung there. Pictures of Aunt Libby at Cane Hill, the family plantation in the low-country where her dad had grown up. And framed opera programs, botanical prints, and even tea labels.

A recent photo of Jory and her was hanging there, too, in a sleek, silver frame. That photo had been taken just this past summer at Uncle Jasper's condo over on Kiawah Island. Theodosia could recall that long weekend perfectly. Uncle Jasper had taken them golfing at the Ocean Course. It had been a magnificent yet difficult course that offered spectacular panoramic views of the Atlantic with several of the holes playing directly along a windswept beach. She and Jory had played a so-so round; Uncle Jasper had come in just a few strokes over par. Afterwards, they'd gone to a restaurant called the Pelican Club for a killer-calorie dinner of crawfish gumbo and fried wild turkey.

That weekend at his condo, Theodosia had formed a real kinship with Jasper Davis. And probably would have gotten to know him a whole lot better if he hadn't always been so darned involved with his work. And if last night's tragedy hadn't changed things forever.

She shook her head angrily, as if she still couldn't quite come to terms with the strange events of last night.

People don't just collapse like that, do they?

Theodosia grimaced. Maybe they did. Jory's Uncle Jasper was sixty-something and men that age often had bad tickers.

But Uncle Jasper was a cardiologist. Wouldn't he have been mindful of his own heart? Wouldn't he have known?

You'd think so. But, then again, doctors often made terrible patients. They were busy, sometimes arrogant, and knew too much. Some even adopted the attitude that, because they dealt in illness and death, they were somehow immune to the ravages of time.

And what of that syringe she'd found? Such a strange, terrible item to suddenly appear. Was it directly related to Jasper Davis's death or was stumbling upon it just a bizarre coincidence? Theodosia knew she'd probably have to wait for a medical examiner's report to answer that burning question.

Theodosia picked up a tea catalog, tossed it onto a pile of others and then watched it slip off her desk and to the floor. Annoyed, she reached over and shoved the whole stack to the floor.

When she'd finally gotten back to Timothy Neville's house last night, she'd felt utterly drained. She'd taken Earl Grey out for a quick walk, but even his doggy exuberance hadn't been enough to hearten or console her. So later, upstairs in Timothy's guest bedroom, she'd spread a spare sheet over the coverlet and allowed Earl Grey to jump on the bed and curl up next to her. Only then did his warm, shaggy body finally provide her with a small degree of comfort.

*   *   *

Theodosia popped out from behind the velvet curtains, a pleasant smile on her face. Although she didn't feel a lot of inner joy today, she knew the inherent comfort and warmth of the Indigo Tea Shop would eventually permeate her consciousness. This former carriage house and tiny treasure on Charleston's historic Church Street never failed to lift her spirits, just as it seemed to cast a magical spell over all who entered.

Theodosia had pondered this phenomenon several times before. Maybe it was the infusion of tea that seemed to hang in the air. An aromatherapy-like blend of cinnamon-scented Nilgiri teas, malty Assams, spicy Yunnans, and rich, smoky Lapsang Souchongs. Or maybe it was the tea shop's pure quaintness and charm that inspired a feeling of well-being. Teapots by Doulton, Royal Albert, and Minton, as well as plain old utilitarian Brown Bettys were stuck in nooks and crannies all over the shop. Behind the counter, where the old brass cash register sat, a floor-to-ceiling warren of cubbyholes held enormous brass tins and glass jars that were filled with teas from around the world. Creaking hickory tables and chairs, pegged wooden floors, sturdy beams, and lovely exposed brick walls gave a sense of cozying in, no matter what the season. Whatever its magical charm, Theodosia knew the Indigo Tea Shop could always pick her up when she felt world-weary and soothe her soul when she was feeling slightly battered.

Haley sidled up next to Theodosia at the counter. "Are you okay?"

Theodosia gave a hearty nod and her mass of auburn hair bounced as she did so. The tea shop was almost full now, and she, too, had a feeling, probably stemming from that sixth sense shopkeepers often develop, that today was shaping up to be a very busy day.

"You were sweet to come in early and bake," Theodosia told Haley. "After last night . . . well, I wouldn't have blamed you if you just didn't have the heart to come in at all."

"I feel just awful for Jory," said Haley. "But moping around never solves anything."

"Just the same," said Theodosia, "I'm very impressed. We're both impressed."

Drayton, who had hustled over to grab a pitcher of ice water, flashed them a quizzical glance. "Since I seem to have been included in that statement," he said, "just what is it I'm supposed to be impressed by?"

"My prodigious baking skills," said Haley. "And my fortitude." Her first statement was said in jest, the latter was uttered with more seriousness.

"But of course," said Drayton. "You're a professional. One would expect nothing less."

"Well, thank you, Drayton," said Haley. "I think."

Drayton cocked an eye toward Theodosia. "You were on the phone with Jory earlier." It was a statement rather than a question.

Theodosia nodded.

"Do the doctors have any inkling as to what happened last night? Was it a heart attack or stroke?"

"He certainly didn't seem all that old," put in Haley.

"In his sixties," said Theodosia.

"Not old at all," was Drayton's brisk reply. "And what about the syringe you found? Do we know yet if it was somehow related to poor Jasper Davis's death or just a nasty coincidence? Meaning, of course, did someone simply drop it there?" Drayton paused for a moment. "Dropped a used syringe. Isn't that a sad commentary on our society?"

"Yes it is," said Theodosia. "But to answer your question, Jory didn't know anything yet. Although, in the cold, clear light of day, I tend to think the syringe *was* just dropped there." She grimaced. "Probably just a strange, sad coincidence."

"Enough about the awful details," said Drayton. "How is Jory holding up?"

"I don't know if it's because he was present at the scene last night or the fact that he's a lawyer, but it seems as if everyone in his family is pretty much counting on him to deal with his uncle's death and, of course, make all the necessary funeral arrangements," said Theodosia.

"Ouch," said Drayton. "Tough duty. Not that Jory isn't completely capable, of course."

"But still . . ." offered Haley. "Wasn't his Uncle Jasper married?"

"To Star Duncan," said Theodosia.

"Then shouldn't she be making the . . . uh . . . final arrangements?" asked Haley.

"It's complicated," said Theodosia.

"It always is," said Drayton knowingly.

"You see," began Theodosia, "Uncle Jasper was in the middle of a divorce."

"Oh," said Drayton. "It really *is* complicated."

"And to quote Star, the soon-to-be ex," continued Theodosia, "while expressing her profound sympathy and full intent to *attend* Jasper Davis's funeral service, she does not feel the actual *planning* of the services should fall upon her shoulders."

"In other words, this Star Duncan is opting out," said Haley.

"More like chickening out," said Drayton, frowning.

"Whatever the case . . ." said Theodosia, suddenly at a loss for words. "Jory's certainly . . ." Theodosia blinked back hot tears.

Drayton reached out and put a hand on Theodosia's shoulder. "If there's *anything* we can do . . ."

"Thank you," said Theodosia. "That means a lot to me." She swallowed hard and shrugged. "Jory and I were supposed to go horseback riding this Sunday at the Wildwood Horse and Hunt Club. Fox hunting . . . you know? With some of the Cardiotech executives." She turned toward the kitchen, pulled up her apron, and wiped at her eyes.

"Oh, Theo," said Haley, stepping around to face her, "if you really insist on being here today, why not just spend the morning in your office? Maybe work on inventory and reorders? You know we're out of almost *everything*. DuBose Bees Honey, sugar swizzle sticks, even those lavender tea candles. Drayton and I can handle the morning and luncheon crowd. No problem."

"She's right," offered Drayton. "We're the dynamic duo."

Theodosia managed a weak smile. "I'm fine, really. Better than fine."

Haley suddenly glanced past Theodosia toward the front door. "Are you sure?" she asked.

Theodosia turned to gaze at the solid, wooden door with a window of shimmering leaded glass. A large bulky form seemed to hover there for a moment, then waver slightly. "What?" said Theodosia.

"I think we have a visitor who probably wants a word with you," said Haley. "And who could upset you even more."

"A customer?" asked Theodosia, wiping at her eyes.

Now Drayton cast a quick glance toward the door and his look of compassion suddenly shifted to one of concern. "Not exactly," he said.

Detective Burt Tidwell lowered his bulk into a wooden captain's chair and gazed about the Indigo Tea Shop. And as he did so his shoulders seemed to relax, his eyes taking on an anticipatory gleam. But this was not an unnatural occurrence. For the Indigo Tea Shop was a place awash in sunshine and brimming with sweetness and innocence. Most visitors readily succumbed to the lure of tinkling teacups, starched table linens, fresh flowers, shiny spoons, heavenly teas, and delicious baked goods. Here everything was genteel and lovely and very proper. An atmosphere separate and apart from anything else.

Tidwell unfurled a starched napkin and laid it across his lap expectantly. In his younger days, he had cut his teeth working for the FBI. Back when his fighting weight had been a good hundred pounds less than what it was now, he had bulled his way through the sixteen-week training program at Quantico like an NFL linebacker breezing through Cub Scout camp. Graduation had found Tidwell young and idealistic, raring to match wits and knock heads with serious bad guys. But, alas, the FBI was not the brilliant, crackerjack organization its PR spinmeisters made it out to be. Rather, it was old school. Plodding and slow, woefully deficient in the intricacies of fieldwork. If you needed a tricky warrant served on a tax-evading corporate scoundrel, the FBI was utterly whiz-bang. If you wanted a RICO-type conviction, the FBI excelled. But when it came to going out on the mean streets to hunt down and apprehend major-league criminals? A lot of street-smart detectives with far more bluster than academic training were hands-down superior.

With a sense of trepidation, Theodosia slid into the chair across from Tidwell. His coming here today seemed to validate the sense of unease that hung over her head like a dark cloud. On the other hand, one could always hope. Perhaps this was purely a social call. She had dealt with him on earlier matters and a sort of guarded, tacit friendship had developed between the two of them.

"Detective Tidwell," Theodosia said pleasantly, gazing into his slightly protruding eyes, noting once again the strange bullet-shaped head that seemed to perch at an odd angle on his bulbous body. "May I offer you some tea?"

Tidwell's bushy eyebrows crinkled like fat, furry caterpillars pulling themselves into a ball for protection from the cold. Theodosia started to rise to fetch some tea, but Tidwell held up a hand to stop her. "There's a problem," he said in a low rumble.

Theodosia sank back down into her chair and glanced about the tearoom. Drayton and Haley were busily pouring tea and serving scones, and she wished fervently that she were bustling about with them, smiling and chatting with customers as if the day were new and fresh and filled with promise.

"What's wrong?" Theodosia finally asked.

"I have a few questions concerning last night."

Now it was Theodosia's turn to crank her eyebrows up a notch.

"*You're* looking into this?" she asked, the feeling of dread beginning to seep into the pit of her stomach.

"The untimely death of Dr. Jasper Davis has come across my desk, yes," said Tidwell.

"But you are a *homicide* detective," said Theodosia.

Tidwell's dark eyes met hers and didn't waver. "Quite correct."

"Something's wrong," she said. Her mouth felt dry and she fervently wished Tidwell had taken her up on her offer of tea.

"Something has come to light, yes," said Tidwell.

"I'm almost afraid to ask," said Theodosia. "Does it have to do with the syringe?"

Tidwell nodded.

"Does Jory Davis know about this yet?"

"No, but I promise he shall soon," said Tidwell.

Theodosia exhaled in a giant *whoosh* and forced herself to look deep into Tidwell's eyes. "Tell me."

Tidwell didn't mince words. "We believe someone administered a lethal injection to Dr. Jasper Davis."

Theodosia winced. That had been the dark thought that lurked in the back of her mind, too, but she hadn't dared let it permeate her consciousness. Now the full effect of Tidwell's words swept across her, stunning her at first, then angering her. Because Detective Burt Tidwell had just confirmed that a cold-blooded murder had taken place last night. Not a heart attack or stroke or diabetic coma or some sort of *natural* thing . . . if that was even the word for it. But a homicide. A murder.

"This was confirmed at the hospital?" Theodosia stared at Tidwell anxiously. "In the emergency room?"

Tidwell nodded slowly. "And by the coroner."

"Could the doctors tell anything about . . . what would you call it . . . the drug . . . the toxin?" asked Theodosia.

Tidwell shook his head and his jowls sloshed sideways. "It's far too early to make any sort of judgment call on this. But the ME did bring in a consulting toxicologist. A Dr. Leo Gallette from the Medical University of South Carolina."

Founded in 1824, the Medical University of South Carolina was one of the South's oldest schools and enjoyed a stellar reputation. If anyone could deduce what had killed Dr. Jasper Davis, Theodosia knew it would be one of their fine doctors.

"Is this standard procedure?" asked Theodosia. "To bring in someone from the outside?"

Tidwell lifted his massive shoulders imperceptibly.

"Does this Dr. Gallette have any initial ideas?" asked Theodosia.

"I don't like to . . ." began Tidwell.

"Come on," coaxed Theodosia.

"Best guess would be fentanyl," said Tidwell.

"Fentanyl," repeated Theodosia. "Sounds nasty."

"Trust me, it is," said Tidwell. "Fentanyl is a highly potent drug used by anesthesiologists. It's what's referred to as a twilight drug. There's also an analog called sufentanil that's ten times more potent than fentanyl." Tidwell paused. "Used in heart surgery, the drug can actually stop the heart in a matter of seconds."

"Heart surgery," said Theodosia as she stared intently at Tidwell. "Do they use fentanyl at Cardiotech?"

Tidwell leaned back suddenly and his chair uttered a mighty protest. "Possibly. I'm almost positive their research and development department is outfitted with a small surgical suite." He held up a hand. "It's crystal clear exactly where you're going with this. Which is why, as a routine matter of course, I shall exercise a search warrant."

"Good," said Theodosia.

"According to Dr. Gallette, more than twelve different analogs of fentanyl have been produced clandestinely in recent years," continued Tidwell.

"Clandestinely produced?" asked Theodosia.

"By illegal drug traffickers," said Tidwell. "And these new fentanyl versions are supposedly hundreds of times more potent than heroin."

Theodosia digested Tidwell's last bit of terrifying information. With this kind of fast-acting drug, poor Uncle Jasper had probably been dying by the time the needle was being withdrawn. Was gasping his final breath as he crumpled to his knees, his heart barely fluttering. And he was probably clinically dead by the time his head struck the hard earth. Theodosia shuddered.

Tidwell shifted in his chair, uncomfortable now, as Theodosia stared down at the table, suddenly lost in thought. "Do you perchance know of any enemies Jasper Davis might have had at Cardiotech?" he asked. "In high pressure work environments there tend to be the inevitable rivals."

"Not really," said Theodosia. "From what I could tell, Jasper Davis was one of the big honchos."

"So I've been told," said Tidwell. "Anyway, I need to speak with Jory Davis ASAP. I've tried calling his apartment as well as his office, but nobody seems to have a clue as to his whereabouts."

"Better just give him a buzz on his cell phone," said Theodosia. "It's . . ."

Tidwell pulled a small black leather notebook from his jacket pocket and slid it across the table along with a sterling silver pen. "Write it down for me, will you?" he asked.

Theodosia scribbled Jory's number into Tidwell's notebook, then slid it back across the table to Tidwell. "You're going to catch this person, right?"

"As always," said Tidwell, "we at Robbery Homicide shall put forth our very best effort." He nodded as if to punctuate his sentence. "But *you*, my dear Miss Browning, are to remain firmly ensconced on the sidelines. No poking around this time. No investigating. Is that clear?"

Theodosia mumbled a noncommittal sound as Tidwell slid his chair back with a *screech* and struggled to his feet.

"I mean that," he said, his eyes blazing a warning to her. "I want you to give me your solemn word that you'll remain completely removed from this."

Theodosia nodded unhappily. "Okay . . . yes."

Tidwell seemed to accept her grudging answer. For even as the words came from her mouth, he was plowing his way across the tea shop, deftly dodging tables and moving at an amazing speed for such a large man.

Theodosia stared at the door long after Tidwell had slipped out, feeling as though she'd been left in the choppy wake of an enormous battleship.

And as she continued to stare, she realized that this was the first time Detective Burt Tidwell had stopped by the Indigo Tea Shop without indulging in a scone or muffin.

3

Haley outdid herself with the lunch she prepared that day. Cream of asparagus soup accompanied by ham and apricot preserve tea sandwiches.

"My goodness," said Theodosia as she stood poised over the simmering pot with a spoon in her hand. "You made this cream of asparagus soup from scratch?"

Haley shrugged. "No big deal." It was nothing for Haley to show up at the farmer's market at the break of day to scoop up artisan butter, fresh brown eggs, just-picked mushrooms and morels, and newly harvested fruits and vegetables and a few imported ones, too. Today she had scored a major hit on asparagus.

"Haley," said Theodosia, "it is a big deal." She dipped her spoon into the steaming, bubbling pot for a sample, then rolled her eyes at the creamy taste and luscious texture. "A *very* big deal. This soup is sinfully delicious."

"Just one of my sweet Granny Odette's recipes that I

adapted," said Haley. She tossed off her response casually, but she was clearly delighted by Theodosia's reaction to her soup.

"Are you ever going to jot down some of these recipes so we can publish an Indigo Tea Shop cookbook?" asked Theodosia. "Of course, we'd have to get Drayton to divulge some of his tea secrets, too."

Haley studied Theodosia carefully. "You've mentioned that before. Were you serious? *Are* you serious?"

"Haley, your recipes are treasures," said Theodosia. "People are always asking for them."

"Receipts," said Haley, holding up a finger. "We'd for sure have to call them receipts." For some reason, recipes were always called receipts in the Carolinas.

"We'll subtitle our cookbook *Haley's Receipts,* then," laughed Theodosia as she reached for the wall phone that had suddenly started to ring. "And make sure you get the lion's share of the profits." Theodosia picked up the receiver and held it to her ear. "Hello?"

"Theodosia." It was Jory.

"Jory," she said, suddenly sobering. "Have you . . . did you . . .?"

"Speak with Tidwell?" said Jory. "Oh yes, I did."

"Oh, honey, I'm so sorry," said Theodosia. She looked over at Haley, who mouthed "Jory?" at her. Theodosia nodded and Haley made a sympathetic face.

"Shocking, isn't it?" said Jory.

"I was stunned when Tidwell told me," replied Theodosia.

"Theo!" said Jory, his strident tone changing to an anguished whisper. "Someone wanted Uncle Jasper dead!"

"It looks that way," she said, as Haley slipped by her, discreetly leaving Theodosia alone for her phone conversation with Jory.

"I've been assured by the police that they are launching a highly aggressive investigation," said Jory.

"They will," said Theodosia. "I know they will." She bit her lip, willing herself not to cry.

"I have something to ask you, Theo," said Jory. "A favor. A *big* favor."

"You've got it," she responded. "Anything you need, you know I'm here for you," she added, thinking Jory was probably going to ask her to help with the funeral arrangements.

"I want you to help me figure out who killed Uncle Jasper," said Jory.

Theodosia hesitated. Burt Tidwell's words still rang in her ears. What had he told her? No poking around, no investigating. Stay on the sidelines.

And she had nodded yes. She had pretty much given Tidwell her word that she wouldn't stick her nose into his investigation.

But how could she stay out of the investigation when Jory was asking her for help?

"Please, Theodosia," he continued. "I really need to have you working on this. On the side, on the QT, doing your own thing." Jory paused. "Because you're *good* at solving crimes. You've more than proven that in the past."

Theodosia closed her eyes and dropped the receiver to her chest. What had Jory called her just last night? *His modern-day Sherlock Holmes.*

"You'll help me, won't you?" implored Jory. "For Uncle Jasper's sake?"

Hot tears slipped down Theodosia's cheeks. It killed her to hear such anguish in Jory's voice. Here was a man who was good and kind and generous to a fault. Who volunteered at the People's Law Office in the Riverland Terrace neighborhood over on James Island. Who gave up evenings and more than a few Saturdays to help folks who couldn't normally afford high-priced lawyers fend off nasty creditors, take slum landlords to court, or figure out ways to get their due from home repair companies that had done shoddy work, then tried to royally screw them.

"*Of course* I'll help you, Jory," Theodosia found herself telling him as she felt a few pangs of guilt over her earlier assurances to Tidwell.

"There's going to be a memorial service tomorrow," said Jory. "At Cardiotech."

"Then we'll start there," said Theodosia, her brain already beginning to whir.

"You'll come? Really?" asked Jory.

"Of course I will," said Theodosia. "You know I will."

"Bless you, Theo," said Jory. "I'll probably be a walking basket case. But if you can . . . I don't know . . . keep your eyes and ears open, it might lead to something. Could lead to something."

"Count on it," said Theodosia. "And Jory . . ."

"Yes?"

"The police say they're going to be aggressive . . . but you haven't *seen* aggressive. When Drayton, Haley, and I get our teeth into something, watch out!"

"I know," said Jory, and now Theodosia could hear admiration in his voice. "You guys are like snapping turtles. And that's exactly what we need. Thanks a million, Theo. I *knew* you'd come through for me. I'll call again later, okay?"

"You know where to find me," said Theodosia, wishing she had some more optimistic words to share with Jory.

"Everything okay?" asked Haley, peering in at Theodosia. "Or as okay as things can be at the moment?"

"Jory just asked for my help," said Theodosia. "You know, in trying to solve Uncle Jasper's murder."

Haley slid by Theodosia and began to ladle soup into small, floral print bowls. "Of course he did," she said. "Because you're good at that kind of thing."

"By 'that kind of thing,' you mean solving crimes?"

Haley gave her a funny sideways glance. "Well, yeah. We've all got to be good at something, right? I mean, I'm good at cooking and baking . . . you said so yourself. Drayton's a genius with tea. And a whiz when it comes to stuff like historical facts or cultivating bonsai or competing in chess tournaments."

"And I'm good at solving crimes," said Theodosia, smiling in spite of herself.

"Precisely," said Haley. "Of course, you're good at other things, too. Like marketing and naming products and coming up with new product ideas. But you really excel at sleuthing."

"Sleuthing," said Theodosia. The word sounded funny to her. Old-fashioned and slightly dated. Like the Nancy Drew books she'd inherited from her mother. The ones in which Nancy still drove a spiffy red roadster.

"Sleuthing, investigation, crime solving, whatever," said Haley. "The thing is, your brain is very *adept* at solving puzzles." She looked pleased with her declaration. "Yup, that's it. You've got a nimble brain."

"Someone's brain is going to get beaned if we don't get lunch on the table fast," Drayton interjected from the doorway, looking perturbed and slightly cross. "We have a tea shop full of paying customers and no luncheon entrées to set before them."

"You already served the buttermilk scones?" asked Haley.

"Gone," said Drayton waving a hand. "Finis. Gobbled up immediately by a most appreciative audience. Nary a crumb remains."

"Okay then," said Haley, switching into her version of overdrive. "Theodosia, grab that tray of sandwiches. That's right, the one covered with plastic wrap. Drayton, you put the rest of those little bowls on the plates so Theodosia can nestle two sandwiches right alongside them." She grabbed a big copper ladle. "I'll serve the soup."

The three of them worked busily for the next couple of minutes. Finally, all the luncheon plates were ready to go. "Perfect," declared Haley. "Now let's get this stuff out there while the soup's still hot."

Theodosia and Haley delivered their luncheon entrées to the various tables, while Drayton hustled about pouring tea. Soon the loud buzz of conversation dimmed slightly in favor of the *clink* of soupspoons in bowls and teacups against saucers.

"Ah," said Drayton, standing in his favorite spot behind

the counter. "Once more we register a small success. Don't you love it?"

Theodosia nodded. "I do. Of all the things I could be working at right now, this is what I really love most."

"Me, too," piped up Haley. "Probably because the pay-off's so nice . . . happy customers."

"There's an immediacy to this," mused Theodosia, "that I think is often missing in other lines of work. Here at the Indigo Tea Shop we know right away if a customer is happy. If our product is a success. When I was in marketing, it often took a good six months before we knew if a product had proved itself."

"I don't think I'd like that one bit," said Haley, swooping back toward the kitchen.

By two o'clock things had calmed down considerably. All the lunches had been served and dispatched with. Haley was in the kitchen happily rattling dishes. Two tables of early-afternoon customers sat drinking tea and munching honey pecan scones from Haley's second batch that day.

And just as Theodosia and Drayton were finally able to sit down and enjoy a bite of lunch themselves, Delaine came rushing in.

"Oh, Theodosia," she gushed, "have you spoken with poor Jory?"

Theodosia nodded in the affirmative, while Drayton popped up to grab a cup and saucer so he could pour Delaine a cup of tea.

"Just half a cup, dear," she told him. "I can only stay a minute."

Drayton continued to pour. He'd learned by now that one of Delaine's minutes could easily stretch to the better part of an hour.

"And what is the news regarding Dr. Jasper Davis?" demanded Delaine.

"No good news," said Theodosia. "According to the police

he was apparently killed via some sort of injection. They say they're actively investigating."

"Oh my," said Delaine, taking a sip of tea. "So the rumors are true."

Theodosia blinked rapidly. "Rumors? There are rumors?"

Delaine flashed a bright smile. "Oh, *tons* of them. People have been coming into Cotton Duck all morning with little snippets of news."

"Rats!" said Theodosia.

"The events of last night *were* written up in the newspaper," Drayton reminded her gently. "This is a fairly major story for Charleston."

"I suppose you're right," said Theodosia. She had secretly hoped she might be able to fly under the radar on this one. Investigate some of the people who'd been at the Ghost Crawl last night without setting off too many alarms.

Maybe I'll just have to set off a few alarms after all.

Delaine crossed her legs and adjusted the rather short skirt of her purple knit two-piece outfit.

"You're looking rather slithery," said Drayton as he passed Delaine a small silver bowl filled with sugar cubes. "And quite a vision in purple." He peered at her closely. "Or is that plum?"

Delaine promptly hopped up from her chair and executed a somewhat self-conscious pirouette.

"Mulberry," she replied. "And don't you simply *adore* it? This is the very latest in matte jersey from Marcus Matteo." She smiled prettily. "Know what his nickname is?"

Theodosia and Drayton waited with dubious expressions on their faces.

"The king of cling!" chortled Delaine. "Isn't that marvelous?"

"Hilarious," agreed Drayton.

"Anyway," said Delaine, "The absolutely adorable Marcus Matteo is going to be at my store this coming Wednesday. He's bringing his entire collection in for a very special trunk show." She picked up her teacup and took a delicate sip.

"You heard it here first. Cling is going to be *huge* this season. I guarantee it."

"Then I'll be right in style," said Theodosia. "My apartment is usually so dry, my clothes are constantly charged with static cling."

"Well, there *is* a major difference," said Delaine, frowning and pulling the neckline of her snug-fitting top a little lower. "Marcus Matteo's creations are *designed* to cling."

"Oh, Theodosia clings," said Drayton, much to Delaine's consternation. "Some mornings when she comes downstairs, she's positively *charged* with electrical energy. You could probably run a toaster off her."

Delaine sat back in her chair and pouted. "I didn't come all the way over here to have the two of you poke fun at my new clothing line."

"Sorry," said Drayton. "With all that's transpired, I suppose we just needed a little comic relief." He glanced at Theodosia. "Theodosia does, anyway. It wasn't much fun for her last night."

"Knowing how the two of you like to nose around, I assume you've got your eye on a few likely suspects," said Delaine.

Theodosia decided to ignore Delaine's comment, but Delaine wasn't nearly ready to let things alone.

"I've always had great admiration for Vance Tuttle and his Charleston Repertory Company," said Delaine. "But it *does* seem rather peculiar that ten minutes after his heated argument with Dr. Jasper Davis, the poor man turns up *dead*."

"So you suspect Vance Tuttle," said Drayton.

"Why . . . yes. I suppose I do," said Delaine. "Don't you?"

Drayton shrugged. "To tell you the truth, I hadn't really thought about it."

Delaine's head swiveled in Theodosia's direction. "But *you* have," she said with more than a little confidence.

"Some," admitted Theodosia. "And you're quite correct. Vance Tuttle did seem fairly worked up last night."

"Pray tell, what *was* that all about?" asked Delaine.

"Funding," said Theodosia in a weary tone. "Vance Tuttle was apparently quite upset that Cardiotech had pulled most of their corporate support."

"But that's certainly not a good enough reason to murder someone," remarked Drayton.

Delaine looked smug. "Wake up and smell the scones, Drayton! Don't you know there are insane people out there willing to *murder* someone for less than twenty bucks!"

Drayton shook his head. "I suppose you're right. I *know* you're right." But Drayton was still unwilling to jump to conclusions and appeared considerably more introspective than Delaine. "Tell me again about Dr. Jasper Davis's work at Cardiotech?" he asked Theodosia.

"He helped develop their new angioplasty product," said Theodosia. "Something called the Novalaser."

"Lasers are very big right now," said Delaine. "Especially for removing wrinkles and sun damage." Realizing what she'd just said, she added, "Or so I've heard." She smoothed her skirt and sipped her tea daintily. "Are you two planning to attend that memorial service tomorrow morning?" she asked.

"What's that?" asked Drayton.

"They're holding a memorial service at Cardiotech," Theodosia explained to Drayton.

"In the J. F. Morton Auditorium," said Delaine. "I suppose since the body won't be released for a few days, the company figures this is the least they can do for their dear, departed colleague."

"So you two will be attending?" asked Drayton.

"I'm certainly going," said Theodosia. She looked at Delaine. "I'd love it if you came with me."

Delaine's hand fluttered to her chest. "Well, I'd certainly *like* to, although I'm frightfully busy. Torn to pieces, really, between working on ticket sales for the upcoming Lamplighter Tour and planning my big trunk show." She dropped her voice to a stage whisper. "You know, Cotton Duck just isn't as *profitable* as it once was." Cotton Duck was Delaine's beloved clothing store. Although Delaine was a clever merchandiser and had worked tirelessly to build the shop into one of Charleston's premier boutiques, it, too, had been touched by a sluggish economy.

"Nothing is as profitable as it used to be," sighed Drayton. "Everything's changed. It's certainly not like the good old go-go nineties."

"But women always need *clothes,*" Delaine insisted with a petulant tone.

"Not always," replied Theodosia. As a confirmed clothes horse, Theodosia had firsthand knowledge of what most women had stashed in their closets and dressers, as well as under the bed. She, personally, had probably amassed enough skirts, slacks, dresses, and jackets to rival the inventory at Macy's.

Drayton reached across the table and put his hand atop Delaine's. "It would be a big morale booster if you accompanied Theodosia."

Theodosia, whose sole intent in attending the memorial service tomorrow was to snoop around, lowered her eyes carefully. "It certainly would," she said. With her theatrics and pushy ways, Delaine would make a great smoke screen. Plus, she was socially mobile and knew absolutely *everyone.* And, if you couldn't wangle an introduction to someone, Delaine would just bully her way in.

"Why, Theodosia, I'm truly touched," said Delaine. "Of *course* I'll go with you. What on earth are friends for?" Delaine smiled brightly. "By the way, I wasn't going to bring this up right now, but I want to give my guests some extra special refreshments at my trunk show this coming Wednesday. If you could have Haley whip up a couple pans of her delightful tea cookies plus a cake or two, that would be absolutely peachy." She turned to Drayton. "And Drayton, do you recall that wonderful tea sangria you served at the Heritage Society's lawn party last year?"

"Yes," was Drayton's guarded reply. Like a lamb to the

slaughter, he realized he'd been led into Delaine's trap.

"I'm going to need something like that," said Delaine. "Tasty and refreshing but with lots more pizzazz."

"More pizzazz," repeated Drayton, shaking his grizzled head.

"Good old Drayton, you catch on quick," said Delaine, giving him a knowing wink.

But when Haley heard about Theodosia's plan to be away from the Indigo Tea Shop tomorrow morning, she expressed concern. "Aren't you guys forgetting something?" she asked.

"What's that, Haley?" said Theodosia.

"Besides serving our regular luncheon customers, we're catering that chocolate tea as well." Haley frowned. "For the Below Broad Garden Club." Below Broad was the term used for the elegant, blue-blooded neighborhood located just below Broad Street.

"Lenaia Carter's group," said Drayton.

Two months ago, Lenaia Carter, president of the Below Broad Garden Club, had cornered Drayton and asked him if the Indigo Tea Shop would cater a special tea. A *chocolate* tea to be precise. He had readily agreed and tomorrow was the big day. At precisely two-thirty, thirty-five gardening fanatics, who also had a love for all things chocolate, were going to descend upon the Indigo Tea Room.

"I thought the menu was all planned out," said Drayton.

"It is," said Haley. "Has been for over a month."

"Well, I still intend to brew my special chocolate teas, as well as a few pitchers of chocolate chai," said Drayton, "so I frankly don't see the problem."

Still, Haley wasn't convinced. "Just that we'll be busy," she said. "For the last few weeks our Fridays have been super hectic."

"Why don't we ask Miss Dimple to come in?" suggested

Theodosia. Miss Dimple, their bookkeeper, had helped out at the Indigo Tea Shop a few times before and done a wonderful job.

"Good idea," said Drayton. "I'll call her right now. I think she's working at the Cabbage Patch Needlepoint Shop today."

"No, you brew a couple more pots of tea," said Haley, glancing at their remaining customers. "*I'll* call her."

But before Haley could pick up the phone and dial, it rang once again for Theodosia. This time it was Constance Brucato calling. Constance was the somewhat scatterbrained executive producer for *Windows on Charleston,* a local TV show that ran on Channel Eight.

"Theodosia?" said Constance, almost shouting into the phone, "we're ready to tape that segment."

"Great," said Theodosia. *Segment? What segment?* Then she remembered. A few months ago she'd committed to doing a couple of tea etiquette and tea lore segments for the *Windows on Charleston* show.

"We need to tape soon," shrilled Constance.

"When?" asked Theodosia. Going into a TV studio was absolutely the last thing she wanted to do right now. But maybe she could put it off.

"Next Tuesday," said Constance. "Probably in the afternoon."

Theodosia grimaced. "Is it possible to put this off for a week or two, Constance? I apologize, but I'm deeply involved in some personal matters right now."

Constance Brucato had sent her video crew to the Indigo Tea Shop this past summer to tape footage that was subsequently cut into twenty-second promo spots. The promo spots had been running for several weeks now, so Theodosia supposed the station pretty much had to produce a show.

"Theodosia," said Constance in her best pushy producer voice, "we're all *involved* in something. Nobody ever has a spare *moment*. Right now I'm trying to figure out how my crew can cover the Charleston Air Expo, a children's festival in Shem Creek, and the first week of the Lamplighter Tour and still produce our daily show!"

"You do sound awfully busy," said Theodosia, figuring it was probably now or never for her TV segment. A five-minute tea segment on *Windows on Charleston* would be fabulous PR for her tea shop. There was no way she could say no.

"Besides," said Constance, sounding exceedingly pleased with herself. "I plan to air the first tea segment during day-time sweeps-week."

"Then Tuesday it is," said Theodosia. "As far as content goes, do you want to begin with the tea etiquette concept we brainstormed? Or maybe the tea blending?"

"Let's definitely start with tea etiquette," said Constance. "I see that whole fancy-schmancy tea service thing as a huge hot button right now. Something with beaucoup appeal for our audience."

Hot button. Beaucoup appeal. Good old Constance. Nothing like parlaying the gentle art of tea into a vehicle for sweeps-week.

"Okay, Constance," said Theodosia. "I'll be there."

4

❧

The J. F. Morton Auditorium at Cardiotech was your typical big company auditorium. Plush chairs, lots of burnished wood paneling, and a malfunctioning audio/video system.

Though Dr. Rex Haggard possessed a deep and well-modulated speaking voice, a voice that certainly carried throughout the entire auditorium, the microphone on the podium kept cutting in and out during his memorial speech. Which left Cardiotech's three hundred or so employees fidgeting in their seats, and Dr. Jasper Davis's contingent of relatives in the front row looking rather quizzical and forlorn.

While Rex Haggard eulogized Jasper Davis rather eloquently, calling him a "valuable asset that can never be replaced," he also used his speech as a rallying cry for his company. Rex Haggard talked about "moving ahead," about "setting new benchmarks," and "achieving heretofore-only-dreamed-about goals." His speech was moving, but, at the same time, very rah-rah. And started Theodosia thinking about the somewhat brittle exchange that had taken place between Jasper Davis and Rex Haggard the night of the Ghost Crawl.

Will the company move ahead faster now that Jasper Davis is no longer playing a watchdog role? she wondered. *Possibly. And will the Novalaser be launched sooner rather than later? Absolutely. Rex Haggard said as much in his address.*

Toward the end of Rex Haggard's speech, Theodosia tuned out his platitudes and studied the crowd. After all, people-watching was one of the real reasons she was here.

Besides Jory and his relatives, there was Jasper Davis's Novalaser team, looking rather somber. She'd been introduced to all of them earlier. As well as to a woman named Lois Kimbrough. Lois, it seemed, was the CFO at Vascular Systems Medical, a rival firm of Cardiotech. Still, she and Rex Haggard seemed on friendly terms, probably because they both sat on the board of the Medical Triad.

And then there was the soon-to-be ex-wife, Star Duncan.

Sitting next to Jory, wearing a bright pink couture suit, Star was a bit of a mystery. A successful realtor with her own agency over in Mount Pleasant, Star Duncan and Jasper Davis had been married some three years ago and estranged for the last two. Jory had told Theodosia that theirs had been one of those mad, passionate encounters in which the two of them really had no business getting married. They should have just carried on and let the flame burn out naturally. Now, of course, in the eyes of the State of South Carolina, Star Duncan was still the legal wife of Dr. Jasper Davis. And, aside from any provisions in his last will and testament, entitled to all his real property and moneys.

There was another loud click and an annoying buzz, and then Dr. Rex Haggard motioned toward the back of the room, where a table had been set up and two lunch-room employees stood by to serve coffee, punch, and cookies. The service had obviously drawn to a conclusion.

Theodosia jumped to her feet, eager to get a good look at Star Duncan. "Do you know her?" she asked Delaine. "Star Duncan, I mean."

"I've met her, if that's what you're asking," said Delaine.

Peering over a few heads, Theodosia could see Star Duncan smiling and shaking Rex Haggard's hand. Probably thanking him for the memorial service.

Delaine followed Theodosia's glance. "I love her suit. Hot pink is such a vibrant color."

"More like haute pink," said Theodosia as she began edging out of the row of seats. "Let's go say hello."

But Theodosia and Delaine had barely traveled ten feet when they were waylaid by a large man with a wide, crooked grin and a bright yellow and blue window-pane-checked jacket.

"Say now," the man said, beaming at Theodosia, "you wouldn't be Miss Theodosia Browning, would you?"

Theodosia politely acknowledged that she was.

The man stuck his hand out. "I'm Ben Atherton, president of Vantage PR. We do investor relations as well as handle all the public relations projects for Cardiotech."

"Of course," said Theodosia as Ben continued to pump her hand with great enthusiasm. "Nice to finally meet you. This is my friend Delaine Dish."

"Pleased to meet you," said Delaine as she swiveled her head, scanning the crowd. Theodosia grinned to herself. Delaine was probably hunting for eligible doctors. *Cardiologists.*

Ben Atherton motioned toward a slim, attractive, dark-haired woman who stood a few feet from him chatting with a small clutch of people. "That's my assistant, Emily Guthro," he said.

"I know Emily," said Delaine as Emily began to edge toward their group. "She's one of my customers. One of my *good* customers."

"Well, *hello,* Delaine," said Emily, grabbing Delaine's hand and giving her a warm smile. "I'm certainly looking forward to your trunk show next Wednesday. Thanks so much for the invitation."

Then Emily Guthro turned her full attention on Theodosia. "Tell me, are you the same Theodosia Browning who outfitted a runner in the Boston Marathon with one of Comsense Corporation's wearable computers?" she asked with a mischievous twinkle in her eye.

"Guilty as charged," Theodosia responded as she studied the woman. Emily was younger than she'd originally thought. Maybe twenty-four or twenty-five. But in her tailored navy suit, with her quick smile and sleekly styled shoulder-length hair, Emily certainly gave the impression of a buttoned-up PR professional.

"You're a *legend,*" Emily exclaimed. "PR doesn't get any better!"

"Except when it's handled by Vantage PR," said Ben Atherton with over-the-top enthusiasm. Ben seemed a perpetual jovial sort. Big, friendly, with an open face and almost boyish charm. The kind of guy who had probably perfected the art of the schmooze and could parley with the media as well as hobnob with corporate execs.

"I really loved your concept for the Ghost Crawl," Theodosia told them.

Ben and Emily murmured thank-yous.

"It sure was a shame they decided to cancel the Ghost Crawls on Friday and Saturday night," said Ben Atherton.

"I didn't realize the whole thing had been scrapped," said Delaine. "What a pity."

"Now that's an example of bad publicity," said Ben philosophically. "Shows how critical it is to control the spin." He hooked his thumbs in his belt and rocked back on his heels. "Funny thing about publicity . . . it's a lot like a football. If you don't handle that thing just right and give it a careful boot in the proper direction, the whole thing can skew out of bounds!"

Emily nodded eagerly. This obviously wasn't the first sports analogy her boss had uttered. "Damage control," she chimed in. "That's what was sorely needed. Of course, Vantage PR was never even given the chance. The press got hold of the story and ran with it."

"Grabbed onto it like a rat terrier with a filet mignon," added Ben. He hung his head and shook it slowly. "A darn shame."

Emily gave Theodosia a shy smile. "It was so sweet of you to volunteer your tea shop's catering services the other night."

"It was nothing," said Theodosia. "Maybe we can make it work again next year."

"I hope so," said Emily.

"Such a sad business," said Ben. "Have the police been able to tell you anything at all?"

"Only that they're fairly confident Jasper Davis was given a lethal dose of drugs," said Theodosia. Since the newspapers had run that story this morning, she figured she was safe talking about it here.

But Emily looked stunned. "Oh no! Are you serious? How awful."

"Terrifying," purred Delaine. "Makes me want to stay home and lock all the doors." She flashed Theodosia a sympathetic glance. "Poor Theo. House sitting for Timothy Neville all by yourself in that enormous mansion. It's gorgeous but must feel terribly *empty* when you're alone."

"Tell me," said Emily, still looking stricken, "do the police think this was accidental? Or do they believe a person or persons actually targeted Dr. Davis?"

"I'm afraid they haven't really determined that," said Theodosia.

"The police haven't determined much of *anything*," said Delaine, rolling her eyes, happy to be part of the conversation.

"But they are actively pursuing this," said Ben Atherton, with a hopeful tone.

"They've assured us they'll do everything possible," said Theodosia.

"Good . . . good," said Ben, giving a weak smile.

"And Theodosia is going to look into things, too," volunteered Delaine.

Ben Atherton studied Theodosia closely. "You are?"

"Not really," demurred Theodosia.

"She's extremely *clever,*" announced Delaine, much to Theodosia's consternation.

"I can believe that," said Emily, a kind smile on her face.

"Say now, Theodosia," said Ben Atherton, as though the proverbial light bulb had just gone on over his head. "Since you used to work with a few old friends of mine, I almost feel like I know you. Which means I'm about to step out of line here and ask a small favor."

Theodosia cast a quick glance toward Jory. He was still standing at the front of the auditorium, shaking hands and talking with people.

"What's that?" Theodosia asked Ben.

"My wife is a member of the Charleston Ceramics Guild. And they're having this big art show tomorrow."

Theodosia nodded. She'd heard about the show.

"Anyway, the Ceramics Guild is holding it in their studio in the Tolliver Building," said Ben. "It's supposed to be a big, fancy juried show. Problem is . . . they're a might short on jurors."

Delaine clapped her hands together in delight. "Theodosia would be *perfect*. You know, she helped judge an art show over in Goose Creek last year."

But Theodosia was searching her memory. *The Tolliver Building. Isn't that the same building where the Charleston Repertory Company is located? Sure it is. In fact, a whole group of nonprofit organizations moved in there recently.*

The Tolliver Building, formerly an old textile mill, had been rehabbed using a grant from the State Arts Commission. With the codicil that only nonprofit organizations be allowed to occupy studio and gallery space there.

"Theodosia," said Ben, "is there *any* way I could implore

you to come to our aid tomorrow? The Ceramics Guild is *desperate* to find someone knowledgeable enough to help judge the teapot category."

"Teapots?" said Theodosia. "You just said the magic word."

Twenty minutes later, Theodosia and Jory were walking down a wide, carpeted corridor in Cardiotech's executive wing and heading toward Dr. Jasper Davis's office.

"I really don't relish doing this," Jory was saying. "But *someone's* got to go in and collect his personal things."

Theodosia nodded. The morning's events had been difficult for Jory. He had, indeed, emerged as the family spokesman. As such, he found himself commiserating with Uncle Jasper's former team members and on the receiving end of condolences from many other Cardiotech employees who had known and respected Jasper Davis.

But Jory had used his "cool training," as he liked to call it. His poise and composure, gleaned from many hours spent in courtrooms and taking depositions, had come in handy now that he had to accept so many condolences and murmur his thanks.

Theodosia had been ferociously proud of Jory. Even in the way he had been so kind and solicitous to Star Duncan, whom the rest of the family seemed to regard as a bit of a pariah.

But as they'd sipped fruit punch and mingled with the other attendees after the memorial service, Theodosia had caught more than a few glimpses of Star through the crowd. And she had gotten the distinct feeling that Star might actually be enjoying herself. Might even have used this as an occasion to socialize and pass out a business card or two.

Had Star really been pitching business? At her dead husband's memorial service? If so, it would certainly represent a new low in memorial service etiquette.

"Here's his office," announced Jory. He stopped abruptly

and scanned the walnut-veneer nameplate that hung to the right of the door: "Dr. Jasper Davis, Vice President of New Product Development."

Jory put a hand on the doorknob and turned it. As the door swung inward on its hinges, Star Duncan gazed up at them with a cool, somewhat aloof expression on her face.

"Hello, Jory," she said. She favored Theodosia with a remote smile. "And you must be Theodosia, Jory's special friend. We haven't met yet." Star Duncan looked supremely confident even as she poked through the desk of her estranged husband. Her *dead* estranged husband.

Jory was stunned. What little color he had quickly drained from his face. "What are you doing in here?" he blurted out. The presence of mind he had maintained for the last few hours suddenly eluded him.

Star Duncan gripped the leather journal she held in her hands and Theodosia noticed that Star's fingernails were painted the same brilliant pink as her suit.

"Probably the same thing you were planning to do," replied Star.

"I don't *think* so," said Jory. He was rapidly regaining his composure. "Star, the family has greatly appreciated the concern you've shown in the face of this tragedy, but I must tell you, as executor of Jasper Davis's estate, I'm the only person who has the authority to take charge of my uncle's personal effects."

"No problem," said Star Duncan. She snapped the leather journal closed and assumed a somewhat bemused expression.

Theodosia could not help but notice that, even though Star Duncan was in her early fifties, she was still a *very* attractive woman. Lots of blonde hair and tanned, gleaming skin, good bone structure, and a great figure. Then there was all that jangling gold jewelry and, of course, the hot pink suit. Star looked extremely "va-voom" and knew it. Played to it, in fact.

Tilting her head coquettishly to one side, Star Duncan gave Jory a pussycat grin. "You know, I'm *still* Jasper's wife.

Somehow we just never got around to finalizing that little old divorce." She wrinkled her shapely nose, studied her shellacked nails. "I suppose it was simply a case of two professionals who were wrapped up in their own pursuits." She turned her megawatt smile on Theodosia. "You know how *that* goes."

"Of course," said Theodosia, who decided there were probably more layers to this woman than a prize-winning Vidalia onion.

"I realize you were still married to Uncle Jasper," said Jory. "And I certainly meant no disrespect. It's just that . . ."

"Yeah . . . yeah . . ." said Star Duncan. She took a step backward, flipped a hand to casually indicate the nest of clutter inside Jasper Davis's top drawer.

Theodosia eased herself up on tiptoe to take a peek. Jasper Davis was not exactly what you'd call a neat freak. There was a jumble of paper, pens, and postage stamps, plus a cell phone, checkbook, and Palm Pilot. All personal items that Jory would have to go through.

"Knock yourself out," said Star. She stepped around the desk, flipped open the leather journal again. "This is killer stuff," she said, turning to what looked like the last page on which Jasper Davis had made an entry. "XKE to Bim." She looked up. "Bim's the only guy he'd ever allow to tune his Jaguar." She pronounced all three syllables of the word Jaguar. "Our Jasper was extremely particular about his precious motor vehicles." She gazed down at the book again. "Now let's see if there are any *real* clues to be found."

"Star . . ." said Jory, really beginning to lose his patience.

But Star continued to read from Jasper Davis's notes. "Cardiology journal notes to team . . . laser demo . . . check ECG." Star glanced up. "Pretty scintillating stuff, huh?"

"Okay, Star, that's enough." Jory reached out, wrested the book from her, passed it back to Theodosia.

Theodosia, who was carrying an oversized black nylon Prada bag, slipped the book inside.

Star held up her hands in mock surrender. "No problem,

I'm out of here." But as she brushed by Jory, she put a sun-freckled hand on his arm. "Take it easy, kiddo," she said. "It wasn't me."

Then she was gone. Leaving Theodosia and Jory to stare at each other.

"Is she always that brash?" asked Theodosia. If Star Duncan wasn't so maddening she'd be amusing. She certainly seemed to have a weird sense of humor.

Jory nodded. "She seemed to be on her best behavior during the memorial service, but now she's reverted to . . ." he stopped suddenly and his eyes slid toward the doorway.

Theodosia turned to see what had caught Jory's attention. And saw Emily Guthro, looking extremely flustered and unsure, standing there, giving them a very wide-eyed look.

"Theodosia?" Emily said tentatively. "I'm *so* sorry to interrupt, but Ben wanted you to have this." She pressed a white envelope into Theodosia's hand, then quickly spun on her heels and disappeared.

Oh dear, how long had Emily been standing there? wondered Theodosia. *Probably just a few seconds. But judging from the stunned look on her face, long enough to have witnessed the final stages of our rather embarrassing confrontation with Star Duncan.*

5

❧

"*Thank goodness you're* back!" screeched Haley as Theodosia let herself in the back door to her office. "Get to work!"

Theodosia dropped her handbag, stepped out of her high heels and into a pair of comfy flats, then quickly draped a long white apron around her neck. "Sorry to be so late," she told Haley as she slipped into the kitchen. "Are we frightfully busy? Were you able to get Miss Dimple to help?"

"I'm here, honey," called Miss Dimple, bumping her way into the kitchen with a big silver tray stacked high with dirty dishes. Barely five feet tall and beyond plump, with a cap of pinkish-blonde curls, Miss Dimple was seventy-something and always upbeat. "I wouldn't miss this for the world," she chattered to Theodosia. "When you live with your bachelor brother and a pair of old cats named Samson and Delilah, you take your fun where you can get it." She paused, a broad grin on her pink face. "My goodness you folks have a land-office business going on here today."

"Really," said Theodosia, impressed. "I wonder what's up."

"For one thing," said Haley, planting hands on slim hips, "Drayton dragged those wrought iron tables and chairs around from the back. It's so sunny and warm today, he thought some of our customers would like to sit outside."

"And they did," said Miss Dimple as she exchanged her tray of dirty dishes for another one stacked with Haley's perfect tea-smoked chicken salads. "The problem is, they sat *inside,* too!"

"I think they'd perch on the counter if we let them," grumped Haley as she drizzled peanut sauce over mounded servings of tea-smoked chicken that sat crisp and golden atop little nests of field greens.

"There must be a lot of tourists in town for the Lamplighter Tour," said Theodosia. The Lamplighter Tour was Charleston's annual tour of historic homes. A very special event, when some of the elegant private homes in the historic district threw open their doors for public viewing.

"*Zillions* of tourists," agreed Miss Dimple. "Angie Congdon over at the Featherbed House is full up." Indeed, Charleston was always popular with the tourists. Something like eight million people made their way to Charleston each year to wander her cobblestone streets, gaze at magnificent architecture, soak up the romantic atmosphere, and indulge in such Carolina offerings as rice, grits, fried oysters, chicken perloo, squash puppies, and cooter soup.

"I can't believe you had time to make your special tea-smoked chicken today," Theodosia told Haley. "Especially since we're hosting that chocolate tea right after lunch." Tea-smoked chicken was one of Haley's specialties. She marinated chicken thighs in garlic, ginger, honey, and soy sauce, then actually *smoked* them in a hot cast-iron skillet over tea leaves and brown sugar.

"Tea-smoked chicken isn't as complicated as it looks," said Haley. "Once it's smoking away on the stove, you just throw open the windows and let it do its thing."

"Maybe we better hurry up and do *our* thing," interrupted Miss Dimple. "We've still got a few hungry customers to serve."

"This tray's ready to go," said Haley, placing a final sprig of Italian parsley on a plate.

"I'll help Drayton serve tea," offered Theodosia.

"Good," said Haley, "because I need a little breathing room if I'm going to get those chocolate sour cream muffins baked."

"Lord, love us," exclaimed Miss Dimple, rolling her eyes as if to advertise her weakness for anything sweet.

"How was the memorial service?" asked Drayton as Theodosia joined him behind the front counter.

"Nice," said Theodosia. "Sad but dignified." She watched as Drayton poured hot water into a teapot, swished it around, and dumped it out. Then he ladled six heaping teaspoons of aromatic black tea into the nicely warmed teapot. "You're brewing some of that marvelous Thai oolong?" she asked.

Drayton nodded. "The woodsy and fruity notes should pair nicely with Haley's smoked chicken." This particular Thai oolong, which Drayton had picked up on his most recent buying trip, was grown in the hilly regions of northern Thailand, the so-called Golden Triangle that was also notorious for its poppy production.

"And what else?" asked Theodosia, who, after the rather bizarre behavior of Star Duncan, was deriving great satisfaction in surveying a scarred wooden counter lined with teapots and tea tins and strewn helter-skelter with tea accoutrement like brewing baskets, thermometers, strainers, and timers.

"My old favorite," said Drayton, "Ti Kwan Yin." Also known as the Iron Goddess of Mercy, Ti Kwan Yin was a Chinese oolong with a flavor reminiscent of fresh plums.

"You're a marvel," said Theodosia, giving Drayton a good-natured pat on the back. "Always knowing which tea to pair with what food. But, I have to admit, I'm curious as to which teas you're going to serve at our chocolate tea this afternoon. If it were left up to me, I'd be more than a little intimidated. I mean, these ladies are expecting chocolate *everything*!"

Amusement danced in Drayton's eyes. "Ah, my dear Miss Browning," he said. "Good things come to those who wait."

Theodosia didn't have to wait long. Once the luncheon crowd cleared out around half past one, her team set to work. "Chocolatizing" the Indigo Tea Shop, as Drayton so aptly put it.

Theodosia, Drayton, and Miss Dimple laid fresh, white linen tablecloths on all the tables, then draped them with squares of cocoa-colored organza. For centerpieces, Theodosia had ordered a case of small chocolate flowerpots from a specialty chocolatier. These were hastily lined with foil, then filled with white tea roses. Chocolate-scented candles set in crystal candle holders were added to the tables as well as tiny gold ballotins filled with four miniature chocolates to serve as a favor at each place setting.

"What about dishes?" asked Haley, who had popped out of the kitchen to survey the tables.

"I was planning to use as much of the Countess Grey as we have," replied Drayton. "It has such a pretty café au lait color, as well as that classy crest adorning it."

"And if we don't have enough?" asked Haley, tapping a foot nervously.

"We'll just mix and match where we need to," replied Drayton. "Like we always do. Oh, and let's be sure to use those gilded three-tiered stands."

"How very elegant," offered Miss Dimple.

"Yes," said Drayton, "but all this is icing on the cake. Or, in this case, chocolate squiggles on the cake. Because the food is supposed to be the real star today." He turned toward Haley with an expectant look. "Are you *finally* going to share your menu with us? Tell us what's going to be the order for serving?"

A piece of paper clutched in her hand, Haley bustled over to Drayton. "I wrote it all out for you so there won't be any slipups." Haley was an absolute stickler when it came to serving tea courses in correct order.

Drayton slipped on his reading glasses and scanned the menu. "Good . . . good," he murmured, then squinted at Haley's cramped writing. "What's this course here?"

She snatched the paper away from him. "Here, better let me walk you through it." Haley was clearly dying to share her special chocolate menu with everyone. She waited until she had their undivided attention, then cleared her throat self-consciously. "First course will be chocolate sour cream muffins."

Drayton nodded. "A sublime offering." Not usually given to gastronomic overindulgence, Drayton had been known to devour three or four of Haley's chocolate sour cream muffins in a single sitting.

"Second course," continued Haley, "chocolate zucchini tea bread spread with cream cheese and orange marmalade."

"Perfect," said Theodosia.

"Then what?" asked Miss Dimple, genuinely loving this.

"Poached pears drizzled with chocolate sauce," said Haley. "Followed by jasmine tea truffles."

"Infused with real jasmine tea?" asked Miss Dimple with a smile. She knew the answer.

"Of course," replied Haley. "I use this super-simple truffle recipe that lets you toss in almost anything for added flavor. Grand Marnier, raspberry jam, even tea."

"You've put together a wonderful menu, Haley," said Theodosia. "Congratulations, you've really outdone yourself."

Haley beamed with satisfaction. "But what about the tea?" she pressed Drayton. "After all, it's been billed as a chocolate *tea*."

Drayton removed his glasses and favored them with a wicked grin. "I promised I wouldn't disappoint and I shan't." He held up three fingers. "To hopefully delight our guests, we shall serve three rather lovely teas today. A chocolate cinnamon hazelnut tea, a chocolate orange tea, and one that's slightly unorthodox . . . a chocolate chai."

"Wow," said Miss Dimple, clearly in chocoholic's heaven now. "There really are chocolate-flavored teas?"

Drayton nodded. "An amazing number of different blends in fact. The first two I mentioned came from Woods and Winston, a wonderful tea wholesaler we use. But I've seen all manner of chocolate teas available from various suppliers."

"And," said Theodosia, holding up an intriguing little brown clay teapot for all to see, "Drayton's agreed to let us serve our teas in a few of his special Yi-Shing teapots." Chinese Yi-Shing teapots were fashioned from a lovely dark, chocolatey-looking clay that came from Kiangsu Province in China. Master potters had been turning them out for centuries, often designing them to resemble gourds, bamboo, and melons. Yi-Shing teapots were much prized by tea drinkers the world over for their ability to retain the taste, color, and aroma of tea leaves.

"These are adorable," cooed Miss Dimple, holding up one of the Yi-Shing teapots to admire. "I wish I had a couple of these myself."

Delaine Dish, who was an on-again off-again member of the Below Broad Street Garden Club, pushed through the door first.

"Drayton, sweetheart," she called, "we missed you this morning." True to form, Delaine, whom Drayton had once dubbed "the chameleon," had changed her outfit. This morning, for the memorial service at Cardiotech, Delaine had worn an elegant gray cashmere sweaterdress and dangerous-looking gray suede stiletto heels. Now Delaine was dressed more casually in a knee-length brown suede skirt and creamy silk blouse with a gold lariat chain draped around her neck.

"You're looking very chocolatey," said Theodosia as she bustled into the tearoom with a tray full of tea favors.

Delaine's hand brushed at her skirt. "The skirt you mean? Yes, I *suppose* it is rather cocoa colored."

Theodosia smiled. *Is it possible Delaine just happened to choose a cocoa-colored skirt to wear to the Garden Club's chocolate tea? Naw, there aren't too many clothing coincidences where Delaine is concerned.*

Consulting Drayton's reservation list, Miss Dimple asked, "Is the reservation in your name, dear?"

Delaine shrugged as though she couldn't be bothered with everyday conventions, especially things as mundane as reservations.

"We'll put Delaine over here by the fireplace," said Theodosia, stepping in before Delaine could make a scene. She glanced at her friend. "You're sitting with Brooke, right?"

"Yes," said Delaine. She selected the chair that faced the front door, then plunked herself down. "I must say," she said to Theodosia, "I'm in a bit of a twitter. Marcus Matteo called and . . ."

"The king of cling," said Theodosia.

"Exactly," said Delaine, thrilled Theodosia had remembered. "He's going to be coming in early for the big trunk show . . . and he's asked me out to dinner tonight! Isn't that exciting?"

"Sounds like fun," said Theodosia.

"Fun?" barked Delaine. "This is a man who attends runway shows in Paris and Milan and New York! It will be an absolute joy, a breath of fresh air to discuss fashion with someone who really *understands* it." She stopped suddenly and cocked an eye at Theodosia. "Of course, I didn't mean that you *don't*, dear."

"Of course," said Theodosia. *Trust Delaine to open mouth and insert foot at least once a day.*

Flustered, Delaine waved frantically at Haley, who was

speeding by with a tray of small crystal bowls filled with Devonshire cream that today had been topped with chocolate
shavings. "I'm a little concerned about *calorie* count, dear,"
Delaine told Haley once she had her attention. "Hopefully,
not everything on today's menu is completely *loaded* with
butter and eggs."

"Of course not," Haley assured her. "Not to worry." Then,
once she was out of earshot, Haley muttered: "Today everything's loaded with sour cream and buttermilk and chocolate."

"What are you mumbling about?" Drayton asked. At the
last minute he had also decided to add a Sri Lankan black
tea with a rich mocha undertone to his repertoire.

"Delaine can be so maddening," said Haley. "She talks
about calorie count like it was leprosy."

"I hope you informed her that imbibing moderate
amounts of chocolate is really beneficial," said Drayton.

"That's right, it's the *im*moderate amount that packs on
the pounds," quipped Haley.

"Actually," said Drayton, "scientists have discovered that
chocolate is chock full of theobromine, a feel-good chemical
that stimulates the activity of neurotransmitters in the brain.
So you get a genuine feeling of contentment and well-being
from eating it."

"Theobromine," repeated Haley. "Sounds like it should
be the name of Theodosia's sister, doesn't it?"

Theodosia shook her head at Haley's little joke. "I think
you've been *sniffing* chocolate, Haley. Because you are in *rare*
form today."

"She's always in rare form," added Miss Dimple. "She's
young and cute and feisty as all get out." She chuckled
heartily and her whole body shook with merriment. "An en-
viable combination."

Twenty minutes into their chocolate tea, Theodosia and
Drayton knew they had a runaway hit on their hands. The
chocolate sour cream muffins had been eagerly snarfed, the
two chocolate-infused teas hailed as surprisingly delightful,

and more than a few people had implored Theodosia to *please please please* add a monthly chocolate tea to her repertoire of special event teas.

Theodosia decided that probably wasn't a bad idea. She and Drayton were always looking to add more specialty teas. So far they had done mystery teas, holiday teas, a lavender tea, children's teddy bear tea, chamber music tea, and even a Great Gatsby tea. So why not offer a chocolate tea on a regular basis?

"And this is Haley's chocolate zucchini tea bread," Theodosia told Delaine and Brooke Carter Crockett as she placed two small plates in front of them. Each plate held two finger-sized tea sandwiches, but what made the presentation so spectacular was the chocolate butterfly perched on one of the sandwiches.

Brooke smiled in sheer delight. "A chocolate butterfly?" she exclaimed. "How delightful!" Brooke Carter Crockett, who was in her mid fifties and utterly stunning with her sleek mane of white hair, was a jewelry maker by trade. She also owned Heart's Desire, one of Church Street's premier jewelry shops. Besides crafting delightful pendants, bracelets, and earrings from sterling silver and eighteen-karat gold, Brooke did a brisk business in estate jewelry.

Theodosia had also been blown away by the two-toned butterfly. It was one of those little extras that Haley had added without telling anyone. She had dribbled melted chocolate onto waxed paper in the form of butterflies. Then, when the chocolate butterflies had cooled, Haley had added drips and dabs of white chocolate to create a pattern on the wings. The butterflies were wafer-thin and looked very elegant perched atop the small sandwiches.

"Someday I'm going to steal Haley away from you," Brooke cautioned Theodosia. "Put her to work on some jewelry designs for me." Brooke was particularly famous for her silver oyster pendants and her gold charm bracelets that featured tiny Charleston images such as bags of rice, carriages, wrought iron gates, sweetgrass baskets, shrimp, and palmetto leaves.

"Haley would probably be a whiz at jewelry making, too," laughed Theodosia. "She's a whiz at everything else."

"I was just telling Brooke about the memorial service this morning," cut in Delaine. Nervous over calorie content, Delaine had resorted to pushing her food around on her plate instead of eating it.

Brooke suddenly looked sober. "So sad," she murmured to Theodosia. "Give Jory my sympathies will you? And, of course, I'll send along a card to his family as well."

"That's sweet of you," said Theodosia.

"I was telling Brooke," said Delaine, "that Star Duncan, Jasper Davis's widow, if that's what you'd technically call her, is quite the character. Extremely vivacious and outgoing, with a marvelous sense of style. Did you know she's supposedly the grandniece of Isadora Duncan! Isn't that an absolute kick?"

"You mean that poor, unfortunate dancer from the twenties who got her silk scarf caught in the wheel of a Bugati?" asked Drayton as he stopped by to pour another cup of tea for Delaine and Brooke.

"My goodness, Drayton," purred Delaine, "you're certainly up on your history."

"That isn't history," scoffed Drayton. "Napoleon is history. Charlemagne is history. *Julius Caesar* is history," he added with a flourish as he headed back across the tearoom.

"Excuse me," said a woman at the table next to them. "Did I just hear you ladies talking about the memorial service this morning at Cardiotech?"

Delaine arched a single eyebrow at this interruption. "Yes, we attended. That is, Theodosia and I did."

The woman stood up and crossed the few feet to Delaine and Brooke's table. She was rail thin in her brown tweed suit and deeply tanned with a slash of dark eyebrows and a cap of short dark hair.

"I should have introduced myself sooner," said the woman. "I'm Peaches Haggard. Dr. Rex's better half."

"Good heavens, hello." She shifted her silver serving tray

to her hip and shook hands. "Nice to meet you. This is Delaine Dish and Brooke Carter Crockett." Theodosia hesitated. "But then, y'all probably know each other, you're in the same club."

Peaches Haggard waved a hand. "Are you kidding? I haven't been to a meeting in three years. I'm only here today 'cause my friends threatened to disown me." She grinned. "And I'm a confirmed chocoholic."

"We're glad you made it," said Brooke.

But Peaches Haggard was staring intently at Delaine. "You own Cotton Duck, don't you?"

Delaine looked as though she were suddenly being accused of committing a felony. "Yeees," she said slowly. One of her eyebrows continued to quiver and Theodosia decided that, with her sharp eyes and expectant air, Delaine looked like a coyote. Sniffing the wind, wondering which direction the danger might be coming from.

"I've been meaning to look you up." Peaches Haggard flashed a toothy smile at the group that was suddenly regarding her with great curiosity. "I just opened a little shop called Petite Provence."

"Oh, my goodness," exclaimed Brooke. "Are you talking about that lovely shop over on King Street? Next to Lady Parish's Silver?"

Peaches nodded. "That's me."

"You have a *marvelous* shop," gushed Brooke. Now she was swept up in excitedly telling Theodosia and Delaine of her recent experience at Petite Provence. "I dropped by the other day and, let me tell you, that shop is *packed* to the rafters with authentic French goods, just like a Paris flea market!" Brooke's face was alight as she related this to Theodosia. "You know, beautiful porcelain dolls, French tea towels, antique laces and linens, famille rose plates, hand-milled soaps from Provence, and the most marvelous linen dresses."

"You don't say," sniffed Delaine. She was staring at Peaches Haggard with about as much warmth as someone would exhibit if they found a poisonous snake curled up in their garden. "How interesting."

"Getting Petite Provence up and running has been an absolute blast," said Peaches. "We've only been open a short while, but we've already sold almost half our inventory. We not only had to reorder on antique hat boxes and hand-knit sweaters in our *third week,* but I'm going to have to go back to France and hit the flea markets again. And I have to seriously think about expanding my clothing line."

"More clothing," said Delaine. "Imagine that." Her eyes blazed and bright circles of color appeared high on her cheeks. Noticing this, Theodosia decided Delaine might be dangerously close to a meltdown.

"Oh, not the kind of items you stock," said Peaches, hastening to reassure her. "This would be French clothing. A smattering of haute couture and more of those sweet dresses from Provence. Probably some of those adorable French-made silk camisoles and underpinnings, too. Sweet garments that look almost convent-made. Very exclusive."

"Exclusive," said Delaine, who seemed to have entered a trancelike state.

"Anyway," said Peaches Haggard, moving back toward her table. "I'm sorry I wasn't able to make it this morning, but I was called into an emergency meeting with my merchandise manager. We've got a huge shipment stuck in a customs office at the Port Authority terminal. She chuckled. "No wonder I never have time to tend my garden!"

"That's right," said Brooke, still impressed by Peaches. "You're the one whose entire yard is banked with that marvelous Lady in Red salvia."

"Poor Delaine," said Theodosia as she joined Drayton at the counter. "She's scared to death Peaches Haggard will expand her line of clothing and seriously cut into her business."

"That's fairly doubtful," said Drayton. "After all, Delaine's been in business for quite a good while, something like four or five years. She's fairly well established."

"Six years," said Theodosia. "And you're right, she's not going to get swept aside, but I can still see her point. An exciting new shop opens up, customers can get a little fickle."

"She's jumping at shadows," said Drayton.

"Do you remember when that other tea shop almost opened down the street from us?" asked Theodosia. "In the Ormand Building?"

"Now *that* was different," said Drayton, suddenly frowning. "They weren't even billing themselves as a tea shop. They were going to be a tea *bar*." Drayton curled his lips in a look of sublime disdain. "It was going to be a rush-rush type of place where you just grab the goods, then dash off willy-nilly. Imagine that."

"We do take-out," said Theodosia.

"But most of our take-out customers are busy shopkeepers from up and down Church Street," argued Drayton. "Folks who are in dire need of a pick-me-up. No, tea is meant to be savored. Taking time for tea has always been a highly civilized repast."

"Interesting that the tea bar people were never able to hammer out the terms of their lease," said Theodosia.

"Hmm . . . yes," said Drayton. "Well . . . I've heard Tom Wigley is a real stickler when it comes to leases." Tom Wigley was the landlord of the Ormand Building, as well as an antique dealer and old friend of Drayton's. Tom often called upon the Indigo Tea Shop for catering help when his antique shop was hosting an open house.

Theodosia had always figured that Drayton had enjoyed a private word with Tom Wigley, prompting Tom to skip over the tea bar in favor of leasing to Le Nest, an upscale linen shop that carried Pratesi and Porthault sheets, pillowcases, and duvet covers.

Flustered now, Drayton's eyes roamed toward the kitchen. "Where *is* Haley with those poached pears? It's time to serve our final course."

"Cool your jets," hissed Haley as she and Miss Dimple came hustling out, carrying trays. "Here they are." Haley tipped her tray slightly to show Theodosia. "What do you think?"

"Perfection," breathed Theodosia. The poached pears, elegantly golden and luscious, were drizzled with squiggles of dark chocolate sauce.

"We've got to serve our chocolates, too," said Haley. "There are the handmade jasmine tea truffles, as well as some cameo-shaped chocolates I ordered at the last minute. But I didn't want to just stick them on the same plate as the pears, so I arranged the individual chocolates on a tiered tray along with edible flower petals. I figured Drayton could take it around and serve them."

"But of course," said Drayton, who liked nothing more than to mingle with the crowd. "Lenaia Carter, the president of the Below Broad Garden Club, has already pronounced this a resounding success. In fact, she wants to chat about the possibility of our doing a holiday tea for the Garden Club as well."

"Go for it," urged Haley.

But as Drayton made the rounds of the tables, passing out the chocolate cameos and jasmine tea truffles, he received the inevitable barrage of questions about tea. *Is pekoe really a tea or is it a blend? How many families of tea are there? What about first flush versus second flush?* And so, as he often did, Drayton fell back on reciting a verse from a marvelous poem by T. S. Eliot.

> The naming of teas is a difficult matter,
> It isn't just one of your everyday games.
> Some might think you as mad as a hatter
> Should you tell them each goes by several names.
> For starters each tea in this world must belong
> To the families of Black or Green or Oolong;
> Then look more closely at these family trees—
> Some include Indians along with Chinese.

"He loves this, doesn't he," said Haley as enthusiastic applause for Drayton filled the tea shop.

"More than anything," said Theodosia. Her eyes shone with pride. For, to her, Drayton and Haley were far more than employees or even colleagues. They were family.

6

At the end of a long week, Theodosia would ordinarily scoot upstairs to her cozy apartment above the tea shop. There she would luxuriate in a hot bubble bath (using her own tea-infused T-Bath products, of course) and then get ready for her date with Jory (usually out to dinner or a concert).

On the other hand, if Jory was absolutely swamped with work, she'd clip the leash on Earl Grey's collar, take him out for a quick ramble through the cobblestone lanes and streets of the historic district, then cozy up back home with a bowl of popcorn and a good book.

But Theodosia was still house-sitting for Timothy Neville. Would be for the next week, in fact, while Timothy and his butler, Henry, continued their genealogical research in Bath, England. And try as she might, Theodosia was finding it difficult to cozy up in a thirty-six-room Italianate mansion.

It wasn't that the house wasn't lovely, because it was. Two flanking parlors contained Italian black marble fireplaces,

Hepplewhite furnishings, and ornate chandeliers. Oil paintings and copperplate engravings adorned the walls. The
kitchen gleamed with restaurant-quality appliances; a showy
solarium was stuffed with plush furniture. And should one
desire a few moments of Zen contemplation, there was even
an Asian-inspired garden out back.

But the house was big. Cavernous, in fact. And, truth be
told, awfully lonely.

Whenever Theodosia had been a guest here, Timothy's
house had always exuded a feeling of bustling warmth and
old-world charm. Making it the ideal venue for a cocktail
party, small music recital, or a Heritage Society reception.

But with just her and Earl Grey padding through these
elegant, oversized rooms, the gleaming marble floors suddenly seemed clattery, the huge rooms a little lonely, and
the high ceilings just a touch foreboding.

Woof.

Earl Grey stuck his furry snout under Theodosia's hand
and gave her a rather insistent "hey, don't forget about me"
nudge.

"*You* like it here, don't you?" she asked the dog as she
scratched under his chin. Earl Grey especially seemed to favor
Timothy's cypress-paneled library where they were camped
out now. Luxuriating on the deeply plush Aubusson carpet,
Earl Grey had surrounded himself with his toys. A half-
chewed shoe, a gnarly tennis ball, and a plush yellow chicken
squeak toy that was ubiquitously known as Chickie Poo.

As if in reply, Earl Grey stretched his noble head upward
and sighed contentedly. His normally shiny brown eyes
were half-closed as though he were concentrating fully on
Theodosia's gentle scratches.

Theodosia had been sitting at Timothy's vast leather-
topped mission-style desk for the last half hour, nibbling bits
of cheese and crackers and sorting through all the items Jory
had cleared out of his uncle's desk this morning. Because
she'd had her big Prada bag along, they'd piled everything
into that. Then Jory had asked her to please hang on to the

whole shooting match, since he was up to his eyeballs in family matters. Which was his subtle way of telling her he was busy making funeral arrangements and dealing with the police.

Theodosia hadn't actually gone through everything yet, but it had become apparent to her early on that, besides being a pack rat, Jory's Uncle Jasper had also been a bit of a technology junkie. The man had an MP3 player, a Palm Pilot, and a camera phone that she assumed would also do text messaging.

Well, why not? He was a scientist after all. One who adapted a laser to actually assist in a new form of angioplasty.

Picking up the neat-looking silver cell phone, Theodosia punched it on and studied it carefully. Then, as an idea took shape in her head, she stood up and motioned to Earl Grey.

"Hey there, big fella," she said to the dog, "jump up in this chair, okay?"

Earl Grey, never one to quibble with the generous lady who fed him so well, immediately jumped into Timothy's leather tufted chair as per instruction.

"Hmm," said Theodosia. Gazing about Timothy's library, she spied a gray felt fedora hanging on a brass hat rack. "Perfect," she declared as she snatched it up, then plunked it atop Earl Grey's head. And, since Earl Grey's Dalbrador head was rather ample and Timothy's head fairly small, the hat fit perfectly.

"Smile now," she told the dog, who was definitely beginning to resemble Sam Spade. "We're going to take a picture and try to send it. Let's see if we can cheer up Jory."

Moving around to the front of the desk, Theodosia aimed, framed, and clicked the shutter. Then it was just a matter of pushing a few buttons before the photo was digitally speeding its way to Jory Davis's laptop computer.

Timothy's desk phone rang twenty minutes later.

"Thank you for making me laugh," said Jory, without preamble.

"You got it!" exclaimed Theodosia, rocking back in the leather chair. "I wasn't even sure I did it correctly."

"Oh, I got it all right," said Jory. "Tell Earl Grey he looks better than most of the private investigators our law firm hires. Except for one fellow who seriously does resemble a bloodhound."

Theodosia's heart warmed to hear Jory sounding so chipper again.

"Gosh, I wish I were there with you instead of sitting in my office dealing with things," said Jory.

Oops. Now he sounds a little down again.

"Sorry," she said. She'd meant to cheer him up, not make him feel even more lonely and estranged.

"No, no, I'm fine," he said. "Glad to see you're fooling around with that stuff. I was hoping you would."

"Are you sure?" asked Theodosia. She reached out and touched the little silver phone. "Actually, I'm kind of knocked out by this camera phone. It's so tiny and techie."

"Then consider it yours," said Jory.

"Really?" said Theodosia, pleased. "Are you sure? Is that even legal? Doesn't everything have to go through probate or something?"

"Don't worry about it," said Jory. "Let's just say I've got an *in* with the executor of the estate. And listen, you're doing me a huge favor by going through Uncle Jasper's stuff." He paused. "I *did* ask for your help, remember?"

"Okay," said Theodosia. "I don't presume to find any glaring clues, but, hey, I'll keep pawing through and see what I can find."

"I thank you," said Jory. "With all my heart. Oh, and Theo?"

"Yes?"

"It looks like Uncle Jasper's two brothers won't be arriving until Monday, so I was thinking maybe we'd still go riding this Sunday."

"Are you sure you really want to?" she asked. "You're not

just saying that because you think I'll be disappointed if we don't go?"

"Actually," said Jory, "I was thinking it might be nice to run away from all this for a few hours and blow the cobwebs out of my head. And it'd be nice to be among Uncle Jasper's friends, too."

"There *is* something highly therapeutic about that," agreed Theodosia, thinking about how much positive energy she drew from just being around Drayton and Haley.

"Then it's a done deal," said Jory. "I'll call you tomorrow, and I'll for sure *see* you Sunday morning. Okay?"

"Perfect," said Theodosia. "In fact, now I'm really looking forward to it."

"Take care then," said Jory as he hung up. "And *please*, keep looking through Uncle Jasper's stuff."

"Okay," she replied. "I will."

The Palm Pilot turned out to be brand spanking new. No notes, no addresses, no schedules stored on it yet. So that device was a complete dead end.

The camera phone was just that. A spiffy new camera phone. But there were already a couple dozen or so numbers stored on it. Probably the ones Jasper Davis had called most frequently, Theodosia decided. She copied them all onto a sheet of paper so she could pass them along to Jory when she saw him on Sunday.

The MP3 player was maybe ten percent filled with music that Jasper had downloaded from the Internet. Mostly jazz. Some Miles Davis and Charlie Parker, a little Thelonius Monk.

That left the leather journal. The date book that Star Duncan had been perusing just this morning.

Flipping through the journal, Theodosia quickly found the last page that seemed to bear any of Jasper Davis's handwritten notes. That was the page for this past Wednesday. The day he'd died.

Jasper had blocked out the entire morning for a staff meeting, but had not written in any appointments for the afternoon. Presumably he'd just been at work. But at the bottom of the page he'd scrawled the word "Jasmine" in red ink. "Jasmine" for Jasmine Cemetery.

Theodosia stared across the room at one of Timothy Neville's vast bookcases and allowed her thoughts to wander.

What if Uncle Jasper hadn't shown up for the Ghost Crawl two nights ago? Would someone still have been out to get him? Maybe. Probably. But who? And where else would they have tried to waylay him?

Tapping a finger on Timothy's desk, Theodosia knew she still didn't have a thing to go on.

Turning her attention back to Jasper Davis's journal, Theodosia paged back to the previous day. Tuesday. As she scanned the pages, the few jottings that were there jumped out at her. "XKE to Bim. Cardiology journal notes to team. Laser demo. Check ECG."

These were the notes Star Duncan had read aloud to her and Jory this morning. Notes that Star had seemed to find amusing but not terribly . . . what was the term she'd used? *Scintillating.*

Theodosia stared at Jasper's notations. They did seem like straightforward business notes about fairly garden-variety stuff. Certainly nothing you'd stare at for a while, then smack your forehead and yell "Aha!"

Feeling slightly let down, Theodosia paged ahead in the book.

Was there something Jasper Davis was supposed to have done today?

There was. Right next to the 10:00 A.M. notation he'd written the words "Sojourner Enterprises."

Sojourner Enterprises? What's that? It could be a company, but it doesn't sound medical. Could Jasper have been going to meet with a potential investor?

Theodosia thought about that possibility for a few seconds, then decided it was pretty far-fetched. Jasper Davis had been a VP in charge of new product development. Securing investors just wasn't his territory. Ferreting out "angels" or silent investors would have more likely been handled by the chief financial officer or chief executive officer, who, of course, was Dr. Rex Haggard.

Sliding open a desk drawer, Theodosia pulled out the Charleston phone directory and slapped it down on the desk. She wet a finger, then paged through the business listings.

Sojourn Inn. Sojourn Motel. Here it is. Sojourner Enterprises.

The company was listed in bold type along with its address, 2749 Greeley Mill Road, and phone number.

Seems to me Greeley Mill Road is outside Charleston proper. Quite a ways out. Maybe . . . past the Edisto River?

With a slight frown, Theodosia picked up her pen and added Sojourner Enterprises to the list of numbers she was planning to give Jory. Maybe *he'd* have some insight into what his Uncle Jasper had been up to.

Wandering into Timothy's vast kitchen some twenty minutes later, Theodosia brewed herself a small pot of Angel Oak, Drayton's own blend of relaxation tea that contained chamomile, rosehips, papaya, and vanilla.

And as Theodosia crawled into bed later, she wondered sleepily how Delaine's date with the designer Marcus Matteo had gone. Or if it was still going on.

7

~❧~

The Charleston Ceramics Guild occupied a large, sunny space on the second floor of the historic Tolliver Building. Since the structure had once been a textile mill, the original oak flooring was still in place, as were the ocher-colored brick walls and floor-to-ceiling windows.

Theodosia arrived a little after two o'clock to find a gaggle of amateur potters and their well-wishing guests milling about the front third of the space, where they were sipping wine and nibbling bits of cheese, talking excitedly about the judging. Here, a gallery of sorts had been created. Heavy-duty Parsons tables and wall shelving of unfinished pine had been erected to display the various wares that guild members had produced over the past year.

Theodosia found the scene surprisingly impressive. She hadn't been sure what she'd gotten herself into when she accepted Ben Atherton's invitation to judge the teapot category.

But now she felt reassured by the high level of skill and artistry that she saw displayed here.

The wooden shelves and tables held all manner of ceramic vessels. Tall, graceful urns, squatty pots, large bowls, and even squared-off ceramic vases with basket-like handles. Gazing at this marvelous array of ceramics, Theodosia was also struck by the variety of glazes the potters had employed. A red oxblood glaze spilled down the side of a small cylindrical vase. Gray-green celadon glaze adorned a pair of tea bowls that to an untrained eye could almost pass for Ching Dynasty. Cream-colored crackle glaze added interest to an elegant, elliptical bowl.

And there were pots with unusual and often amusing surfaces and glazes, too. Pots that had bubbled and buckled during the intense firing process until they resembled mirthful modern creations. Jars that were wonderfully pitted and dotted with free-form patterns caused by serendipitous flare-ups of ash in the kiln.

But what impressed Theodosia most were the teapots.

A teapot isn't an easy vessel to create. The right thickness (or thinness, really) of clay is essential. The wall must be engineered to retain heat, yet not be so heavy that it's prohibitive to lift. A good, workable spout that pours but doesn't drip is a must, and the handle must be comfortable and user-friendly. On top of all that, a teapot's simply got to have personality.

Theodosia was a firm believer that everything brought to the tea table should somehow add to the experience. A teapot could be elegant and slightly aristocratic, simple and functional, or even amusing—but it had to exude *some* sort of personality or character. After all, the whole goal in taking time out of the day for tea was to have an enjoyable, enriching experience.

In Theodosia's mind, three key elements were necessary for a successful tea time: outstanding tea and treats, meaningful conversation with friends or a serene and contemplative sip by yourself, and the perfect tea accoutrements.

And teapots certainly counted as tea accoutrements.

"Theodosia!" Ben Atherton had spotted her from twenty paces away and now pushed his way through the artsy-looking crowd to greet her. "You made it," he enthused. "Wonderful!" He grabbed Theodosia's hand and pumped it with hearty exuberance.

"This is such a great space," said Theodosia, still gazing around the industrial-space-turned-gallery.

But Ben was far from finished with his greeting.

"And this," he said, somehow magically producing a small woman in a bright yellow jumpsuit, "is Cleo!"

Theodosia smiled tentatively at Cleo. "Hello," she said to the woman with a wide, bright smile and spiky, razor-cut hair that gave her the slight appearance of an artichoke. She wondered whether Cleo was a potter, the Ceramics Guild's executive director, or one of the show volunteers. But Ben Atherton immediately jumped in to answer that question.

"Cleo is a board member and one of the Ceramics Guild's foremost potters," he announced with pride. Then he added: "She's also my wife."

Bingo, thought Theodosia. *The wife. Well, Ben is certainly over-the-top enthusiastic about her. They must be a good match.*

"I've heard so much about you, Theodosia," bubbled Cleo. "Ben's told me all about your marketing career, your wonderful tea shop, and, of course, your very close friendship with Dr. Jasper Davis, God rest his dear departed soul."

Theodosia blinked. *Very close friendship? Not really.*

"Dr. Davis and I were acquaintances," she explained. "I'm not sure I'd say we were close . . ."

But Cleo suddenly grabbed Theodosia by the arm and pulled her toward one of the long Parsons tables. "This way, dear," she said, her grip amazingly strong for such a small woman. "The teapots you'll be judging are over here."

Theodosia gazed back over her shoulder, looking for help from Ben Atherton, but he seemed to have disappeared into the crowd. So she decided to make the best of the situation and focus her attention on the tables laden with teapots.

"Judging on the other categories started ten minutes ago," Cleo instructed briskly, suddenly switching to a no-nonsense, businesslike demeanor. "So you'll need to make your selections fairly quickly." Cleo picked up a clipboard from the table and thrust it into Theodosia's hands.

"There are eleven teapots in all and each one is numbered," continued Cleo. "What we're looking for right now is a first-, second-, and third-place winner in each category." She smiled sweetly as Theodosia digested all this. "Once those ribbons are awarded, we'll take all category first-place winners, conduct a second judging, and award a best in show. Nice, big purple ribbon." Cleo suddenly stopped and took a gulp of air. "What more can I tell you?" she asked.

"I think you've pretty much covered it," said Theodosia. She decided that Cleo seemed like a well-meaning, buttoned-up volunteer. The kind any organization would be lucky to have. "And thank you. You seem to have everything very well organized and set to go."

"Hopefully," said Cleo, narrowing her eyes and carefully perusing the row of teapots. "As you can see, we've got a little bit of everything here."

"And they all look gorgeous," said Theodosia, her eyes drinking in the shiny glazes, lovely contours, and artfully arched handles. "I'd say judging is going to be fairly difficult."

Cleo curled a finger for Theodosia to come closer, and Theodosia, who was a head taller than Ben Atherton's wife, inclined her head downward in response.

"If you *really* get stuck," whispered Cleo, "just keep in mind that my teapot is number seven."

And with that, Cleo Atherton spun on the heels of her matching yellow wedgies and sped off.

Theodosia groaned inwardly.

Awww. Did Ben Atherton's wife just set me up or what? Give me a break!

Theodosia's first impulse was to walk out. To set the clipboard down on the table and forget the whole thing.

But . . . there were ten other potters here who had made lovely teapots and *hadn't* tried to sway her opinion. Didn't they deserve a fair shake? Sure they did. Of course they did.

Trying her best to put the whole incident behind her, Theodosia set to work eyeballing the teapots. She decided that she probably needed to employ some sort of methodology in her judging. So, at the bottom of the page, she hastily scrabbled out the gist of how she'd form her decision.

She would award one to five points for overall functionality. How did the teapot feel when you picked it up? Did it balance nicely? Was the lid seated properly? And she would give another one to five points for sheer artistic flair and originality. Did the teapot intrigue her or make her smile? Was it sensuous-looking or whimsical? Did the teapot project its own unique personality?

It took Theodosia about fifteen minutes to inspect each and every teapot and come up with her numerical scores. The one that stood head and shoulders above all the others turned out to be a round, almost pumpkin-colored ceramic teapot with a dark brown twig-shaped handle. It had a plasticity to it that was intriguing and unique, and the teapot itself just begged to be handled. Surprisingly, Cleo Atherton's teapot, a small turquoise-colored vessel with a stubby spout, weighed in at number three.

Heading back to the judges' table, Theodosia wondered if Cleo Atherton would hold her third-place designation against her. Or, worse yet, would Ben?

Interestingly enough, it wasn't an issue. Cleo glanced at Theodosia's final tally sheet, nodded briskly, then passed it on to another volunteer for tabulation. "Thanks, Theodosia," she said. "If you're interested, there's a demonstration just starting. A couple of potters from Edgefield."

Edgefield County in the northern Piedmont Region, or Pee Dee, was renowned for its thick deposits of sticky gray clay. In the early eighteen-hundreds, pioneers who'd settled there began fashioning bowls, platters, and water jars from the clay, kicking off a thriving industry. Today, contemporary Edgefield potters were still recognized for their artful pottery.

But Theodosia was more interested in inspecting the dozens of unfired bowls, plates, and sculptures that rested on drying racks in the back of the studio, next to the half dozen or so pottery wheels, large plastic clay bins, and firing kilns.

"Don't you just love green ware?" Cleo asked Theodosia, following her gaze. "It's so raw and rustic and full of promise."

"I know what you mean," agreed Theodosia. "Once clay is molded and shaped, it's still only half done. Color and glaze and texture are what really impart the final personality." She turned to face Cleo. "Does your husband enjoy this as a hobby, too?"

"Ben?" laughed Cleo. Her face filled with amusement. "Good heavens no. He's far too busy with work. That man has lots of irons in the fire. And I do mean *lots*."

"Oh really?" said Theodosia, detecting something in Cleo's voice. Something unsaid, but something Cleo was dying to divulge just the same.

"Would you believe," said Cleo, dropping her voice to a stage whisper, "that Ben just nailed down a monthly column with an extremely prestigious magazine?"

"Very impressive," said Theodosia, letting a couple of beats pass. "Which magazine is it?"

"*Medical Innovations,*" said Cleo. "Do you know it?"

"I do," said Theodosia. She had once handled an account that manufactured a line of diabetes products and had placed their print ads in the publication, *Medical Innovations*.

"It's a fabulous coup for Ben," enthused Cleo, obviously bursting with pride over her oh-so-successful husband.

"It certainly is," agreed Theodosia, even as the words *conflict of interest* bubbled up in her brain. Should a PR professional whose job it is to promote a medical products company also be carefully aligned with a publication that deals with the medical industry and its reports on product news? Hardly.

"Ben's new column kicks off next month," confided Cleo. "He was just telling me that the Novalaser is going to be his first big story. Now that it's going to be released a little ahead of plan, of course."

"Of course," said Theodosia, thinking back to the subtle disagreement that took place between Dr. Rex Haggard and Dr. Jasper Davis the night of the Ghost Crawl. Rex Haggard had been hot to release the Novalaser, Jasper Davis had seemed hesitant. Now Jasper was dead and Ben's wife was chortling merrily about what a big scoop the Novalaser story was going to be.

Is Ben Atherton a yes-man for Rex Haggard? Theodosia wondered. *Maybe. Probably. Okay, then, here's the real biggie. Could the two of them have conspired against Jasper Davis? Or did Ben perhaps have a personal agenda that might have included getting rid of Jasper Davis?*

Theodosia shivered. She had come here to judge teapots for the Ceramics Guild because she thought it would give her an opportunity to scuttle upstairs and snoop around the Charleston Repertory Company. After all, Vance Tuttle was the one who'd engaged Jasper in a nasty argument the night he was killed.

And now . . . now an entirely new possibility had presented himself. Jovial, forty pounds overweight, gladhanding, PR big shot Ben Atherton. *Ben a suspect? Yeah, maybe.*

"Oh, Theodosia," said Cleo, breaking into her thoughts. "You *will* stick around to help us judge best in show, won't you?"

"Sure," said Theodosia. "No problem. When do you think that will be?"

Cleo glanced at her watch and pursed her lips. "Maybe . . . another twenty minutes?"

Great, thought Theodosia. *Time enough to run upstairs and have a quick look around. Then come back down and maybe have a little chat with Ben. If he's still here, that is.*

Loud, boisterous laughter erupted from a group of people across the room and Theodosia saw that Ben Atherton was, indeed, still present and accounted for. The perfect PR guy, yucking it up with the volunteers.

It was sublimely quiet and a good ten degrees cooler in the hallway as Theodosia made her way down the wide corridor. Heading toward a short flight of wide stone steps, she was determined to get a peek inside the Lebeau Theater, home to the Charleston Repertory Company.

The Lebeau Theater itself had come under fire from other arts groups a year ago when the Charleston Repertory Company had spent well over a million dollars to complete the renovations.

Theodosia had one foot balanced on the first step when a voice suddenly called out to her: "Having a good snoop?"

Startled at the words, Theodosia's initial reaction was to flinch. Then, trying to compose herself as best she could, she turned and glanced over her shoulder. When she saw who it was, she let out a self-conscious laugh. Emily Guthro, Ben's young assistant, had just emerged from the ladies' room. A small camera on a leather strap dangled from one hand.

"Emily . . . hi there," said Theodosia. "Actually, I'm just playing curious visitor. I've never been in this building before and was wondering how the architects went about turning the other half of this space into a theater."

"Oh, it's really neat," said Emily, hustling over to join Theodosia. "This old textile mill is a marvelous place. It just goes on and on." She grinned as she slung her camera around her neck. "Come on, let's go take a look."

"You're taking pictures today?" asked Theodosia.

Emily made a face. "Ben tapped me to take photos of the Ceramics Guild's big hoo-ha. He's going to try and get

them in the *About Town* section of *Charleston Magazine*."
Maybe even the newspaper, too."

The two women climbed the wide staircase and pushed
open the double doors that led into the Lebeau Theater.

"Wow," enthused Theodosia as she gazed around. "This
is terrific."

"Isn't it?" said Emily.

The Lebeau Theater yawned before them. Entering from
the main lobby as they had, put them at the top row of seats.
From there, rows of plush midnight blue theater seats
stretched out to either side of them and descended rather
steeply until the rows flattened out and the first row of theater seats was just about even with the low-rise wooden
stage.

"I love this theater-in-the-round concept," said Emily. "It
means there isn't a bad seat in the house."

Slowly, the two women descended toward the stage.

"I'm glad I ran into you today," said Theodosia as their
footsteps echoed in the deserted theater.

Emily waved a hand. "If Ben's involved, then I'm involved.
He's always dragging me into things. But it looks like this
Ceramics Guild project is going to be fun after all. Ben
completely turned the reins over to me—asked me to handle all the promotion and PR."

"He must feel you're very capable," said Theodosia.

"I guess so," said Emily. "At least I *hope* I am. I was able to
get the Ceramics Guild mentioned on a couple of radio shows
earlier this week and I think that really helped boost today's
turnout. Anyway, I think it did."

"Sure it did," said Theodosia, encouragingly. "Every little bit of media exposure helps. I've been doing PR for Spoleto the past couple years and I'm thrilled when even a
teeny, tiny radio station over in Goose Creek or Moncks
Corner wants to do an interview or list events in their community calendar."

"But Spoleto is Charleston's major art festival," said
Emily, impressed. "That must be *tons* of work."

"It is," said Theodosia. "But it's fun. And I always love a challenge," she laughed.

"So how did the teapot judging go?" asked Emily.

"It went well," said Theodosia. "I was impressed. There certainly seems to be a wealth of talented potters in these parts." She didn't bother to tell Emily that her boss's wife had tried to curry favor with her.

When Theodosia and Emily reached the stage, they gazed at the three-sided open stage edged with footlights.

"This is a wonderful theater," said Theodosia. "I can understand why Vance Tuttle is worried about finding money to keep this place open."

"I think all arts organizations are going through a bit of a crunch," offered Emily. "At least all the ones I've done PR for."

"I guess Vantage PR does its fair share of pro bono work," said Theodosia.

Emily nodded. "Yes, but thank goodness we also have *real* clients like Cardiotech," she said just as a door slammed shut somewhere backstage. "I'm still a 'newbie' in the business, but it doesn't take a genius to recognize that times are tough."

"Is there a large backstage area, too?" asked Theodosia, continuing to look around.

Emily flashed a conspiratorial smile. "Don't know, but I assume so. Let's have a look, shall we? It *sounds* like somebody might be home."

The two women crossed the bare stage, then ducked behind the back wall. After wandering through a staging area that was surprisingly open and expansive, they hooked a right and turned down a long corridor. A window-lined brick wall ran along the left side. On the right was a row of offices. What looked to be a sort of "green room," a small costume department, and a large room filled with phone banks, where volunteers undoubtedly staged fund-raisers and conducted telephone ticket sales.

"I think I hear voices," said Emily. "Somebody's back here."

They stopped at another door and peeked in. This work room was stacked with office supplies and contained a copier and fax machine.

"No," said Emily. "Guess I'm just hearing things."

Theodosia, who happened to glance out of one of the nearby windows, suddenly caught sight of two people walking across the back parking lot. "No, a couple people *were* here. But now they're . . ." She stopped midway through her sentence, surprised that she recognized the two people she was gazing down upon.

"Theodosia?" said Emily, sounding worried.

Theodosia continued to stare out the window, and watched as Vance Tuttle pulled open the door of a bright red Porsche 911, then held out his arm to help Star Duncan climb in.

"Hey," said Emily, glancing out the window and frowning. "I remember her from the memorial service. Isn't that Jasper Davis's wife?"

"Star Duncan," said Theodosia in a flat tone. *What is she doing here? And with Vance Tuttle?*

"Who's that with her?" asked Emily.

"The director of the repertory company," said Theodosia, still in a state of mild shock.

"*That's* Vance Tuttle?" asked Emily, peering down at him. "Hmm."

"You know him?" asked Theodosia.

Emily shook her head. "I really only know *of* him." She stared at Theodosia and suddenly looked uncomfortable. "I mean . . . just from what I heard happened the other night. The infamous *argument*. Which I guess makes it all the more weird to see those two together."

Theodosia bit her lip and continued to stare.

"You don't think he . . . ?" Emily's eyes suddenly widened and her voice dropped off.

"Had something to do with Jasper Davis's death?" said Theodosia, picking up what had to be Emily's unspoken thought. She stared at Vance Tuttle as he slammed the driver's side door on the Porsche, then waved a merry good-bye to Star. He turned, started across the parking lot toward an older model Mercedes-Benz, then glanced up at the window where the two women peered out. Both instinctively took a step backward but not before a gleam of recognition flashed in Vance Tuttle's eyes.

"Listen, I gotta get back," said Emily. "Ben's going to be looking for me."

"Me too," said Theodosia, thinking to herself: *Whatever Vance Tuttle is up to with Star Duncan, I need to get to the bottom of it.*

"Are you really looking into things like Delaine Dish said?" Emily asked as the two of them retraced their steps.

"A little," Theodosia admitted. "For Jory's sake."

Emily gave an encouraging nod. "You go, girl," she said. "Jasper Davis was one terrific guy. Even when we managed to screw up a few technical details in his press releases, he was always very patient."

"Jasper Davis got along with everyone?" Theodosia asked. "Ben Atherton? The rest of the people in your firm?"

"Oh, sure. Dr. Davis was always a real gentleman. Not like *some* people at Cardiotech," said Emily, making a face.

"By some people, I'm guessing you might mean Rex Haggard?"

"The big poobah," laughed Emily. "Or at least that's what we call him back at the office. *He's* not exactly a picnic to deal with, although Ben never seems to have any problems. Then there are a couple guys in R and D who are total jerks."

"Which ones are those?" asked Theodosia.

"Sam Hillary and Donald Beim," said Emily. "And are they ever *nasty*!"

"Were Hillary and Beim at Jasmine Cemetery Wednesday night?" asked Theodosia.

"Sure," said Emily. "Ben shanghaied me to work at the front gate collecting tickets, so I'm pretty sure I remember seeing them come in."

Theodosia thought for a minute. "Tickets to the Ghost Crawl were pre-sold, right?" she asked.

"That's right," said Emily.

"So you'd have a list of names?"

Emily shook her head. "No. Sorry. Names were never attached to any tickets. We just sold them to whoever wanted one. It's not like we had a raffle or anything."

"Too bad," said Theodosia. "Then we might at least have had a list of suspects."

8

❧

Night had a firm grip on Charleston. No birds stirred save a few barred owls, nocturnal city dwellers that floated soundlessly on outstretched wings, searching backyards for small prey. An occasional star glimmered as the clouds shifted and parted over the harbor. On Patriot's Point a foghorn emitted a low moan, warning incoming ships of nearby shoals.

On Archdale Street, just a few blocks from the famed Battery, Theodosia emerged from sleep like a diver coming up for air. She gasped, her eyes flew open, and she glanced about the dark room in surprise. Heart jittering inside her chest, Theodosia felt a sense of unease suddenly engulf her.

Something woke me up. What?

There had been a noise somewhere in the depths of Timothy Neville's old house. Not really a *creak,* not quite a *clunk.* But a subtle sound nonetheless.

That's it. A sound. From . . . somewhere downstairs?

Propping herself up on one arm, Theodosia squinted at

the alarm clock that sat on the nightstand. The old brass clock read 5:30 A.M. She grimaced, knowing the calm, cool light of dawn was still a good hour away.

Okay now. Did I hear a real sound or was it something I dreamed?

Cocking her head and listening hard, Theodosia didn't hear the sound repeated. All seemed quiet.

Still . . .

Theodosia pushed back a mound of goose down comforters and sat up quietly. Then, as a kernel of an idea formed in her head, she leaned expectantly over the side of the bed.

I'll bet Earl Grey is having a nocturnal romp. Enjoying a rousing game of toss the chickie.

Peering down, squinting in the darkness, she saw that Earl Grey was sprawled out on his tartan dog bed, snoring contentedly, his big paws twitching. His furry, yellow Chickie Poo toy lay on the floor next to him.

Maybe it's Dreadnought, Timothy's old Manx cat. Although he's an awfully quiet fellow, hardly ever seen or heard from. So . . . maybe someone really is prowling around downstairs?

Quietly, stealthily, Theodosia slipped out of bed. She crossed the bedroom, her feet inches deep in the plush pile of Timothy's Chinese carpet. Her hand was on the doorknob before she realized she didn't have any sort of weapon. Timothy had amassed a fine collection of antique pistols, but those were downstairs, recently put on display in a new glass case in his library.

A lot of help those pistols are to me now!

On impulse, Theodosia reached over to the dresser and wrapped her hand around a thick, brass candlestick.

Why do I suddenly feel like a character out of an Agatha Christie mystery? Padding about in my pajamas, wielding an antique candlestick?

Then, when Theodosia realized Earl Grey wasn't beside her, she went back and gave his dog bed a gentle nudge with her bare foot.

Psst! Get up, faithful companion. I could use a little moral support.

Earl Grey peered up at her, stuck his rear end in the air, and stretched languidly. Then, with one graceful movement, he eased himself out of bed.

That's more like it. Good dog.

Together they slipped out of the bedroom, tiptoed down the hallway, then descended the grand staircase to the main level.

Arriving on the main floor seemed anticlimactic. No boogey man popped out to terrorize them. No disconcerting bright lights suddenly flashed in their faces. No clattering footsteps scrambled hastily for the nearest exit.

Instead, Theodosia turned on all the lights, room by room, as they conducted a thorough search of the premises. Main salon, solarium, library, living room, dining room, breakfast nook. By the time they finally reached the kitchen, the last room in the house, Earl Grey figured he had worked hard enough for one day. He padded over to his stainless-steel dog dish, stared steadily at it for a few moments, shifted his meaningful gaze to Theodosia, then stared back at the dog dish. It was his way of telling her *You woke me up pretty darned early. Don't you think I deserve a nosh?*

Theodosia decided she probably wasn't going to log any more sack time herself. And that after their big false alarm, *she* probably deserved a good breakfast, too.

Rattling around in Timothy's large, amply supplied kitchen, she chopped onions and red pepper, snipped chives, and grated some nice Gruyère cheese. Then she whipped it all together with a couple of the fresh brown eggs that Haley had sent home with her. As her omelet sizzled on the big blue Wolf six-burner stove and she sipped a cup of Ceylon breakfast tea from the Kenilworth Estate, she fixed breakfast for Earl Grey.

Being the picky eater that he was, Earl Grey had inspired Theodosia to come up with an interesting mix that was similar to GORP—the granola, oatmeal, raisins, and peanut concoction that hikers and campers always seemed to swear by.

Only Earl Grey's canine version was called KRBY. Kibbles, raisins, banana, yogurt. The recipe wasn't all that complicated: One cup of dry dog kibbles, a sprinkle of raisins, two slices of banana, and a small scoop of plain yogurt.

And the dog loved it. Adored it to be more precise. And since Theodosia had stumbled upon this magic concoction, Earl Grey's fussy eating habits had vanished and his fur had become less bristly and more lush. Even his shedding had let up to the point where she no longer had to sweep the kitchen floor every single day.

Two hours later, Theodosia was zipping herself into a pair of jodhpurs and yanking on a pair of black English riding boots. Directly following breakfast, she'd taken Earl Grey for a jog through the historic district. Since it had still been awfully early, she'd enjoyed the morning fog that seemed to give everything a slightly softer edge: the giant mansions, the wrought iron lamps, even the lovely, live oak trees that met to form a bower over many of the streets. Returning to Timothy's house, she'd luxuriated with a nice hot shower, then hurriedly dressed.

Theodosia checked her watch. Jory would be swinging by to pick her up in about ten minutes and she was eager for their day to begin. First a nice, scenic drive to the Wildwood Horse and Hunt Club, then a tour of the clubhouse and the stables. They'd probably be offered a groaningly huge hunt breakfast, which she'd only pick at. And then it would be time for the actual fox hunt!

But first . . .

Theodosia assessed herself in the mirror. She certainly looked like she belonged to the horsey set with her khaki-colored jodhpurs and tailored white shirt. But would the black riding jacket she'd borrowed from Delaine really work?

Theodosia slipped into the tight-fitting jacket and studied her image.

Hmm. Very Ralph Laurenish and ready-for-the-hunt.

She reached for the Meadowbrook hunting helmet and seated it on her head. Her full auburn hair spread out around her face Medusa-like.

I can do better than this.

She gathered her hair into a ponytail, then twisted it into a chignon, and pinned it low on her neck. She put the riding helmet back on her head and assessed herself one last time. What she saw pleased her.

Much better. Definitely more formal, maybe even bordering on severe. Just what the Wildwood Horse and Hunt Club is all about.

Twenty minutes later Theodosia was sitting in Jory Davis's BMW, breezing down Highway 17 and heading into the heart of the low-country.

Geographically, the low-country includes the coastal plain from Pawley's Island, just south of the North Carolina border, all the way to the Savannah River, which is also the Georgia state line. Extending inland for approximately eighty miles, the low-country comes to a natural conclusion at a geographical divide known as the Fall Line, where South Carolina's hills begin to appear.

And the low-country, with its palmettos, live oaks, swamps, tidal flats, and often subtropical climate, was dear to Theodosia's heart.

Her father had grown up out here on Cane Ridge Plantation, a former rice plantation. Her Aunt Libby still lived there. And Theodosia had developed a deep and abiding love for its pine thickets, hardwood forests, marshland, and sinewy rivers filled with oysters, shrimp, and crawfish.

"You're awfully quiet," Theodosia said to Jory when he hadn't uttered a peep for a good ten minutes. "Are you sure you want to do this?"

"I'm hoping it will clear my head," replied Jory.

"You don't *look* very happy," said Theodosia. "And that was meant as a caring remark, not a criticism," she added quickly.

"I know," said Jory, still looking glum.

"Something's wrong," she said.

"Something's come to light," said Jory.

"Tell me," Theodosia said, watching him watch the road.

Jory sighed. "It turns out Uncle Jasper's estate is far larger than we originally thought it was."

"Because of real estate holdings?" asked Theodosia.

"Not exactly," said Jory. "He had the condo on Kiawah Island and the house on Ashley Avenue, but the bulk of his estate really lies in stocks and bonds. A *lot* of stocks and bonds." Jory turned to her and raised his eyebrows a notch.

"Are we talking a balanced portfolio?" asked Theodosia cautiously. "Or did your Uncle Jasper control a lot of Cardiotech stock?"

"Fairly balanced," said Jory. "But he did hold around a hundred thousand shares of Cardiotech, plus warrants for another hundred thousand shares."

"Wow," said Theodosia, doing some quick calculations and realizing that Jasper Davis's Cardiotech stock had easily been worth eight hundred thousand dollars. Double that if he'd exercised his warrants.

"I'd imagine that's going to be Star Duncan's reaction, too," said Jory.

"It will all go to her?" asked Theodosia, looking surprised. For some reason, the serendipitous inheritance felt unfair. Like Star hadn't really *earned* it. Hadn't really been Jasper Davis's wife. She'd simply been in the right place at the right time, whereas Jasper Davis had certainly been in the *wrong* place at the wrong time.

"From what I've been able to determine so far," said Jory, "Uncle Jasper never changed his will after they separated."

"Do you suppose Star knew that?" asked Theodosia.

"Don't know," said Jory.

Theodosia was quiet for a few moments as she watched stands of cypress fly by. Smiling to herself when they crossed over a narrow creek, she spotted two boys in a flat bottom boat known as a jonboat. She loved it out here, especially on this road. There were lots of little farm stands that sold fresh-caught crabs, Sieva beans, alligator meat, homemade angel biscuits, and calabash, also known as gourds and pumpkins. There were even those ubiquitous low-country treasures that Charleston women utterly adored and couldn't seem to get enough of: sweetgrass baskets. Yes, Theodosia was *bon yeuh,* or born here, as they say. And she reveled in it.

"I saw Star Duncan yesterday," Theodosia said to Jory as a split rail fence came into view.

"You ran into her?" asked Jory. He eased his foot off the accelerator, turned under a rustic wooden arch with a sign that read "Wildwood Horse and Hunt Club," then bumped down a gravel road, the split rail fence still running along on either side of them.

"Not exactly," said Theodosia. "Remember I told you I was going to help judge teapots for the Charleston Ceramics Guild? In the Tolliver Building?"

Jory nodded. "Yup, I remember. In the same building where Vance Tuttle has his repertory group or whatever the heck he calls it."

"That's where I saw her."

Jory swerved into the parking lot and suddenly slammed on his brakes as a large silver horse trailer suddenly backed into the road. The stop sent the two of them rocking forward.

"She was at the theater?" he asked, once the danger was past and they were able to pull into a parking space.

"Actually, I sort of spotted Star out the window," said

Theodosia. "Vance Tuttle was walking her to her car. A very hot little Porsche, I might add."

"No kidding." Jory sat there with a slightly quizzical look on his face. "Hmm . . . maybe she's on their board of directors or something."

"Or they're dating," offered Theodosia.

"Are you serious?" said Jory, surprised. "Those two?"

"I only caught them for a split second," said Theodosia. "But I had the feeling there was *something* between them. Chemistry, I mean."

"I'll be darned," said Jory. He sat with his hands on the steering wheel for a few moments, pondering this information, then he peered over at Theodosia. "You've got that note of suspicion in your voice," he told her.

"Do I?" She didn't really think she did.

"Yes, you do," said Jory.

"Actually," said Theodosia, "I was beginning to think Ben Atherton looked awfully suspicious."

Now Jory wore a look of puzzlement. "You're talking about Ben Atherton the PR guy?"

Theodosia hastily told Jory about her conversation with Ben Atherton's wife, Cleo. And Ben's big coup at getting his own column in *Medical Innovations* magazine and his plans to lead off with an announcement of the Novalaser.

"It seems like a lot of folks at Cardiotech are eager to push the release of that Novalaser," sighed Jory. "Especially now that Uncle Jasper isn't around to sound a cautionary note."

"Especially Dr. Rex Haggard," said Theodosia.

"Speak of the devil," said Jory, giving a nod.

Theodosia followed Jory's gaze toward a large paddock where a dozen or so horses and riders were milling about. Dr. Rex Haggard, wearing a scarlet riding coat, had just vaulted onto the back of a large chestnut horse and was chatting with someone astride a dappled gray horse.

"Who's he talking with?" asked Theodosia. Whoever it was had her back to them.

Jory watched for a moment, then the rider on the dappled

gray horse turned in the saddle and he could finally see who it was.

"I believe that's Lois Kimbrough," said Jory. "You know, the CFO at VSM. You met her Friday, didn't you? At the memorial service?"

Theodosia's eyes sought out Lois Kimbrough. She wore a dark blue hunt coat and a black velvet riding cap pulled low on her forehead. Leaning forward in the saddle, Lois stroked her horse's shoulder with her right hand. In her left hand she held the reins and a braided leather riding crop. Lois Kimbrough looked crisp, confident, and extremely capable. Pretty much the same way she'd looked two days ago at Cardiotech.

"They certainly seem friendly," said Theodosia. The phrase *thick as thieves* popped into her head, but it seemed inappropriate and premature to voice that thought. Instead she said: "Especially since they work at rival companies."

"They do," agreed Jory. "But they're also members of the Medical Triad."

"Which is why Lois Kimbrough attended Uncle Jasper's memorial service," said Theodosia.

Jory shrugged. "It was nice of her."

"Was she at Jasmine Cemetery the night he died?" asked Theodosia.

Jory put a hand up to the side of his face. "I . . . I don't know."

From the tone of his voice, Theodosia knew Jory was still feeling tired and more than a little down. It was definitely time to change the subject. Jory had told her he wanted to go riding today to clear his head, so that's exactly what they would do. Nothing more.

The Wildwood Horse and Hunt Club occupied more than four hundred acres that was once a flourishing rice plantation just east of the small town of Adams Run. The main house, a large, rambling white-columned structure, had long since been renovated to serve as a club house. There was a large horse barn and outbuildings had been converted into storage sheds. And the land, with its ponds, rice dikes, fields, and forests, had pretty much been allowed to return to the wild. It provided the perfect setting for riding to the hounds.

Of course, most hunt clubs didn't actually set their hounds after a real fox these days. What with housing developments, "No Trespassing" signs everywhere you looked, and a very real shortage of red foxes, that era had pretty much passed. Now, the hunt of choice was a drag hunt. The scent of fox was dragged along a course designed to lead horses and riders through woods and fields, splashing across streams, and over natural jumps. The hounds were encouraged to pick up the scent, so to speak, and give chase with a field of riders following close behind.

As Theodosia and Jory climbed the steps of the old mansion, Ben Atherton met them on the wide portico. Dozens of riders were already there, sipping mint juleps and sparkling cordials made from mulberry wine. No doubt, Theodosia thought, the mulberry wine had been made from the fruit of the mulberry trees that grew all over the low-country.

"Welcome, you two, welcome," Ben proclaimed. "This your first visit to Wildwood?"

"I've been here before," said Jory. "But it's Theodosia's first time."

"Surely you've ridden to the hounds, though," he said, smiling broadly at her."

"I've done my share of tearing through the low-country astride a galloping horse," admitted Theodosia. "But I've never had the advantage of baying hounds to lead the way." She smiled warmly at Ben, wondering what was really behind all that hail hearty good humor.

Ben Atherton tilted his head back and let go an enormous belly laugh. "Well said," he chortled. "And I predict an utterly *marvelous* hunt today. Good food, strong drink, fast horses. To really make things interesting, Sam Sickert has brought in his Bywater Hounds. They're an outstanding pack, leggy and tough. It'll be all you can do to keep up with them."

"You're not riding?" said Theodosia.

"Not today," replied Ben.

"Theo's a fantastic rider," said Jory, remaining neutral against Ben Atherton's almost manic good humor. "She's seated in the field today. I'm just going to be a hilltopper." Hilltoppers were riders who followed the action at a slower pace and didn't do any jumping.

"I'm sure you'll have an outstanding hunt, just the same," said Ben, slapping Jory on the back. "Say there, Theodosia, I want to thank you again for your help with the judging yesterday. Everyone at the Ceramics Guild certainly appreciated your time and effort."

"Not a problem," replied Theodosia. "It turned out to be lots of fun. And I think it's wonderful that Vantage PR does so much pro bono work for the Ceramics Guild, although your wife tells me you're not really a potter yourself."

"Oh, once in a while I stick my hands into a mound of wet clay," Ben laughed as he took another long draw on his drink.

"*Ben Atherton certainly* seems like the quintessential PR guy," said Jory, once they were out of earshot.

"He is," admitted Theodosia. "One from the old school who believes in serious glad-handing and plying everyone with lots of liquor. Kind of a lethal combination." She stopped when she saw the look on Jory's face. "I didn't mean *that* kind of lethal," she told him, feeling flustered.

"But you do view him as a viable suspect," said Jory.

"Maybe," said Theodosia. "I know I get some kind of vibe off him."

Jory put a hand on her shoulder. "Sorry, honey. I didn't mean to push so hard. I wasn't really expecting you to nail

Uncle Jasper's murderer cold. Things just don't happen that way."

But sometimes they do, Theodosia thought to herself as they strolled over toward the buffet table. *They do if I can shake something loose.*

"Say now," said Jory, as he picked up a large white plate and studied the contents of the table that stretched out before them. "This hunt breakfast looks mighty good!"

Partaking of a large hunt breakfast was pure tradition. And the spectacular spread that the Wildwood Horse and Hunt Club had laid out this morning was no exception. In fact, it was a gastronomic feast.

She-crab soup, shrimp pilaf, duck and sausage gumbo, sliced ham, barbecued chicken, blueberry pancakes, red rice, and Chicken Bog beckoned enticingly from various highly polished silver vessels lined up on the buffet table.

"Look at this," enthused Jory. "Chicken Bog. One of my absolute favorites."

Chicken Bog was one of those quintessential low-country staples. A cross between a casserole and a stew, Chicken Bog featured chicken, rice, and sausage cooked with onion, carrots, and celery. Theodosia wasn't exactly sure why the dish was called Chicken Bog, except that it was classic Carolina comfort food and probably helped improve your outlook when you were feeling all "bogged" down.

"You're not eating?" Jory asked Theodosia as he enthusiastically helped himself to a large dollop of sweet potatoes and a thick slice of ham.

"I had an early breakfast," she told him, recalling her 5:30 A.M. wake-up call.

"Have some more," said Jory, eyeing the shrimp pilaf. "Once the hunt begins, you're going to be burning calories like mad."

"Good point," said Theodosia as she watched Ben Atherton stride across the room and sidle up to the rustic pine bar where Rex Haggard was seated. After waggling a finger to signal the bartender for another drink, Ben leaned in close to Dr. Haggard and murmured something in his ear. Fervently wishing she could be a mouse hiding in that corner, Theodosia said, "I think I *will* have something to eat after all."

9

"What's in there?" asked Theodosia as she and Jory were exiting the clubhouse, ready to head over to the stable.

"That's the gun room," said Jory, indicating a wood-paneled room lined with trophies and gun cases. "The club has a trapshooting stand nearby."

Curious, Theodosia took a few steps into the room and looked around. "Oh," she said, startled, as someone whirled toward her. "I didn't know anyone was in here."

"Theodosia?" A woman smiled tentatively at her. "It's Peaches. Remember me?"

"Of course," said Theodosia, rapidly regaining her composure. Rex Haggard was here today. It was only natural that his wife, Peaches, would accompany him.

"And you must be Jory," said Peaches Haggard, crossing the room and extending her hand. "I was so sorry to hear about your Uncle Jasper. He was a wonderful man. Such an asset to the company."

"Thank you," said Jory. "It's nice to hear he was so well thought of."

"I'm sorry I wasn't able to attend the memorial service at Cardiotech," said Peaches. "But I understand there'll be a funeral this coming week," she said.

"Tuesday," said Jory. "At St. Michael's Episcopal."

"A marvelous edifice," murmured Peaches. "So steeped in history."

"Are you riding today?" Theodosia asked her. Somehow, she'd gotten the idea that Rex Haggard and Lois Kimbrough might be riding together.

Peaches gave a throaty laugh. "Afraid not. I'm not much of a rider, especially after I broke my collarbone two years ago while taking a water jump. Now I just tag along for the socializing." Peaches tipped her glass of amber liquid toward Theodosia and ice cubes clinked softly against the side of the crystal glass.

Maybe, thought Theodosia, *Rex Haggard and Lois Kimbrough are riding together.*

"The club certainly has an impressive collection of trophies," said Theodosia as she studied the array of gold loving cups, silver bowls, and engraved plaques that lined the walls and sat in glass display cases. She peered at a tall silver urn with the figure of a hunter posed on top of it. The engraved sentiment read: "Skeet Shooting Champion, 2002, 2003, and 2004." Underneath the championship title, a single name was engraved: Rex Haggard.

"Your husband must be one heck of a shot," said Theodosia, "to have been awarded this trophy three years in a row."

"You better believe it," said Peaches Haggard, swelling with pride over her husband's accomplishments. "Rexy's a dead shot."

Inhaling the scent of leather, hay, and horses, Theodosia felt instantly at home as she and Jory stepped inside the large wooden horse barn. Gleaming tack hung from pegs, colorful wool horse blankets were slung over box stalls, and a dozen or so riders fussed with their horses.

Theodosia drank in the gentle horse sounds that accompanied the activities. Low nickers to stablemates, sharp snorts, impatient stomps, grunts as saddle cinches were pulled tighter.

A gray-haired man wearing khaki slacks and a battered brown suede jacket led a large roan horse out of a box stall. "Easy now," he told the horse in a calm, reassuring voice. "Stay easy." The roan shook his head and shuddered, a horsey response to the stableman's admonition.

"You must be Gus," said Jory as the man clipped a lead onto the big horse's bridle.

Gus cocked an eye at Jory. "That's me." He patted the horse on the flank, then slid a camel-colored pad onto his back. "Bet you're Jory, the fella was related to Dr. Jasper Davis."

Jory nodded. "He was my uncle."

"Sorry for your trouble," muttered Gus, tossing a black leather saddle on top of the quilted pad, then ducking down to grab the cinch.

Theodosia, a confirmed horse lover, could barely contain herself. "Is this one of the club's horses?" she asked, allowing the horse to nuzzle at the pocket of her jacket.

Gus nodded as he pulled the cinch tight and the big horse suddenly shifted his weight. "Dr. Rex told me you two were gonna be riding today. Most members trailer in their own horses for a hunt," said Gus. "But the club still keeps half a dozen here."

"I know. Lucky us," said Theodosia, who had moved on to scratching the big roan on his stubbly chin.

"You can ride?" Gus asked, eyeing Theodosia. "You can handle yourself on a horse?"

"I've been riding pretty much all my life," said Theodosia as she fished an apple slice cadged from the buffet table out of her jacket pocket. Holding her palm flat so there was no chance of getting nipped, she fed the treat to the horse.

"You can take Romanoff then," said Gus, unsnapping the lead and handing the roan off to Theodosia. "See, he's taken a liking to you already." Gus turned his gaze on Jory. "And how 'bout you?"

"I'm what you'd call your novice rider," said Jory with a sheepish grin. "I'm going to be a hilltopper today."

Gus grunted. "Follow me. My guess is old Sea Spray might be just right for you." He led Jory into one of the box stalls and helped him saddle a big brown horse.

Theodosia was already riding Romanoff around the grounds when Gus and Jory emerged from the barn leading Sea Spray. She reined her horse sharply and clattered over to them.

Nervously, Jory stepped out of the way. "What's that for?" he asked, pointing to a red ribbon that had been tied to Romanoff's tail.

"Means he kicks," said Theodosia, and Jory suddenly swerved to give the horse a wide berth.

"Better put this on your head," said Jory, handing Theodosia's black velvet riding cap up to her before Gus helped him mount his own horse.

As cute and stylish as riding caps looked, they were really hard hats in disguise. Inside that black velvet was a Kevlar helmet engineered to protect the rider's head. You never knew when a horse would stubbornly refuse a jump and the rider would go pitching forward anyway. Or when low-hanging branches would give a rider a good swipe.

Aroooh! Aroooh!

Baying hounds suddenly signaled that the hunt was about to begin. So Theodosia and Jory dug their heels into the sides of their horses and trotted over to the paddock to join the rest of the field.

Fox hunting upholds certain protocols. The field masters

and the master of the hounds, so designated by their red coats, were always in charge. In this case, Rex Haggard, the president of the Wildwood Horse and Hunt Club, was one of the field masters today. The rest of the riders, known as the field, were in less formal "ratcatcher" attire. That is, rather than wearing very formal clothing, they were in riding jackets, riding breeches, and black leather boots.

The twelve foxhounds, or six "couples," were attended by the huntsman and his assistant, the whipper-in.

Although Theodosia was riding with the regular hunt field, she was a visitor and thus relegated to stay in the rear of the pack. Jory, of course, would follow along at a slower pace with the group of six other hilltoppers.

Ta da da. Ta da da.

The sound of the hunting horn echoed the length of the valley and the pack of hounds were suddenly in full cry, baying loudly. Then, with a signal from the huntsman, the brown-and-white dappled hounds were off and running, their lanky bodies stretched out, their ears flying behind as the dogs flew swiftly across the field.

"Hi ho!" yelled the rider to Theodosia's right, and then they were off, too.

Hoofs thundered, leather squeaked, and bridles jangled as two dozen riders raced pell-mell after the baying hounds.

As they tore across a field of alfalfa, the riders fanned out. Bent low over Romanoff, Theodosia could see the hounds surging ahead and scrambling up a hill that would soon lead them into the woods.

The first jump came before she was ready for it. A drainage ditch filled with water, maybe three feet across. Theodosia leaned forward, lifted her horse off, then sat back in the saddle, coming down textbook perfect, except for a little splash. Romanoff's back feet had hit the edge of the water. Leaning forward again, she and Romanoff charged up the hill into the woods with the rest of the pack.

Theodosia loved horses dearly and had always been crazy about riding. She'd started out riding western style. When she was in high school, she'd switched to English-style riding and jumping. She didn't have the patience for dressage, but jumping had won her heart. Galloping along on a powerful horse, hooves kicking up clods of earth, flying over split rail fences and bushy hedges, was magical. It was like being on the winged horse Pegasus. Every girl's dream. Every woman's, too.

Now branches swatted her face as they skimmed along under the trees. Romanoff was a powerful animal who loved to run. In fact, it was all she could do to keep him toward the rear of the pack.

More jumps loomed ahead and by this time Theodosia was more than ready for them. First a low hedge, then, maybe a thousand yards beyond that, a split rail fence. Romanoff cleared the split rail fence with more than a foot to spare. He was a big, powerful animal and not even breathing hard.

The baying of the hounds had let up some now, and the pace gradually slackened to a fast trot. Theodosia shifted to a posting motion, rising up in the stirrups then coming back down in the saddle to offset the horse's jarring gait.

The field was clumped together now and a good-looking man on a jittery white horse passed her his silver flask. She accepted it, enjoyed a small sip of what had tasted like very fine cognac, then passed it back to him, feeling exhilarated.

After following the hounds for a good half hour or so, they came to a clearing where some of the riders dismounted and led their horses over to an old metal watering trough. There had clearly been an old farmhouse here once. Though only a pump and water trough remained, there were remnants of an old foundation made of tabby, the precursor to concrete that blended oyster shells, sand, lime, and sea water.

Rex Haggard raised his hand in greeting as she rode up. "How goes it?" he asked. "Enjoying the first hunt of our cubbing season?" Cubbing season was the preliminary season when horses and hounds were trained and conditioned.

Theodosia wondered just how many of the hounds used today would pass muster and "graduate" to the formal fox hunting season.

"This is wonderful," she told him. "I'm having a great ride."

"Jory's Uncle Jasper would have approved," said Rex Haggard. "He was one of our most avid riders. He would have been joint master with me this year."

"Such a shame," said Theodosia.

Rex Haggard gave a shrug. "Life goes on," he said, jiggling the reins, moving the bit around inside the mouth of his large chestnut horse to keep it focused.

"Indeed it does," said Theodosia, somewhat surprised by his brusque attitude. "And I understand your company is proceeding full speed ahead with the Novalaser."

Now Rex Haggard looked ebullient. "Two weeks, thirty days tops," he told her. "Then Cardiotech is back in the headlines again." His horse danced in place as he squinted off into the distance. "Damn," he shouted. "Two hounds just broke away from the pack!" And Rex Haggard spurred his horse on so he could consult with the huntsman and the whipper-in.

A moment later, Lois Kimbrough rode over to Theodosia as she was allowing Romanoff to drink from the trough.

"It's nice to see you again," Lois told Theodosia. "These are certainly better circumstances than last Friday."

"It was kind of you to attend the memorial service," said Theodosia.

"Nonsense," said Lois. "Jasper Davis was a friend." They both reined their horses around and began following the pack leaders down a rutted trail.

"Had the two of you worked together?" asked Theodosia.

"No, no, we just knew each other as rivals," Lois Kimbrough told her. "And through our association with the Medical Triad."

"Then you probably attended the Medical Triad's fundraiser," said Theodosia. "In Jasmine Cemetery."

"No, I wasn't there," said Lois Kimbrough, narrowing her eyes. "But I understand you were nearby." The two of them rode along together in silence for a while. "Ben Atherton tells me you're looking into things," said Lois, urging her horse into a hard trot as the pace began to pick up.

Did I tell Ben I was looking into things? No, Delaine was the one who mentioned that. Last Friday at the Cardiotech memorial service.

Theodosia urged her horse forward, staying along side Lois, mulling over her words.

And now that little story is making the rounds at Cardiotech? And at Lois Kimbrough's company? Hmm.

"That Ben's a real PR guy," said Theodosia finally, deciding two can play at this game. "Always trying to put a spin on things."

"PR guy," snorted Lois Kimbrough, pulling her cap low on her brow. "If you ask me, I'd say Ben Atherton's an out-and-out huckster."

Theodosia didn't respond as she rode along side Lois.

"And now I hear Ben Atherton is doing a little double-dipping," continued Lois. "Handling Cardiotech's PR and contracting to write a column for *Medical Innovations.*" Lois laughed harshly, as though she found this all highly amusing. "Well, why not? A person's got to make a living, right?" she said as a blast from the huntsman's horn once again pierced the air.

Flasks were stashed and riders quickly picked up the pace as the hounds rooted out the scent again and launched into a full cry. The hunt was back on.

Tearing down a grassy lane between two fences, Theodosia glanced off to her right, wondering if Jory and the other hilltoppers would appear. There was no sign of them yet, but they were doing just as their name implied—staying atop the hills and enjoying a bird's-eye view.

Then the field of riders was back in the woods and dealing with all manner of jumps and obstacles: fallen logs, dead falls, and old dirt-constructed dikes, left over from when the surrounding countryside was a flourishing rice plantation.

Finally, after ten minutes of hard riding, the woods thinned out and horses and riders crossed a soggy field, being mindful of sinkholes. They cantered across a narrow wooden bridge, horses' hooves producing miniature thunder, then around the edge of a small pond where marsh wrens and warblers darted from cattails to scraggly pond pines.

When the hounds dove into a forest of bald cypress, the field of riders gamely followed them in.

The forest was loamy smelling and darker, with springy ground that was easy on the horses' legs and very little wire grass or underbrush to obstruct their mad dash. Here were also large clusters of chanterelles, those distinctive apricot-colored South Carolina fungi, that seemed to pop up whenever autumn moisture and cooler temperatures came to the low-country.

As the field of riders spread out, Theodosia could see Rex Haggard and Lois Kimbrough up ahead of her. Riding close together, she had the distinct feeling they were subtly trying to edge each other out, exercising their competitive natures in sport as well as in business.

She'll be the field master next year, thought Theodosia. Or at least joint master.

Chunks of wet mud that smelled like rotten eggs flew by Theodosia, kicked up by the horses directly in front of her as they galloped a soggier portion of forest. And, for once, Theodosia fervently wished she wasn't riding at the back of the pack. *Gonna have to get this jacket dry-cleaned,* she decided, noticing that the trees were thicker here and kudzu wound its way up many of the trunks.

"Stone wall," cried out a rider up front.

Uh, oh.

Checking Romanoff's speed, Theodosia spied an open space to the right of the stone wall and decided the most judicious thing to do was take her horse over that way. All the other obstacles she'd jumped so far were fairly forgiving. A stone wall was not.

She reined Romanoff toward the right and brought him down to a lazy canter. He fought her, tossing his head angrily as if he knew he could easily clear the stone jump. But he was a well-trained horse, and he responded to her, slowing and turning to the right exactly as she asked.

Just as they passed a dense copse of mulberry, a brown-and-white hound sprang out in front of them.

One of the runaway hounds?

Startled, Romanoff shied, crab-stepped frantically to the left, and slammed himself and Theodosia's leg into a nearby tree trunk.

Ouch!

Theodosia reined the frightened horse to a stop, then glanced down, searching the earth for the poor hound dog that most certainly had been trampled to death. Yet no furry, crumpled body lay under her horse's powerful hooves. Or anywhere nearby.

He got away? Theodosia put a hand down and rubbed at her sore leg. *Well . . . good. I guess.*

Romanoff stood quietly, switching his tail, as the baying of hounds faded into the afternoon and the sounds of the forest, the chirp of birds, the gentle rustle of wind through leaves overhead, the buzz of a few insects, suddenly took over.

"Hey," she said, clapping a hand reassuringly on her horse's ample shoulder. "Let's not try *that* again."

She eased her heels into Romanoff and spurred him into a trot.

Got to catch up with the field.

Coming to the edge of the forest, she turned down a narrow trail that bore faint signs of recent hoofprints and looked fairly well traveled. Then again, so did the trail that led off in the *opposite* direction.

Trying to get a fix on the faint baying of hounds, Theodosia reined her horse in. Unfortunately, sounds seemed to bounce around out here. A slight feeling of trepidation began to insinuate itself, and Theodosia leaned forward in the saddle to give Romanoff another reassuring pat on the shoulder. A reassuring pat that was mostly for *her* benefit.

Pop.

Startled, Theodosia spun in her saddle, looking left then right.

"What?" she cried out, even though there was no one around to hear her.

The sound echoed again. Another loud *pop.* Then something *whooshed* past her head.

What the . . .?

Thinking fast, Theodosia kicked free of the stirrups and dove off her horse. She might be a city girl now, but she'd grown up in the country and still recognized the sound of a gunshot.

Holy smokes! Did somebody just take a shot at me?

Ducking her head, Theodosia crouched down beside an enormous live oak, thankful for its generous girth and powerfully grateful to be wearing her hard hat. Wondering just how good its stopping power really was.

Shot at me with a . . . what? Rifle? Handgun?

She dropped the reins, letting Romanoff wander off a few yards on his own. The horse stared at her with mild curiosity, then moved another fifty feet away to where a particularly tasty clump of green grass had sprouted. He pulled at the tendrils, munching contentedly, and ignored her.

Come on hilltoppers, thought Theodosia. *Where the heck are you? This is the part where you're supposed to come galloping in and scare the bad guy, or bad guys, away. If that's what they really are.*

They didn't come. Nobody came. But, thank the Lord, no one fired another shot either as she crouched behind the sheltering oak.

Twenty minutes later, when she *still* hadn't heard a shot or detected any movement in the woods around her, Theodosia brushed herself off and headed out to round up Romanoff. After a minute or two of coaxing, she caught the big horse and hopped onto his back. She'd also made up her mind that the important thing to do now was try to find her way back to the hunt club.

Besides, what were her options, really? Try to catch up with the hunt field? They had to be miles ahead by now.

As Theodosia wound her way back through the forest and circled the pond, she thought about what had just happened.

Did a hunter blunder his way onto Wildwood's property? Or did someone from the nearby shooting range veer off course? Because I'm awfully sure somebody was using live ammo.

It took Theodosia a good fifty minutes to negotiate the return trip through the woods and fields. And when she and Romanoff finally arrived back at the barn, there wasn't another horse and rider in sight. Although, once again, she could detect the faint sound of baying of hounds in the distance.

Breathing a sigh of relief at arriving at the clubhouse safely, Theodosia slid out of the saddle and led her horse into the barn. It wasn't until she was in Romanoff's box stall, pulling the saddle off him, ready to give him a good rubdown, that she became aware of low voices.

Someone else must be in the barn. Jory and some of the other hill-toppers came back early perhaps?

She slipped the bridle off Romanoff, then swung the stall door closed, eager to tell someone . . . anyone . . . about her strange episode.

"Gus?" she called. "You in here?"

There was a grunt, then a murmur of voices.

Two voices?

Theodosia made her way down the center aisle of the barn to the last box stall. Gus was there all right. And Lois Kimbrough was with him. Her big horse stood in the stall with its right foreleg cradled in Gus's gnarled hands. A black cat with shiny green eyes stared at Theodosia from outside the stall, then slipped away as she approached.

"What's wrong?" Theodosia asked. She was tired and

dusty and cranky from having the life scared out of her.

Lois Kimbrough and Gus stood in the stall, their heads together. As Theodosia came closer, she saw that Gus's callused hands held a dripping syringe.

"Rob Roy pulled up lame," Lois Kimbrough said without turning to glance at Theodosia. "Gus thought he might need a shot of cortisone."

Lois glanced Theodosia's way, then reached up and put her hand on the stall door. "Hold off, Gus," she said as Rob Roy began shifting about inside his stall. "Best to close this first."

The door swung shut on the box stall. But not before Theodosia spotted a black leather bag, half buried in the straw, filled with glass vials and other syringes.

10

Sitting in the passenger seat next to Jory, Theodosia was in-
ordinately quiet on the drive home. Jory, who was still exhilarated from his ride with the hilltoppers' group, didn't
seem to notice Theodosia's thoughtful, if not distressed,
state of mind.

Truth be told, Theodosia was worried sick that Jory
would ask her what was wrong. Then she'd have to tell him:
I think someone took a shot at me. But didn't Jory have enough
on his mind? Enough to worry about?

Theodosia knew the answer was a resounding yes. Which
was why she'd decided to remain quiet for the time being
and not tell Jory about the shot someone might have fired at
her. Or about the cache of vials and hypodermic needles
she'd spotted.

"You're awfully quiet," said Jory, looking over at her.

Startled, Theodosia took a big gulp and stared at him

with what she hoped was wide-eyed innocence. "I am? You think so?"

"I don't blame you," said Jory. "After galloping all over the countryside today, anybody'd be exhausted and sore. I know my own backside is starting to feel more than a little lame. And I didn't do nearly the amount of hard riding you did."

"I hope this really did help clear your head," said Theodosia, worrying that some of her earlier musings to him might have opened up a few cans of worms.

"Oh, it did," said Jory effusively. "I had a terrific time. Riding Sea Spray, as cantankerous as that animal was, was great therapy."

"I thought Sea Spray was supposed to be gentle," said Theodosia. "Maybe even a little plodding," she added with a grin.

Jory swerved his car around a crow that was picking away at a freshly hit squirrel. "Well, he seemed pretty unruly to *me*."

Theodosia stared out the window watching the countryside fly by and thought about Rex Haggard, who was supposedly a "dead shot." And about Ben Atherton, who was trying to parlay the release of the Novalaser into his own personal triumph. And about the very aggressive Lois Kimbrough.

Then there were the glass vials and hypos in Gus's horse-doctor bag.

All of this information she'd gleaned, all of this so-called *evidence,* was circumstantial at best. Yet none of it boded well.

Theodosia put a hand to her neck and massaged the sore spot right at the base of her skull. This was the same spot that used to plague her after ten or twelve hours at the office. When unreasonable deadlines or frantic clients got to her. That silly spot on her neck burned like a hot coal right now.

Theodosia turned her head to the right, trying to stretch her tired neck muscles. Willing herself to relax, she stared out the window just as Jory slowed for a stop sign and a red-tailed hawk came gliding out of a pine tree.

"We just passed Greeley Mill Road," she cried. "Stop!"

Gravel crunched under their tires as Jory stomped on the brakes and brought the car to a slow stop at the side of the country road. "What's the problem with Greeley Mill Road?" he asked.

"It was in your uncle's appointment journal," Theodosia told him excitedly. "He was supposed to have an appointment near here last Friday." She closed her eyes, bit her lip and tried to recall the address. "I think it was something like twenty-seven forty-something Greeley Mill Road," she told Jory. Theodosia opened her eyes, pleased she'd been able to fish an approximation of the address from her memory. "Yes, that's it!"

"What's it?" asked Jory, accelerating slowly and guiding his BMW in a tight U-turn.

"Sojourner Enterprises," replied Theodosia.

"Really," said Jory. "Okay." They had arrived back at the crossroads. "Which way?" he asked. "Right or left? Your call."

Theodosia made a fast guess. "Um . . . left." This was what she loved about Jory. The trust factor. She yelled "stop the car" and he did. No questions asked. Of course, if she'd have yelled to stop the car because she wanted to buy a jar of country-raised honey, he still would have slammed on the brakes and pulled the car over.

Two miles down the road they hit pay dirt. A wooden sign for Sojourner Enterprises rose up from a thicket of wax myrtle.

"Want to turn in?" Jory asked her.

Theodosia didn't hesitate. "Of course," she said. "We need to check this out."

A sour smell assaulted them the minute they stepped out of the car.

"Eeyuh," said Jory, wrinkling his nose. "What on earth is that smell?"

Theodosia, who'd grown up in the low-country and had been around farm animals, knew instantly what kind of business was carried out at Sojourner Enterprises.

"Pigs," she told Jory as she scanned the farmyard and caught sight of two long, low buildings. "This is a pig farm."

Their arrival hadn't gone unnoticed. Someone was walking slowly toward them from one of the buildings.

"Hello there," said Theodosia, waving a greeting to the man. She knew a friendly approach would net far more information than if they came cowboying in, demanding answers to questions. Besides, this was the heartland of the low-country. Everybody was friendly out here. At least she hoped they were.

"I think you missed your turn," said the man as he approached them. "The Weidemeyer auction's being held a mile or so down the road. Although I'm guessing it's probably over by now." The man was tall and thin, about sixty years of age, with sun-bronzed skin and deep blue eyes. The kind of deep, pure blue the Atlantic Ocean was once you got your boat out a good six or seven miles.

"No," said Theodosia, we're in the right place. I'm Theodosia Browning. And this is . . ."

"You related to Eldon Browning?" asked the man suddenly.

Her father had been gone a good twenty years now. To hear someone speak his name in a slow, gentle accent was infinitely pleasing.

"Yes, I am," she said. "He was my father."

"The lawyer." A faint smile played at the man's mouth.

"And I'm Jory Davis." Jory stretched out his hand.

"Oh, my goodness." Now the farmer seemed genuinely befuddled.

"Jasper Davis was my uncle," said Jory.

"Aha," said the farmer, but this time there was sadness in his voice.

"We know he was supposed to have a meeting here this past Friday," said Theodosia.

The farmer nodded. "He was. With me. I'm Pete Tureau, General Manager here at Sojourner Enterprises. When he didn't show up, I phoned his office." He turned his gaze to Jory. "I'm sorry for your loss, sir. Dr. Jasper was an awfully nice man."

"We were just curious, Mr. Tureau," said Theodosia, "as to what your meeting was about."

Pete Tureau gave them a careful look. "You sure you're really who you say you are?" he asked.

Theodosia and Jory both nodded.

"You're not from one of those left-wing animal rights groups?"

This time they shook their heads and Theodosia asked: "Why do you ask?"

"Because of the pig hearts," said Pete. "The ones used in cardiology testing."

"Are you serious?" said Jory, suddenly looking pale.

"You think they should practice on *human* hearts?" asked Pete.

"Well . . . no," stammered Jory.

"Some of the animal rights people don't see it that way," said Pete. "We had a gang of 'em protesting up a storm a few months go. The Animal Liberation Protectorate. ALP they called themselves. They were singing songs and splashing blood all over everything. Darned near scared my two hired hands to death."

He peered at Theodosia. "You *sure* you're not one of those radical types?"

"I believe in animal rights, but I'm also a meat eater," said Theodosia. *And a fish, chicken, and dairy eater,* she thought to herself.

"Okay then," said Pete Tureau to Jory. "Sorry for your loss."

"Thank you," said Jory.

"So you'd worked with Jasper Davis for a number of years?" asked Theodosia.

Pete nodded. "Five, maybe six years. Three years ago we

came up with a genetically modified hybrid for Cardiotech researchers to work with. These are hearts that very closely approximate human hearts. Everything is still in clinical trials, of course, but pig hearts look extremely hopeful for patients who can't cope with certain immunosuppresive drugs that are needed to prevent the human body from rejecting artificial hearts."

"Fascinating," said Theodosia, meaning it.

"It really is amazing," admitted Pete. "Especially when you think about how many lives could potentially be saved."

When they got back to Timothy Neville's house after a mostly silent ride home, Theodosia turned to Jory. "You want to come in? Have a bite to eat or something?"

"Of course I do," said Jory. "But I can't. My two uncles are arriving tomorrow for Tuesday's funeral and I've got tons more legal mumbo jumbo to plow through." He grinned ruefully. "And I really hate to admit this, but I'm feeling awfully creaky and sore. What's really on my mind is going home and filling my bathtub with hot water."

"Then you might also want to brew up some meadowsweet tea," advised Theodosia.

"To drink?" asked Jory.

Theodosia gave him a look of commiseration. "To soak in."

11

❧

Theodosia was halfway through the second chapter of the newest Mary Higgins Clark thriller when breaking glass suddenly shattered the silence.

A split second later something bounced hard on the carpet. Startled, she watched as a strange object spun wildly in front of her, then caromed off and thudded loudly along the wooden floor of Timothy Neville's elegant library.

Earl Grey was instantly on his feet, barking fiercely before whatever it was stopped rolling. Theodosia wasn't far behind him.

"What was *that?*" she yelled, angry, surprised, and more than a little rattled.

As if in reply, Earl Grey tilted his head back and let loose an accusatory howl. He, too, was unhappy at having his evening so rudely interrupted.

Whatever it was . . . glass bottle, stone, hunk of metal . . . the darned thing had come to rest beneath a massive wooden library table. Grabbing a small wrought iron shovel from a stand of fireplace tools, Theodosia dropped to her hands and knees and put her head flat against the floor. She squinted though dim light and dust bunnies.

There it is. I see it.

Manipulating the clunky little shovel, Theodosia fished out the object.

The errant missile that had just been tossed through Timothy Neville's library window turned out to be a rock. A rock with a note wrapped around it and secured with dull gray duct tape.

Theodosia scrambled to her feet and held out the shovel that contained the lumpy rock to Earl Grey.

"Look at this," she said to the dog, her heart still pounding. "I thought things like this only happened in old black and white movies."

Earl Grey rolled his eyes, stretched out his snout, and sniffed the object gingerly. As if it were something nasty. Like a dead rat.

Theodosia carried the rock over to Timothy's desk and set it down carefully. She didn't want to touch the thing because there might be valuable fingerprints to be had. But she *did* want to read the note or whatever it was that was scrunched and taped around the jagged rock.

Selecting from a ceramic jar filled with pens and pencils, Theodosia poked gently at the note and sticky tape. After ten minutes of judicious prodding, Theodosia freed the note.

"This was not meant for us," she told Earl Grey, who sat by her side looking deeply concerned. "Someone is undoubtedly ticked off at Timothy Neville." But deep in her heart, Theodosia had the sinking feeling she was whistling in the dark.

And she was.

Because the note, what little there was of it, was clearly intended for her.

It read: *Next time I won't miss.*

She stared at Earl Grey, who stared back at her.

Okay. Now what do I do? she wondered. *Pick up my book and keep reading? Call a hardware store to come fix the window? Grab my dog and run screaming out the front door? After all, this is the second rather nasty incident today.*

Theodosia dug her phone directory out of the purse she'd dumped nearby. Leafing through it quickly, she found the number she was looking for and dialed with a slightly trembling hand.

"Good lord!" cried Tidwell, once she'd explained exactly what had taken place. And been forced to reveal the exact contents of the note. "Someone takes a potshot at you this afternoon and tonight you receive a rather ominous special delivery warning! You've been *investigating*!" he thundered.

"Well . . . yes," replied Theodosia. "Some. A little bit." She cringed, knowing she sounded weaselly and a trifle bubble-headed.

"Even when I advised you *not* to."

"Uh . . . that was probably good advice," Theodosia told him, thinking she probably should have phoned Jory Davis instead.

There was a sigh on the other end of the phone. Deep and accusing. Filled with unsaid admonitions.

"All right," Tidwell told her. "Sit tight, I have to make a call. And when I tell you to sit tight I mean *do not move* under any circumstances. Do not pass go, do not collect two hundred dollars." There was a click and a faint buzz on the line while Theodosia remained on hold for a minute or so, then Tidwell came back on the line again. "Archdale Street, correct?"

"That's it," said Theodosia.

"A patrol unit is on its way," growled Tidwell. "They're just a few blocks over so it won't be long."

"Okay," said Theodosia. She glanced back over her shoulder at the shattered window, then down at the floor where shards of jagged glass lay scattered. "Good. Great," she added.

"I dare say, Miss Browning, you sound rather upset."

Theodosia drummed her fingers on the highly polished desk. She could hear Tidwell's wheezy breathing, knew he was still upset. "I was hoping the warning, or whatever you'd call the darn thing that came smashing through the window, was intended for Timothy Neville . . . he can be a fairly sizable target, you know."

"Hah!" roared Tidwell. "Time to face reality, Miss Browning. Now *you're* the target."

"But I haven't really done any *concrete* investigating," said Theodosia. "Asked a few questions, maybe, but . . ."

"You're chattering," Tidwell told her, but there was kindness in his voice.

Theodosia clamped her mouth shut and frowned. Tidwell was right. This sensation of being rattled, this slight lapse in courage, simply wasn't like her. She prided herself on being tenacious and bold. And a little bit fierce.

"I'm okay," she told him. Theodosia knew that one of her quirks was being unable to back off. In fact, when someone warned her to back off, she generally took their admonishment as a signal for a headlong charge. Theodosia Browning, whose mother had died of cancer when she was just eight, who'd cut her teeth in a marketing firm populated by slick-talking fast-track males, had discovered early on that living life to the fullest was definitely not for the meek.

"Listen," Theodosia said to Tidwell, because she wasn't sure what else to say. "Has the lab come up with any fingerprints on the syringe that turned up in Jasmine Cemetery?" Fresh in the back of her mind was the vision of the syringes and vials she'd seen spread out in the horse barn earlier today.

When Tidwell hesitated for a long moment, Theodosia pounced on him. "They did, didn't they?" She could almost see him nodding reluctantly. That strange bullet-shaped head doing a "bobble-head" motion atop his big body.

"The fingerprints were rather badly smudged," replied Tidwell. "But the lab did recover a partial. Enough for maybe a seven or eight point match."

"Well?" said Theodosia. She knew this was good news. Great news, in fact. These days local and federal fingerprint databases were huge and easily accessed via computer. And they were amazingly comprehensive.

"Nothing yet," said Tidwell. "The person whose prints were on that syringe is definitely not in our database. Actually, they don't seem to be in *any* database."

"They're not in the AFIS?" she asked. The AFIS was the Automated Fingerprint Identification System, a comprehensive database that local, state, and federal agencies could easily access via computer. "Isn't that unusual?"

"Not really," said Tidwell. "If there hasn't been a previous arrest or a person hasn't served in the military, then they're simply not there." He paused. "We're still not to the point where everyone's prints are simply loaded into a national database for security purposes."

"I understand," said Theodosia, fervently hoping the country would *never* get to that point.

"Kindly listen up," said Tidwell. "You simply must abandon this Jasper Davis investigation you seem to have launched and exercise extreme caution. This is a *homicide* we're dealing with. Do you understand?"

"Yes." *My goodness, Burt Tidwell is in a foul mood tonight.*

"Mmn," said Theodosia, wondering briefly if her call had perhaps interrupted him. Taken him away from something important. She thought about that possibility and quickly dismissed it. Burt Tidwell lived and breathed detective work. *Loved* the thrill of it. In fact, he had probably been sitting in his living room, staring at a blank wall, deep in a blue funk when she called. The man had probably been *ecstatic* to get her call. Eager to break the tedium of his humdrum Sunday evening.

"Are you even listening?" Tidwell asked, just this side of shouting.

"The police are at the house now," Theodosia told him as she heard car doors slam outside then footsteps echo on the wooden verandah.

"Then I shall leave you in the very capable hands of the Charleston Police Department," responded Tidwell. "Whose officers will hopefully exercise extreme care when it comes to collecting the evidence."

"I'll give them a plastic baggy," said Theodosia.

"Excellent," said Tidwell. "I'm sure they'll be forever grateful."

Theodosia sensed Tidwell was about to hang up when he added: "Oh . . . and Miss Browning?"

"Yes?" she asked. *This time he's really going to let me have it.*

"You'd best telephone a glazier to deal with that window."

12

~❦~

"*I'm feeling very* Assam this morning," declared Drayton as he stood gazing at the various tins and jars of tea stacked on the Indigo Tea Shop's floor-to-ceiling shelves.

"Good for you," muttered Haley as she crouched next to him, digging in the cupboard under the cash register. "Hey, have you seen those pink votive candles?" she asked. "And our little silver candleholders?"

"I definitely think we should go with the Sessa Estate Assam," said Drayton, fingering the various enameled tins, then finally selecting one. "It delivers that superb malty flavor so characteristic of Assams but in a slightly toned-down version. The Sessa Estate is smooth and rich."

"With the weather so drizzly and overcast today," continued Haley, "I thought a flickering candle on each table might be a welcome addition."

"Are you two even listening to each other?" asked Theodosia. She sat at the round table nearest the kitchen, hunched over last week's receipts. Their financial situation looked good, it was just everything else that seemed a little shaky.

Popping her head up like a gopher, Haley squawked: "What?"

Drayton's head continued to swivel back and forth as he studied their stash of teas. "Pardon?" he mumbled, balancing one tin of tea while continuing to scrutinize the rest.

Theodosia tapped her black fountain pen against the scarred hickory table and frowned. She'd woken up this Monday morning with the distinct feeling she was suddenly in over her head. Jory had asked her to help him, was *counting* on her to help him. But some unknown presence out there was sending her powerful messages to back off. And, truth be known, she was beginning to feel more than just a little nervous.

"Ah," said Drayton, and a smile creased his lined face. "This particular Assam from the Dooars growing region should be highly complimentary. It's slightly less pungent, a little flowery, absolutely ideal for morning sipping."

Every morning Drayton picked two or three different teas for what he called his "daily brew." Those teas became the pouring teas for the day. Of course, if a customer wanted a different kind of tea, say a Formosan oolong, a fragrant Darjeeling, or a Chinese black tea, the Indigo Tea Shop was always happy to oblige.

"Got 'em," crowed Haley as she scrambled to her feet, proudly clutching the box of pink candles she'd been searching for.

"Nothing like a good Assam from India," smiled Drayton. "Nine hundred million tea drinkers can't be wrong."

Theodosia glanced at her watch. There was still a good twenty minutes before the tea shop opened. Maybe she'd run the events of the last twenty-four hours past Drayton and Haley and see what they thought. They were usually excellent sounding boards. Good at listening and quick to render an opinion.

"Drayton . . . Haley," Theodosia called. "Got a minute?"

134 *Laura Childs*

"Always," said Drayton, grabbing a freshly brewed pot of tea. "Now if you'll kindly indulge me and take a sip of this . . ." He stopped mid-sentence. "What's *wrong?*" he asked suddenly.

Theodosia glanced up at him. "Oh dear, is it really that apparent?" she asked.

Drayton nodded solemnly. "My goodness, yes. You look perplexed beyond belief." He glanced over at Haley. "Haley, please come join us immediately."

Haley, who'd been charging around the tearoom like a gazelle, putting candles on all the tables, came bounding over. "What's wrong, Theo?" she asked.

Theodosia grinned crookedly. "I suppose *everything* is if you really want to know the truth."

Drayton and Haley slipped into chairs. "We really want to know," said Haley, suddenly looking nervous.

Taking a deep breath, Theodosia proceeded to tell them all about the shot that went whizzing by her head in the woods yesterday and the rock that came crashing through the library window last night.

After registering horror and exclaiming over her good fortune at not being injured, Drayton and Haley quizzed Theodosia extensively about both incidents. Theodosia, of course, went on to tell them about Rex Haggard winning a gun club trophy for being a crackerjack shot and Gus and Lois handling the syringes. She mentioned her phone call to Tidwell but omitted the part about his yelling at her.

"Yikes," exclaimed Haley, "do you think all of this is related to Dr. Jasper Davis's death?"

Theodosia nodded. "Some of it has to be."

"This whole thing keeps getting mysteriouser and mysteriouser," said Haley. Now that her initial shock had faded, she seemed somewhat intrigued.

"No, circumstances have gone far beyond merely the mysterious," said Drayton stiffly. "I'd say we're veering into extremely dangerous territory."

"Tell me about it," said Theodosia, feeling somewhat heartened by their clucking and commiseration.

"You shouldn't stay at Timothy's house all by yourself," declared Haley. "Maybe you should move back into your apartment upstairs."

Drayton nodded. "I completely agree. To reside in Timothy's vast home all alone seems far too dangerous."

"I have to stay," said Theodosia. "I promised Timothy I'd play house sitter and swore to him I'd watch over his treasured residence. Besides, I have Earl Grey to keep me company."

Drayton cocked an eye at her. "Your dog has many fine talents, but could he wield one of Timothy's dueling pistols in a crisis situation?"

"Noooo," said Theodosia. "But he's proved himself to be a fairly worthy adversary in the past."

"Why not have Jory move in with you?" suggested Haley.

Theodosia shook her head. "Won't work. He's got relatives flying in for the funeral tomorrow and tons of legal hassles still to deal with."

Drayton sighed. "I'm sure Jasper Davis's so-called widow isn't making things any easier for him," he said as he uncharacteristically plopped a lump of sugar into his tea and stirred it slowly.

"Oh," said Theodosia. "Let me tell you about *her*." And she quickly related the Star Duncan-Vance Tuttle walking-to-the-car incident she'd witnessed on Saturday.

"Star Duncan with Vance Tuttle?" shrieked Haley. "Get out!"

"Are those two suddenly *dating?*" asked Drayton.

The bell over the door suddenly *tinkled* and a familiar voice called out "Toodleoo . . . hello there, my dearies!"

"Delaine," said Drayton without bothering to turn and look. He put a finger to his lips and gave a knowing wink.

"Don't worry about me," said Haley, jumping up and scurrying toward the kitchen. "Smell that heavenly aroma?

I've got raisin scones and brioche about ready to emerge from the oven."

"Theodosia, darling," said Delaine, clattering across the floor in her ultra high stiletto heels. "I've got something for you." She waved a white envelope in the air.

"I hope it's a clue," said Theodosia in a droll tone.

The smile slipped from Delaine's face. "Pardon?"

"Don't mind Theo this morning," said Drayton, pulling out a chair for Delaine. "She's just off in her own little world." He said it lightly, as if making a joke.

"But of course," said Delaine. She smiled faintly then set the envelope down on the table and slid it across to Theodosia. "I brought your tickets."

"Tickets?" asked Theodosia, looking slightly puzzled.

Now it was Delaine's turn to look upset. "Don't tell me you *forgot!*" she cried, looking extremely exasperated. "Good lord, Theodosia, you of all people should know I've been working my fingers to the *bone* selling tickets for the Lamplighter Tour!"

"Oh, right," said Theodosia. Every year Delaine was locked in mortal combat with a handful of other women to see who could sell the most tickets for the Lamplighter Tour, a once-a-year event where some of the historic district's most lovely and distinctive private homes were thrown open for public viewing. And every year Delaine sold Theodosia a pair of tickets.

"You could at least show a *hint* of enthusiasm," chided Delaine. "Especially since I'm also working frantically to pull off my big trunk show this Wednesday."

"What's to plan?" asked Drayton. "Your so-called king of cling is bringing in his stretchy dresses and you tapped us to handle refreshments." Drayton stood up stiffly and adjusted his cuffs. "Seems fairly straight-ahead to me."

Delaine threw Drayton a theatrical *I'm-completely-swamped* look. "There are *details,* Drayton. Significant details yet to be worked out."

Drayton arched a single eyebrow and gazed down at

Delaine. "A little bird informed me that the king of cling was squiring a certain someone about town this weekend."

Delaine's face suddenly rearranged itself into a brilliant smile and she positively beamed. "Oh, Drayton, he was! Friday evening Marcus Matteo and I had dinner *a deux* at Café Angelina and then Saturday evening we dined by candlelight at Le Papillon. We enjoyed the most exquisite French dinner . . . champagne, truffle-infused foie gras, and coq au vin. Very romantic and *tres* expensive!" Delaine's eyes danced and her face glowed with excitement. "I must tell you both," she said with a conspiratorial air, "that I find European men so much more . . ." she paused, searching for the correct word . . . "shall we say *worldly?* Yes, that's it. Worldly and cosmopolitan. Completely at the opposite end of the spectrum from our rather predictable local fellows."

"Do tell," said Drayton, rather acerbically.

"Why Delaine," said Theodosia, surprised, "it sounds as though you have a burgeoning romance with Marcus Matteo!"

One of Delaine's hands flew to her chest and pink shellacked nails touched the bodice of her pink silk blouse. "I believe I *do* care for him!" She said these words in such a rush and with such heartfelt sincerity that it was hard for Theodosia not to recall that Delaine had probably been in and out of love at least three times in the past year. Romances heated up pretty fast in Delaine-land. Of course, they cooled off just as rapidly, too. Still, Delaine was a dear soul who deserved to find long term happiness. We all do.

"Just don't rush into things," cautioned Theodosia.

"Oh, honey, I wouldn't do any such thing. You know me better than that."

"Humph," said Drayton.

Delaine swiveled her head and fixed Drayton with a steely-eyed stare. "Pardon, Drayton? I didn't quite catch that."

"Just clearing my throat," said Drayton, reaching to collect his teacup and spoon. "Don't mind me."

"We never do," said Delaine in a saccharine-sweet tone.

By the time Miss Dimple arrived some forty minutes later, Theodosia had finessed Delaine out the door, chatted with a few of her morning regulars, sampled Haley's brioche, and put all of last week's financial receipts in order.

A bookkeeper by trade, Miss Dimple had worked almost forty years for Mr. Dauphine, the elderly gentleman who'd owned the Peregrine Building next door but succumbed to a heart attack two years ago. Distraught over her employer's passing, Miss Dimple had seemed both depressed and at odds and ends until Theodosia came up with the idea of freelancing. Now Miss Dimple was happy as a clam as she handled the books for Heart's Desire, Antiquarian Booksellers and The Chowder Hound, as well as filling in behind the counter at Pinckney's Gift Shop.

"Are you still enjoying your stay in Mr. Neville's lovely home?" Miss Dimple asked Theodosia as the bookkeeper lowered her plump form into a padded captain's chair. "I visited it some twenty years ago and was astounded by the grandness of the decor. But I'm sure old Timothy's done more restoration and sunk more money into it by now."

"He has," said Theodosia noncommittally. She still didn't want to admit that, after the rock and note came blasting through the window last night, staying in Timothy's house made her feel more than a little on edge.

Reaching into her sensible black handbag, Miss Dimple pulled out a pair of gold wire-rimmed glasses and carefully put them on. She peered down at the table where Theodosia had her things scattered.

"What a cute little item this is," Miss Dimple said, picking up the camera phone that Jory had given Theodosia. "I'll just bet this is one of those text messaging phones."

"It is," said Theodosia, slightly amused that Miss Dimple

even *knew* what text messaging was. After all, her former employer's office had been equipped with a manual typewriter,
a Dictaphone, and an old-fashioned intercom. "But it's really a camera phone," Theodosia added.

Haley, who had seen Miss Dimple come in, suddenly appeared with a small plate of brioche. "Try this, Miss D," she
said. "It's a new recipe."

Miss Dimple was clearly delighted. "I'm supposed to be
counting calories," she told Haley, even as she gazed with
wide-eyed anticipation at the goodies set before her.

"Well, you can count on this for melt-in-your-mouth
pleasure," said Haley. She nodded at the camera phone Miss
Dimple still held in her hand. "I want to get one of those
myself. They're totally cool."

"If you ask me," said Drayton, hustling over to place a
minipot of tea in front of Miss Dimple, "I'd say it's a darned
silly contraption."

Haley stared right back at him. "You didn't think Theo's
digital camera was silly the other night."

"What are you talking about?" demanded Drayton.

"Easy," cautioned Theodosia. A few customers had turned
their heads to look over at them, curious as to what was going on in their little cluster.

Haley smirked. "When you were taking pictures at the
Ghost Crawl."

Drayton's right eyebrow lifted and quivered, then he di-
rected his gaze at Theodosia. "That was a *digital* camera?" he
asked. His words dripped with disapproval.

"Of course it was," laughed Haley.

Now Drayton looked just plain hurt. You tricked me,"
he said to Theodosia in an accusing tone.

"I didn't trick you," said Theodosia, suddenly feeling bad
at the brouhaha she'd caused. "I just didn't give you the
complete story."

"You said it was a point-and-click," persisted Drayton.

Haley was enjoying this little scene immensely. "Duh . . .
it *was* a point-and-click. It just wasn't *conventional*."

Gazing over the top of his tortoiseshell glasses, Drayton uttered a huge sigh.

"Look at him," chortled Haley. "Drayton's going to take the high road. Give us a good dose of righteous indignation."

"Of course he is," chimed in Miss Dimple, who was halfway through her brioche. "It's the only way he can win!"

Moving to her office, Theodosia arranged everything in a tidy little stack atop her desk while Miss Dimple sat down across from her in the overstuffed chair they'd dubbed "the tuffet."

"You're making a tidy profit," Miss Dimple informed her as she balanced a large black ledger on her chubby knees.

"Versus just making a living," said Theodosia.

"Exactly," said Miss Dimple. "It's amazing how many small business owners don't seem to understand the difference between making a living and turning a real profit."

"Adding the T-Bath products really made a huge difference," said Theodosia. Last year she had designed the beginnings of her T-Bath line, natural products such as Green Tea Bath Soak, Green Tea Feet Treat, and Lavender Luxury Lotion. All were lotions and potions that incorporated the healing and antioxidant powers of teas and herbs.

"You've also got a couple of years under your belt," noted Miss Dimple. "You're not a rookie anymore. You're able to judge what works and doesn't work. You know which promotions pull customers in. And exactly where your profit margins lie."

Theodosia grinned. To the untrained eye, Miss Dimple might look like a plump little elf in her early seventies, but when it came to keeping the books, generating P&L statements, and filing tax returns, she was a veritable bookkeeping shark. When Miss Dimple started spouting numbers you could almost see the green eye shade appear.

"So we'll keep the wolf from the door for another week or two?" asked Theodosia.

Miss Dimple snapped the ledger book shut. "Till well into next fiscal year for sure," came her confident, business-like reply.

"Wonderful," said Theodosia. Truth be told, she had long since stopped worrying about whether the Indigo Tea Shop was a sustainable entity. The Church Street neighborhood had readily embraced her little tea shop and tourists contin-ued to flock to it. Their catering business was growing by leaps and bounds and the special event teas were always booked solid. Even if business did slack off and they only made enough to cover rent, operating costs, and their three salaries, she'd continue to run it. The Indigo Tea Shop wasn't just a business anymore, it was a treasured way of life.

Miss Dimple struggled to her feet and slid the ledger onto Theodosia's desk. "Oh my goodness," she said, glanc-ing at the Lamplighter Tour brochure and tickets that sat atop a pile of tea catalogs. "The Lamplighter Tour. I haven't been on one of those in a coon's age. Not since Mr. Dodge Burdell of the Goose Creek Burdells was squiring me about," she said with a distant smile on her face. "And I see you bought tickets. Good for you."

"Only because Delaine was selling them," replied Theodosia, wondering what had ever become of Mr. Dodge Burdell of the Goose Creek Burdells.

"So you're not going to attend?" asked Miss Dimple. "Pity to let the tickets go to waste. Surely there must be one or two homes you haven't toured yet. I just adore seeing all the ladies and gents in their turn-of-the-century costumes, the lovely rooms lit by candlelight." Her face seemed to glow when she spoke of it. "Reminds me of when I was a lit-tle girl and we really did use candles during the war. I'm talking about World War II, of course. Not the war folks around here still jabber about . . . the War between the States. Good gracious, no one's *that* old."

Picking up the Lamplighter Tour brochure that Delaine had delivered along with the tickets, Theodosia glanced through it as Miss Dimple gathered up her things. Once again the Pike-Albert Home would be featured. And the Ravenel Home, which Drayton always referred to as a "stunning example of Victorian excess."

Theodosia scanned the rest of the list. Yes, over the years she'd pretty much toured all of the houses. She'd even catered a tea in the back garden of the Avis Melbourne Home. A rather *disastrous* tea where one of the guests had been poisoned!

"Sometimes," added Miss Dimple, "it's fun to revisit those old homes after they've changed hands. You see what restoration projects were done." She paused in her packing. "Theodosia, you should *go*."

"Um hm," answered Theodosia as she continued to flip through the pages, then gave a start as she suddenly recognized Lois Kimbrough's name.

Lois Kimbrough. Hmm.

Scanning the brochure copy quickly, Theodosia soon learned that Lois Kimbrough, the hard-charging CFO of Vascular Systems Medical was now the proud owner of the historic Charles Ferriday home. And that this fine home, a Federal Style over on East Battery Street, would be open for the tour this year for the first time in twenty years.

"You know, Miss Dimple," said Theodosia, thinking about the highly competitive, somewhat enigmatic Lois Kimbrough, "you're right about going on the Lamplighter Tour. I think I will use those tickets after all."

"Knock knock."

Theodosia looked up from her desk to find Emily Guthro standing in the doorway, smiling in at her. Dressed in a short khaki jacket and navy slacks, clutching a dark brown envelope-style leather briefcase, Emily was the picture of a young professional.

"That fellow out front . . . Drayton is it?" said Emily. "He told me it was okay to wander back. Sure hope I'm not interrupting."

"Not really," said Theodosia. Miss Dimple had just left and she hadn't really started on anything else. "I wish I could tell you I've been busy straightening up . . ." She gestured at her famously messy desk. "But I've really just been paging through tea catalogs."

"I can't tell you how civilized that sounds," said Emily. She popped open her briefcase, pulled out a manila envelope, and took a few steps forward. "Do you have time to look at a few photos?" she asked. "They're the ones I took at the Ceramics Guild this past Saturday."

After Theodosia and Emily had concluded their impromptu tour of the Lebeau Theater, they'd returned to the Ceramics Guild for the awards ceremony. There, Emily had snapped dozens of publicity photos.

"I banged out a quick press release to the *Charleston Post & Courier,* too," continued Emily, "and thought I'd send three or four of the photos along with it." She paused. "Since you're in a couple of them, I thought I'd give you copies." She handed the envelope over to Theodosia with a hopeful look. "You can just select the ones you like."

"Terrific," said Theodosia, opening the envelope and pulling out the glossy eight-by-ten-inch photos. "Crazy as it sounds, this is one of the things I kind of miss about marketing and PR."

"Oh please," said Emily as she looked around, fascinated by the teapots, photos, and memorabilia that Theodosia had crammed into her little office.

Thumbing through the black-and-white photos, Theodosia was pleasantly surprised to find that all the shots were quite good. Emily had managed to produce some nice high contrast photos that would probably reproduce well in the newspaper. Each shot was tightly framed and most were two-shots, that is, close-ups of two people interacting with each other. Again, the tighter the shot, the less grainy the newspaper reproduction would be. Plus Emily had managed to convey a "story" in each shot. Very important.

"These are good," said Theodosia. Here were shots of the winners in the various categories, shots of Cleo and the rest of the volunteers, and even a shot of Ben Atherton, grinning broadly, his hands thrust into a mound of wet clay.

"Thanks," said Emily. "Gosh, you've got an amazing office." She was carefully studying Theodosia's collection of teapots that was displayed on an antique bookshelf and probably in need of dusting. "Oh, my heavens!" exclaimed Emily. "You've got a Peter Rabbit teapot!"

Theodosia smiled. Jory had given her that teapot last year for her birthday.

"I'm absolutely crazy over all things Beatrix Potter," enthused Emily as her eyes drank in the creamy white teapot hand-painted with the infamous bunnies: Flopsy, Mopsy, Cottontail, and Peter. "Guess I'm still just a kid at heart."

"Nothing wrong with that," said Theodosia. In her apartment upstairs she also had a Betty Boop teapot and a teapot in the shape of a designer handbag. Novelty teapots were enjoying enormous popularity these days and were being snatched up by collectors everywhere. Obviously, she was no exception.

"I see now you're wildly creative," said Emily, gazing at the framed tea labels, the French poster advertising *Rue de Rivoli Salon de Thé,* the elaborately decorated red hats adorning a brass hat stand, and the stack of cotton T-shirts emblazoned with the words "Tea Shirt." Staples in her store, Theodosia herself had designed these colorful Tea Shirts adorned with a whimsical drawing of a teacup and curlicue of steam rising above it.

"You oughta see my office," wailed Emily. "A twelve-by-fifteen-foot pantheon to corporate mediocrity. Beige walls, beige carpet, beige computer. The only bright spot is a poster for a museum show of nineteenth-century American quilts that I hung on the wall. And a scraggly looking Boston fern left over from the last occupant." Emily gave a wry smile. "I guess I should be happy, though. At least it's a real office and not one of those awful cubicles like they joke about in the Dilbert comics. With pointy-headed weirdos sitting in the adjoining cubicles."

"You got that right," said Theodosia. Her first job right out of college had been a Dilbertesque experience at a direct marketing firm. There her nemesis, a woman by the name of Margot Keyes, who was constantly embroiled in redecorating her home, occupied an adjoining cubicle. Margot loudly harangued interior decorators by phone and continually brought in fabric and drapery swatches, sticking them under everyone's noses to solicit opinions. They had dubbed her Chateau Margot.

"Oh, gosh," said Emily, drifting back to Theodosia's desk. "I forgot to ask how Jory is doing."

"Hanging in there," said Theodosia, glancing down and gesturing at the brown leather journal, the MP3 player, and the Palm Pilot that lay on her desk. "Talk about sad," she said to Emily. "Jory wanted me to hang onto all this stuff that belonged to his uncle." A mournful expression swept across Theodosia's face and there was a slight catch in her voice.

Emily shook her head slowly. "This whole thing is so awful," she said. "I stopped by one of the Cardiotech labs earlier today to drop off some medical product sheets we'd designed and when I walked by Dr. Davis's office somebody new had already moved in."

"That is sad," agreed Theodosia.

The fact that it was business-as-usual at Cardiotech seemed to dampen their enthusiasm slightly and the two women chatted quietly for a few minutes about the marketing and public relations business.

"Truth be told," said Theodosia, "I'm glad I got out when I did. Today budgets are being slashed, clients are even tougher, and media campaigns are expected to deliver more than awareness—they have to impact *sales*."

"It's brutal," agreed Emily. "Then again, I haven't been

in this business all that long. I landed an internship with Vantage PR because I had a degree in clinical chemistry and they handled so many medical accounts. Then a few months ago, when an opening for a junior account exec came up, I jumped. But, believe me, it's been tough. A regular baptism by fire."

"Let me guess," said Theodosia. "You're . . . what? Twenty-four or twenty-five?"

"Twenty-five," said Emily.

"And I bet they've already sent you out to take a meeting with their toughest client." Theodosia paused for a moment, thinking. "Either the CEO of a crumbling online brokerage or a struggling start-up."

"Start-up!" exclaimed Emily. "How did you know?"

"Been there, done that," said Theodosia, once again thankful she was now running her own company, small as it was.

"Don't get me wrong," said Emily. "I'm still loving it, but ask me again in another three years. I might have total burn-out by then."

"I sure hope not," said Theodosia, and meant it.

"Is that you with your dad?" Emily asked, pointing to one of the framed photos on Theodosia's wall.

"Taken when we sailed together in the Compass Key yacht race," said Theodosia, smiling at the memory.

"Great boat," said Emily. "You two still sail?" she asked.

Theodosia shook her head. "My dad's been dead almost twenty years now."

Emily grimaced. "Mine died seven months ago." She put a hand to her heart. "Bad heart."

"Hey, Theo."

Theodosia glanced up. This time Haley stood in her doorway.

"You've got *another* visitor," Haley informed her rather crisply.

Emily instantly began gathering her briefcase and photos. "You're busy. I'd better take off. Sorry to take up so much of your time."

"Don't be silly," Theodosia told her. She glanced at Haley. "Who is it? The sales rep from Figaroa Teas?" She'd been expecting him to drop by sometime today or tomorrow.

"No, no. It's Delaine's *friend,*" said Haley, enunciating carefully, as though she were the bearer of a very special secret. "You know, the *designer*. Marcus Matteo."

Theodosia glanced at her watch. "Did you tell Mr. Matteo that Delaine left here well over an hour ago?" she asked.

Haley shrugged. "I think he wants to talk to you anyway." She furrowed her brow. "You know, he sort of looks familiar."

"I don't think so, Haley," said Theodosia. "Delaine was very clear about the fact that Marcus Matteo works out of Milan. He's supposed to be here for just a limited time, touring a few cities with his trunk show."

"Still . . ." said Haley, turning to leave.

"Miss Theodosia," said Marcus Matteo, bursting into her office, arms extended, a wide smile across his darkly handsome face. "I am sooo happy to make your acquaintance. Miss Delaine has told me sooo much about you."

Marcus Matteo grabbed Theodosia's hands, pulled her close to him, and delivered a series of air kisses before she knew what was happening. Satisfied that she had been greeted sufficiently, Marcus Matteo proceeded to turn his megawatt charm on Emily.

"Hello," he said, brown eyes gleaming and a curl of dark hair tumbling across his forehead. "You are yet another pretty friend?"

"Yes. I mean no," said Emily, blushing.

"Sure she is," said Theodosia, amused by Marcus Matteo's flamboyant and somewhat audacious greeting. With his above-average good looks and charm oozing from every pore, Theodosia decided Marcus Matteo was probably a superb salesman. Flattery would get him *everywhere*.

"Please," Marcus Matteo said to both women, "I am very

late. I was told to meet Miss Delaine right here, but I was unavoidably detained." He gave a boyish grin, as if the reason didn't matter, it was the presentation that was key.

The two women laughed politely, but Emily's eyes sparkled. *I think she likes him,* thought Theodosia.

"Miss Delaine and I were supposed to meet for lunch," continued Marcus, "then I got a message that I am to instead meet her at the floral designer, a place called Camellia Grove." He threw his hands up in the air. "I have no idea where that would be, of course."

"It's not far from here," volunteered Emily. "Why don't I give you a lift?"

He turned on her with great intensity. "You are *too* kind."

"It's no trouble," she told him.

Marcus Matteo dropped his voice a notch to an intimate growl. "You have eaten already?" he asked Emily. "You've had lunch?"

"Not yet," she replied, fixing him with a dazzling smile.

"Then we must first enjoy lunch," said Marcus. "My treat." He paused, flashed a slightly helpless, little-boy look at Theodosia. "You can make a recommendation?"

"I'd invite you both to stay," said Theodosia. "But every one of our tables is filled right now. However . . . the Chowder Hound is just down the street," she added, hoping she wasn't witnessing the beginning of a romantic scenario, Marcus Matteo-style.

"The Chowder Hound," repeated Marcus Matteo. "Such a delightful name. I *love* it! We must go and enjoy!"

13

❧

"*Your carrot bisque* smells heavenly," said Theodosia. She was standing in Haley's woefully small kitchen, inhaling the various intoxicating scents.

"Thank you, ma'am," said Haley as she bent down to take a quick peek at the lemon cream scones that were turning the loveliest shade of golden brown in the oven. She straightened up, pulled open the refrigerator, and grabbed a large silver bowl filled with freshly prepared chicken and chopped apple salad.

"Ooh, what's that?" asked Drayton, suddenly lounging in the doorway.

"That's my crabby apple salad," said Haley. "In honor of you."

Drayton's eyes widened in surprise. "Me?" he said. "*I'm* not crabby."

Haley set the bowl down on the counter, planted her hands on her slim hips, and stared at him. "Let's see now, furrowed brow, short, stiff answers, incessantly tapping foot. What would you call that?" she demanded with a wry grin on her face.

"Focused," said Drayton. "Extremely focused."

"Ah," said Haley, as she snatched up the bowl again and Drayton made a hasty escape into the tearoom. "So that's what that is."

"He's still upset with me about the camera," said Theodosia. "I should have told him it was digital but I didn't want him to get in a twist."

"He would've been, too," said Haley as she plopped a generous dollop of what she'd dubbed Drayton's crabby apple salad onto the luncheon plates that were spread out. "Drayton's just that kind of guy. Stodgy and stubborn."

"Maybe we could look upon his character as strong-willed?" suggested Theodosia.

"I suppose that *is* a kinder assessment," replied Haley as she pulled two pans of lemon cream scones from the oven then, just as quickly, shoved two more pans in to bake. "When these are done," she told Theodosia, "I'm going to bake a couple sweet potato pies. I think we could all use a little comfort food after the hair-raising experiences you shared with us this morning."

"Amen," said Theodosia.

"Gun shots and rocks through windows," murmured Haley. "Not a good thing."

"The worst part of it," said Theodosia, "is that I'm not making any progress on this Jasper Davis murder."

"No real clues, I guess," said Haley, philosophically.

"Actually," said Theodosia, "there are more clues than you'd think. But they don't lead conclusively to any one person."

For the next two minutes, Theodosia and Haley were silent as they ladled carrot bisque into small bowls, tucked the bowls next to a generous dollop of crabby apple salad, then slid a hot lemon cream scone onto each plate.

"The jelly's on the table, so these are good to go," declared

Haley, wiping her hands on her apron. "Drayton!" she called. "Time to serve!"

Drayton was back in a flash. "Wonderful lunch," he pronounced, seemingly none the worse for his sharp exchange with Haley a few moments earlier.

"Thank you," said Haley. "Now you two go knock yourselves out. I'm going to get right on those sweet potato pies. Maybe even whip up a batch of peanut butter biscuits for Earl Grey. Send him a subtle message that he's a very brave guy and we're counting on him to guard Theodosia."

"Subtle?" said Drayton, carrying out a tray filled with luncheon plates. "Have you ever seen that canine eat? There's nothing subtle about him!"

Luncheon service at the Indigo Tea Shop was busy this Monday. There were a number of regulars, some tourists Brooke Carter Crockett had sent over, and three tables of ladies from the Red Hat Society who'd stopped by for lunch before they jaunted off to visit another tea shop over in Mt. Pleasant.

By one-thirty the tea shop was virtually empty and Theodosia knew there'd be a short lull before the afternoon crowd appeared. She and Drayton had been desperately trying to find some free time so they could put their heads together and work on the holiday tea blends . . . and maybe this was it. Working on the teas would be a welcome change and might help take her mind off the harrowing events of the past few days.

Theodosia mentioned this to Drayton.

"Absolutely," he declared. "No time like the present." In a flash Drayton was seated at the table nearest the kitchen, his black ledger open, Mont Blanc pen in hand, poised and eager to get going.

"See what you think of this," said Drayton as Theodosia slipped into the chair across from him. "A holiday tea called Apple Dandy. Black Ceylonese tea blended with a hint of cinnamon, hibiscus, and bits of dried apple."

"I love it," said Theodosia. "You're thinking of using lo-cal apples?"

Drayton nodded. "Probably pink lady apples from Mount McAlpine." Mount McAlpine was the big apple growing re-gion in the northern part of the state.

"And what about Holiday Spice tea?" asked Theodosia. "Our customers always seem to specifically request that type of blend."

"Got it," said Drayton, consulting his notes. "A fine Chi-nese black tea, probably a Keemun, flavored with orange peel, cinnamon, clove, and vanilla."

"You've really been thinking about this," said Theodosia, impressed.

"Someone has to," said Drayton. Then, just as quickly, he gazed directly at her, a crestfallen look on his face. "Oh, Theo-dosia, I didn't intend it to come out *that* way," he stammered. "I just meant that . . . oh, now I've offended you, haven't I?"

"Not in the least," said Theodosia. "You know I always de-pend on you to take the lead when it comes to tea products. After all, *you're* the one who's the master tea blender. You're the one who grew up in China and actually worked at the tea auctions in Amsterdam."

"And the one with a tendency to go charging ahead," laughed Drayton. "Putting his foot squarely in his own mouth. Sorry. I'm sure you have more than a few ideas of your own."

"Actually, I've been focusing more on the T-Bath prod-ucts," said Theodosia. "But I did come up with what might be a fun name. I'd love to call one of our teas Serendipitea."

Drayton closed his eyes for a moment, suddenly lost in thought. "What if," he began, "what if we blended a Chi-nese white tea . . . one with a nice woodsy, fruity note . . . with orange pieces and strawberry leaf?"

"Wow," enthused Theodosia. "You can do that?"

"I can do anything," replied Drayton, pleased that she liked his suggestion. "I'm a master tea blender. Or so they say."

"You are indeed," said Theodosia. "No wonder people come from all over the Carolinas and beyond to buy your blends. Why, just last week, two college professors drove up from Savannah to buy six tins of Earl Green!" Earl Green was Drayton's inspired blend of Earl Grey and Gunpowder Green, with a little hibiscus thrown in for sweetness.

"I've got one more idea," said Drayton, tapping his pen.

"Shoot," said Theodosia.

"A blend called Basic Black. A rich Chinese black tea flavored with rosehip petals."

"Sounds very glamorous," said Theodosia.

"It would be even more so," said Drayton, "if people served it in martini glasses."

"Which you did at our mystery tea last year and everyone *adored* it," said Theodosia.

Drayton nodded. "You know, we've just got to write that tea book," he enthused. "Complete with Haley's recipes."

"Receipts," said Haley, suddenly arriving at their table with two slices of hot, right-out-of-the-oven sweet potato pie.

"Good gracious," said Drayton. "Is that sweet potato pie I see before me?"

Haley nodded as Drayton picked up his fork and plunged it into the still-steaming pie.

"Oh, this is incredible," marveled Drayton, savoring his first bite. "When we put our tea and receipt book together, this should surely be one of the preeminent recipes."

"I agree," said Theodosia, thoroughly enjoying her own slice of pie.

"You've been working on the new holiday teas," said Haley, craning her neck to get a peek at Drayton's ledger.

"We have," said Drayton. "In fact we're just about finished."

"Really?" asked Haley. "What about the hummingbird nests you were telling me about?"

Drayton picked up a napkin and delicately blotted his mouth. "I haven't forgotten," he said.

"What's this about hummingbird nests?" asked Theodosia.

"I thought for the holidays we'd spice up the shop with a few exotic tea offerings," said Drayton. "For instance, I found the most adorable Chinese green tea nests delicately scented with jasmine."

"And they look like hummingbird nests?" asked Theodosia. "How cute."

"Oh, they are," said Drayton. "Tiny, little tea leaf nests that will brew, oh, maybe four cups of tea."

"Sounds like a fun novelty item," said Theodosia. "And the tea is good?"

"First class," said Drayton. "Plus I'd like to add some brick teas, too." Brick teas were cakes of compressed tea. When you wanted to brew a pot of tea, you simply shaved a small amount from the hard black cake and made a sort of paste. Brick teas were generally made from tea leaves that had been fermented, then aged—the most costly having been aged for twenty to thirty years. And unlike most teas which were best when served young and fresh, brick teas, particularly those made of pu-erh tea, got better as they aged, much the same as fine red wine.

"What about the T-Bath line, Theo?" asked Haley. "You said you were going to add to it?"

Theodosia brushed her mass of auburn hair back from her face and smiled. "I've been doing some concocting of my own," she told them. "I have our manufacturer working on a slug of new lotions, many of which will contain white tea in combination with various essences."

"Tell us," said Haley, making a quick check of the tea shop to make sure no one in their spattering of customers needed a refill.

"Okay," said Theodosia. "We're going to have a new T-Bath lotion infused with basil and bergamot."

"Ooh," said Haley.

"Plus a white tea, ginger, and chamomile facial moisturizer," continued Theodosia, "and a lemon verbena and white tea bath oil."

"To die for," said Haley. "Sounds like aromatherapy heaven!"

"Good heavens," exclaimed Drayton, "you'll have people wanting to sip their bath water!"

Which sent them all into gales of laughter.

"And tell us about packaging," said Haley. "We're staying with the celadon green packaging, aren't we? And that dry brush style typography?"

"Absolutely," said Theodosia, "except now we're going to add little silver tags imprinted with a sort of *tea legend*. I found the perfect silver tags online from a little scrapbook shop in New Orleans called Memory Mine. We'll buy the tags in bulk, pen some nice copy, then give the whole she-bang to our printer."

"You guys are *so* good at promotions," marveled Haley. "I think I'm going to try to come up with something, too."

"Go for it," urged Drayton.

Theodosia smiled to herself. Sitting around with Drayton and Haley like this, brainstorming ideas, was a total kick. They worked so well together and completely respected each other's ideas. She knew this wasn't always the way it was inside companies. In some agencies and PR shops, brainstorming was turned into a competition, and people were zealous about guarding their ideas and their turf.

"You know what I've always wanted to do as a promotion?" asked Drayton.

"Tell us," said Haley, caught up in his enthusiasm.

Drayton grinned. "Hold an old-fashioned Irish street tea."

"What exactly is that?" asked Haley.

"We'd set a couple wooden tables out front and put out dozens of sturdy white mugs. We'd half-fill the mugs with hot, frothy milk in one almost-uninterrupted gesture, then top them off with hot, steaming tea in the same robust manner." He gave an enthusiastic nod. "Hopefully everyone would slosh and sip away and have a grand old time."

"Then let's do it sometime," said Theodosia. "Invite all our friends and everyone from up and down Church Street."

Theodosia, Drayton, and Haley were so lost in their grand plans that they barely noticed the lone man who'd entered their shop. It was only when he came within a few feet of their table that Drayton looked up, startled, then set his teacup down with a loud *clink*.

"Mr. Tuttle?" he said.

Theodosia and Haley whirled to see who it was Drayton had spoken to.

They found the lean, somber face of Vance Tuttle staring down at them.

"Hello there," said Drayton, vaulting out of his chair and moving toward the man, his one arm extended in greeting.

Vance Tuttle shook Drayton's outstretched hand. "Yes, good day Mr. Conneley. We met . . ."

Drayton's head bobbed. "Yes, at the . . . well, uh, this is Theodosia Browning," he said, abruptly changing conversational direction.

"Hello," said Theodosia, rising to greet him.

"And Haley Parker," added Drayton.

"Howdy," said Haley. She gave a perfunctory wave then dashed off to grab a teapot and pour refills at the two tables where customers still lingered.

Vance Tuttle regarded Theodosia and Drayton with a somewhat guarded expression. "I suppose you know why I'm here," he began.

Theodosia flashed Drayton a quick glance. She didn't have a clue as to why Vance Tuttle was standing in front of them. And from the expectant, almost shocked look on Drayton's face, it was obvious he didn't either.

"I was afraid you might have gotten the wrong impression the other night," Vance Tuttle said to Drayton. "Jasper Davis and I were not having an argument so much as a disagreement. A *discussion* if you will."

"Uh . . . yes," said Drayton, fumbling to adjust his bow tie which already looked perfect. "Of course you were."

"I certainly intended no harm to come to the man," continued Vance. "Whatever happened following our little *imbroglio* was in no way connected to me. It was simply a hideous and bizarre tragedy."

"Good heavens, man," said Drayton, "you don't have to come explaining yourself to *me*. To any of us."

"I merely wanted to clarify the incident," said Vance Tuttle. "Make sure there was no chance of misunderstanding." He offered them a crocodile smile that seemed to lack any real warmth.

So that's it, thought Theodosia. *Vance Tuttle has found himself to be a prime suspect in Jasper Davis's murder and he's trying to drum up allies. Or, at the very least, character witnesses. Is this little command performance of his rather weird? Yes, I think it is.*

Obviously, Theodosia wasn't the only one who found the situation a little off-kilter, because Drayton was gazing at Vance Tuttle with a good deal of skepticism.

"It seems you and Star have become fast friends," said Theodosia, jumping in. Drayton nodded. He looked like he was dying to pump Vance Tuttle for additional information but was too polite to do so.

"Yes, we're *friends,*" Vance said in a peevish tone. "And Star, dear, smart lady that she is, had disregarded certain unfounded rumors and been kind enough to lend financial support to our repertory company. For goodness sake," he snapped. "*Someone* has to."

Vance Tuttle's visit was the sour note that seemed to signal an end to the enthusiasm and excitement everyone had been feeling.

"What a creep," exclaimed Haley, circling back to Theodosia and Drayton. "You're sure that guy's in theater? It doesn't seem like he has an empathetic bone in his body."

"You can look as though you're emoting, but not really commit emotionally," replied Drayton. "That's why they're called *actors*."

"My granny always said 'never trust an actor,'" said Haley. "You think she was right?"

Drayton looked thoughtful. "Don't know. I'll say one thing, Vance Tuttle certainly strikes me as a strange duck."

"Maybe he's the one who killed Jasper Davis," suggested Haley. "You guys already said Jasper Davis was on the funding committee at Cardiotech. And that he was forced to curtail funding to a whole lot of arts organizations. Maybe Vance Tuttle was so upset and furious, he just had to get back at him."

"So he murdered Jasper Davis, even as he was ingratiating himself to the man's estranged wife?" asked Theodosia. Somehow the whole thing seemed awfully far-fetched. "Now he's trying to get Star Duncan to pony up funding?"

Haley shrugged. "I don't know. Whatever. It *could* hold water."

"Maybe," said Theodosia.

"Stranger things have happened," said Haley.

"They certainly have," said Drayton. "Just look at poor Delaine."

"What about Delaine?" asked Theodosia.

"Twenty-four hours ago she had stars in her eyes at the prospect of being wooed by Mr. Marcus Matteo, the self-proclaimed king of cling," said Drayton. "And now the aforementioned king and Italian couturier has squired Miss Guthro out for what would appear to be a cozy lunch. I might also add that Miss Guthro departed this establishment with a few stars glimmering in her eyes."

"Delaine's gonna be furious," said Haley, grinning wickedly.

"No, she isn't," said Theodosia. "Because the only way Delaine is going to hear about this is if one of us tells her."

"So we don't get to burst her bubble?" asked Haley, looking disappointed.

"Not a word, please," said Theodosia. "Why destroy her for no reason?"

"Theodosia's right," said Drayton. "Their relationship

will undoubtedly come to a natural conclusion anyway."

"Exactly," said Theodosia. "Once Marcus Matteo stages his trunk show on Wednesday he's off on the rest of his ten-city tour. So why burden Delaine by telling her the man is a rapacious flirt? Chances are, deep down, Delaine probably knows the man's true character."

"If you ask me, I think there's more than flirting going on," said Haley, rolling her eyes.

"Perhaps so," said Drayton. "But since we are highly civilized beings, Delaine's personal business is none of our business." He stared at her intently. "Is it, Haley?"

"No," she said, still intrigued. "I guess not."

Theodosia left the tea shop early. Bidding good-bye to Drayton and Haley around three-thirty, she hopped into her Jeep and swung by Gallaghers Food Service to pick up some supplies, then zipped across town to the Quick Print to grab the finished flyers for their upcoming Victorian tea. But at four-thirty, much to her surprise, Theodosia found herself bumping through the wrought iron gates of Jasmine Cemetery.

It had been an impetuous decision on her part to come back here. Return to the scene of the crime, as it were, to satisfy her slightly morbid curiosity with a fast look-see.

Driving up the crumbling road to the top of the hill where she and Haley had served tea and shortbread some five nights ago, she stopped the vehicle, cut the engine, and gazed around.

Jasmine Cemetery was an ancient cemetery. The bones of many fine men who served in the Revolutionary War rested here. Charleston men who'd kissed their wives and children and prosperous lives good-bye, then galloped off to serve with fierce leaders such as Francis Marion, the Swamp Fox, or his aid, Major John James. Most of these brave men had returned not in glory, but wrapped in hasty, makeshift shrouds.

There were Civil War soldiers here as well. Thousands of gallant soldiers who'd fought for the Confederacy, another thousand who'd worn Union Army blue.

Many of these fallen warriors had found a final resting place here, their graves now carefully tended, their battles preserved only in memory.

Stepping out of her Jeep, Theodosia was overcome by the solemnity of Jasmine Cemetery. Last Wednesday night, this had been a place filled with jostling visitors interested in gleaning a few nuggets of history. Now it was deserted and felt almost church-like in its solemnity.

Theodosia walked softly across dry, brittle grass, gazing at the curious mixture of elaborate tombs and simple markers.

"Here lies C. Edward Barnwell, soldier, husband and father," read an ancient carved marble tombstone. Another carried the inscription "Never Forget." But here, in this oldest section of the cemetery, many inscriptions were unreadable, the stones and carvings worn smooth by time.

Theodosia stared at the area where the ghost crawl tableau had taken place. It was quiet and utterly deserted now. Hard to believe almost a hundred people had been milling around here just a few nights earlier.

She glanced at the gnarled live oak that had served as the backdrop for her tea table. Lacy tendrils of Spanish moss floated down from its gnarled branches, giving it a spooky, mournful appearance.

Spooky. Let's not dwell on spooky right now.

Shrugging off a slightly ominous feeling, Theodosia furrowed her brow and gazed around.

Let's see, if our table was set up here, then right over there was . . .

Theodosia paced off the approximate distance. She figured she'd probably wandered six or seven steps toward the stage, jockeying for a better view. Then, when Jasper had staggered out, she'd dashed another ten steps to his side.

So that would take me to right about here.

She walked a few more steps, then paused and stared down in bewilderment.

Strewn on the ground, in the approximate area where Dr. Jasper Davis had died, was a scattering of bright red petals.

What the . . .?

Perplexed, Theodosia stared at the red blossoms. Wondering how they'd gotten there, puzzling over who might have put them there.

Did Jory's family leave them?

Somehow that seemed the most logical. Although a family wreath or bouquet of flowers might be more appropriate. But this random sprinkle of blossoms seemed . . . strange.

Leaning forward, Theodosia plucked a few of the blossoms from the ground. They felt papery and wilted in her hand, like the wings of dead butterflies.

Someone from Jory's family must have left these, right?

Theodosia thought about this for a moment, knew it was certainly possible if not plausible. But there was another possibility. In fact, a rather unsettling one.

What if Jasper Davis's murderer had come back and left these? Had come back to celebrate and . . . gloat?

It was a decidedly ugly thought. One that made Theodosia shiver and pull her sweater tightly about her.

She stared again at the flower petals in her hand.

What the heck are these flowers, anyway? They look familiar.

Something in the back of her mind gave a tiny *ping*. Where had she seen flowers like this?

These are . . . what? Salvia? Who grows salvia?

The answer was, of course, almost everyone. Charleston was famous for its wealth of courtyard and secluded backyard gardens. And with an amazingly benign climate, late blooming salvia was rampant all across the city.

But on the heels of that thought, another came crashing home to her: *Peaches Haggard grows prize-winning salvia!*

In fact Theodosia distinctly remembered Brooke talking about how Peaches Haggard of the Below Broad Street

Garden Club specialized in growing Salvia coccinea, the very distinct Lady in Red salvia.

Peaches Haggard who was married to Rex Haggard. Peaches Haggard who didn't go riding with the rest of the group on Sunday. Who'd stayed behind and . . . done what? Could it be that Peaches was a crack shot just like husband Rexy? Had she gone to the club's nearby gun range and popped off a few shots?

A sudden *crunch* of footsteps on gravel caused Theodosia to spin around on her heels. Panicked, clutching her chest, sure the killer had crept up behind her, she stared straight into the hard, beady eyes of Burt Tidwell.

"You!" she exclaimed.

He pursed his lips, then sipped delicately from a large paper cup that probably contained a double-dose of high-octane coffee.

Relief flooded Theodosia as she watched the detective quaff his brew. Then, he fixed her with an accusatory gaze.

"What are you doing here?" he asked abruptly and without preamble. No greeting, no salutation, no *hello, how are you?*

"Nothing really," she said. "Just looking around."

"Looking," growled Tidwell. "You make it sound so innocent."

"Believe me, it is," replied Theodosia.

Tidwell's dark, accusatory eyes bored into her. "I stopped by the Indigo Tea Shop earlier. Drayton told me you were out checking on a few things."

"Drayton told you that?" asked Theodosia. "Those were his exact words?" *That's not like Drayton.*

Tidwell scowled fiercely. "Of course not. First I had to string the old fellow up and beat him with a rubber hose." He paused, pleased with his little joke. "Actually, Drayton *wasn't* particularly forthcoming. It was only when I expressed dismay over the stray bullet and unsolicited rock and warning note you received last evening that he readily volunteered any information. And even then he said you were just running errands." Tidwell scowled. "Running errands indeed." He then harrumphed.

"So you didn't really beat it out of him," said Theodosia. She was a little in awe of this irreverent side of Tidwell. She'd seen the hard, caustic Tidwell many times, but this was something relatively new.

"No beating was necessary," said Tidwell. "But, please dear lady, why are you out dashing about by yourself?"

Theodosia shrugged. "Sorry. I didn't know I was under house arrest."

Tidwell let loose his infamous sigh. A mighty exhalation that seemed to originate in the depths of his diaphragm and resonate like the cry of a humpback whale. "You're *sorry*," Tidwell parroted back. "You're oh-so-worried about upsetting my delicate psyche."

"No, I'm not that presumptuous," replied Theodosia.

Tidwell took a step toward her, frowning. "What is it you're holding?"

Theodosia opened her hand to show him.

"Flower petals," said Tidwell. He stared at the ground around her. "It's been raining flower petals."

"Salvia," said Theodosia. "Bright red ones. The same kind Peaches Haggard grows."

Tidwell raised an eyebrow. "The same kind a *lot* of people grow," he replied.

"Who do you think put them here?" Theodosia asked. "On this very spot?" *Say something, darn it. Share a theory with me.*

"Perhaps they blew in on an errant wind," replied Tidwell. He had finished his coffee and seemed to be searching for a place to ditch his empty cup. It looked like he was about to stash it next to a grave, then thought better of it.

"You don't think flower petals simply appearing here is a tad strange?" asked Theodosia.

Tidwell smiled a barracuda smile. "Ms. Browning, I find everything strange these days, including wormholes in space, our government's foreign policy, and reality TV. Now, I suggest you climb back into that beastly bright red road warrior vehicle of yours and, as we have so monotonously discussed, leave the investigating to trained investigators."

"But you'll be in touch?" she pushed.

Tidwell pursed his lips once more. "I have a feeling we'll be in contact, yes."

"Do you have anything more on the fingerprints?" Theodosia asked him.

"No," was his brusque reply.

"You know Jasper Davis's funeral is tomorrow?" she asked.

Tidwell nodded. "I intend to make my presence known. Oh, and I took the liberty of phoning the Wildwood Horse and Hunt Club. They're forwarding a copy of their membership list to me as well as topographical maps of the grounds."

"You're checking it out," said Theodosia. *Good.*

"Mm hm," said Tidwell as he walked her to her Jeep. Pulling open the driver's side door for her, he gave a little wheeze, then peered at her carefully. "Mr. Conneley cares a great deal for you," he said. Then, when Theodosia didn't answer, he added: "A lot of people do."

"I know," she said in a whisper. "Thank you."

"Be careful," Tidwell said, then turned on his heels before she could say anything more.

14

❧

The historic district after dark is a sight to behold, the atmosphere wistful and dreamy like a romantic watercolor painting. Grande dame mansions of almost mythic proportions seem to glow with an inner warmth and splendor as lamps come on, fireplaces are lit. Like wedding cakes designed by some fanciful caterer who couldn't resist adding a few extra poufs of frosting, these great homes were decorated with every manner of balustrade, pilastrade, and filigree.

Inside these high-ceilinged masterpieces the French palette of oyster white, salmon pink, and pale blue remains firmly in place. No decorator du jour has ever declared old-world elegance out of style here. Furniture in these homes is plump and proper. Sterling silver, Limoges china, and oil paintings by early Charleston artists such as Thomas Sully and Rembrandt Peale, all lovingly passed down through generations, are still displayed and much admired.

Reflecting a page out of history, Charleston's patchwork

of historic homes also serves as a reminder of an earlier gentried Americana. And during the last two weeks of October, when cooler nights finally prevail, the proud owners of these magnificent mansions that grace Montagu, Queen, and Church Streets graciously open their doors to visitors and become highlighted stops on the fabled Lamplighter Tour.

"Jeepers," Drayton exclaimed to Theodosia in a stage whisper. "Look at that tea service. If I'm not mistaken, it's eighteenth century Chinese grisaille porcelain!"

The two of them had come here tonight to visit Lois Kimbrough's clean-lined Federal Style home in the role of investigators as well as tourists. Investigators because Theodosia had convinced Drayton that something seemed a little off-kilter with Lois Kimbrough. She was too perfect, too competitive, maybe a little too connected to those syringes. But they were tourists, too, since Drayton was a passionate historic district booster. And this house, the former Charles Ferriday house, had always caught the attention of his keen eye.

Also know as Adam Style, after the English-Irish architect Robert Adam, Lois Kimbrough's home featured tall, graceful windows, geometric room layouts, bands of architectural decor around interior rooms, and a large marble foyer.

Theodosia scanned the program she'd been handed by one of the guides on the front piazza, a pretty young woman in rustling silks and an upswept hairdo that looked very eighteen-hundreds.

The program copy proudly declared that "countless upgrades and embellishments have been made within this fine dwelling, yet each has been painstakingly interpreted to remain in keeping with the time-honored Federal Style tradition and this home's historic status."

"I'm blown away," said Drayton, gazing about hungrily. "This almost approaches Timothy's home in terms of grand restoration."

Theodosia had to agree with him. Not many homes could out-grand Timothy Neville's Italianate mansion, but Lois Kimbrough's home came awfully close. An enormous crystal chandelier sparkled overhead, peach-colored silk decorated the walls, yards of peach organza set off the high windows, and plush vanilla-colored upholstery covered the ornate sofas and love seats. A peach and light blue Chinese rug was whisper-soft under foot and everywhere, literally everywhere, were groupings of tasty collectibles. Staffordshire dogs, crystal boxes, handblown glass vases, and miniature antique brass sculptures.

It was dazzling yet highly organized at the same time.

Theodosia decided that Lois Kimbrough must have either inherited a ton of money to afford all this grandeur, or she was a whiz of a CFO who'd negotiated one heck of a compensation package.

"Hello, Theodosia," purred Lois Kimbrough. "Lovely to see you again." Lois Kimbrough, dressed in cream-colored silk blouse, matching slacks, and a gold mesh belt, smiled past Theodosia at Drayton. She stuck out her hand and Theodosia was positive Lois's peach nail color was the exact shade of her silk wall coverings. "Mr. Conneley, is it?" she drawled. "I understand you're on the board of the Heritage Society. I'd love to serve on that board myself some day." She fixed Drayton with a dazzling smile.

"Then you must join us at our next meeting," responded Drayton. "Come as my guest and meet everyone involved."

"What a kind invitation," said Lois. Her eyes wandered back to Theodosia. "Are you on the board, as well?" she asked.

"Not at the moment," said Theodosia. "Drayton keeps urging me to join, but I'm already involved in so many things."

"Theodosia does *tons* of work for the Spoleto Arts Festival as well as with Big Paw, Charleston's service dog organization," said Drayton. "Tell Miss Kimbrough about Earl Grey," he urged.

"Earl Grey is a certified . . ." began Theodosia.

"Maybe I'm just the hyperactive type," interrupted Lois. "But I feel like I can never be *too* involved." She laughed and threw her arms akimbo. "Bring it on, I say."

Okay, thought Theodosia, *change of conversation.*

"I hope your horse recovered," said Theodosia. "Good thing Gus was there to give him a cortisone injection. Will he need another one, do you think?"

"I haven't been back to the stable since Sunday," said Lois. "But Gus tells me Rob Roy is doing just fine. He should be in perfect form for Saturday's hunt." She eyed Theodosia. "You're riding again, I'm sure."

"Probably not this Saturday," said Theodosia.

"Really," said Lois. "Then how about you?" She gazed at Drayton.

"Oh my goodness, no," laughed Drayton. "I'm not a horse person at all."

"Really," said Lois, looking surprised. "Because you certainly have the air of someone who rides. That tweed-and-leather country gentleman look."

"No, sorry," grinned Drayton. "Tweedy, yes. Leathery, no." He shrugged. "At least I *hope* not."

Lois giggled politely at Drayton's little joke. "Well, please do roam about the house and enjoy yourselves," she urged. "Be sure and take a peek at the oval room, then amble out to the back garden. We're serving tea as well as champagne." She fanned herself with one of the programs. "It's nice and cool outside, but awfully warm in here what with all the candles blazing and the warm bodies moving about."

"*Is Lois Kimbrough* always that forward?" Drayton asked once they were out of earshot.

"That was actually subdued for her," said Theodosia. "Then again, this was only the third time I ever really talked to her. But I certainly got the feeling she was impressed with *you.*"

"She seemed awfully predatory," remarked Drayton.

"You say that whenever a woman comes on strong," replied Theodosia.

"Probably because it's true," said Drayton.

They wandered slowly through the house, admiring the library with its shelves of leather-bound books, commenting on Lois Kimbrough's collection of art nouveau vases by Emile Gallé, stopping in to view the oval room which had been turned into a lovely little parlor.

As they wandered onto the back portico, Theodosia turned to Drayton. "You talked to Tidwell about the gunshot."

Drayton suddenly looked stricken. "He brought it up. I didn't think I was breaking any confidences." His fingers twiddled nervously at his bow tie. "Tidwell pushed, I started blabbing. Are you quite upset?"

Theodosia shook her head. "Nope. Not at all. Just in a quandary over how all the pieces and parts fit together."

Drayton suddenly reached into the breast pocket of his camel jacket and pulled out his wallet. He plucked an embossed business card from it and handed it to Theodosia. "Here," he said.

"What's this?" She squinted at it. "Oh, Tidwell's card. With a couple new numbers added, I see."

"He gave that to me today, told me to call him if I came up with anything."

Theodosia nodded. "Which is Tidwellese for 'if Theodosia keeps snooping and gets in trouble, call me pronto.'"

"Quite correct," said Drayton. "And Tidwell was quite emphatic about getting in touch with him, by the way. Said all the necessary data was there to call, e-mail, or text message him, whatever *that* is."

"That's like the phone Jory gave me," Theodosia told him.

"Good grief," said Drayton. "In my day a phone was just that. A simple phone. Now they've been re-engineered to do dozens of different tasks. Send photos, videos, text messages . . ."

A slow grin spread across Theodosia's face. "You're sounding decidedly plugged in, Drayton."

"No, no," protested Drayton. "My knowledge has been gleaned solely from being bombarded by Haley's chatter. She's our resident technocrat."

The two of them stared out into the garden where flickering torches illuminated a large patio surrounded by greenery and scattered with wrought iron tables. Glass hurricane lamps with white flickering candles rested on each table.

"Shall we continue outside?" asked Drayton. "Partake of some refreshments?"

"Love to," said Theodosia, pushing open the door.

A cool breeze swept across their faces as they crossed the brick patio and paused in front of a small pond. A tiny waterfall trickled down from a stand of rocks and small orange koi peered up at them from the depths of the water. Reeds and wire grass surrounded the pond, looking as if they'd grown there naturally, not been dug up from some low-country swamp and transplanted at great care and expense.

"When you told me earlier that you ran into Tidwell today, I was amazed," said Drayton. "Whatever possessed you to go back to Jasmine Cemetery? For that matter, what possessed him?"

"I'm not sure," said Theodosia. "When I left the Indigo Tea Shop I had no intention of going there. It just sort of happened."

"Fate," muttered Drayton. "Karma."

"You know," said Theodosia. "I think you may be right."

Like so many of Charleston's hidden gardens, Lois Kimbrough's patio garden was a lovely, verdant oasis. Enormous crape myrtle and camellia bushes snugged up against the patio. Toward the back, against what looked like a woven wood fence, were dense stands of loquat and oleander. Large ceramic urns contained small palmetto trees that swayed in the gentle night breeze.

A temporary bar had been set up near the koi pond and a young, tuxedo-clad bartender smiled and raised his eyebrows in greeting as Theodosia and Drayton approached.

"Hot tea or champagne?" Drayton asked Theodosia. "You're not going to want the iced tea because it's probably made from powder." He fixed the bartender with a baleful gaze. "*Is* it made from powder?"

"Probably," said the bartender.

"Champagne then," said Theodosia.

"And I'd like a cup of hot tea, please," added Drayton. "With lemon."

Gathering up their beverages, they made themselves comfortable at a nearby table. Seated all around them were Lamplighter Tour visitors, all seeming to enjoy the mild evening and lovely garden setting.

"Look at this," sneered Drayton. "Styrofoam cups. How déclassé."

"My champagne flute's plastic, too," Theodosia told him. "I guess the Lamplighter Tour hosts are getting more practical."

"Or *think* they are," said Drayton. "You know, I watched Lois Kimbrough's face when you made your cortisone shot remark. Nothing seemed to register."

"No, it didn't," said Theodosia. "She's either very cool or very innocent."

"Are we starting from the assumption that everyone is guilty until proven innocent?" asked Drayton. "You realize, that's the basis of the Napoleonic Code."

Theodosia took a sip of champagne and looked around. Probably, she decided, in high summer, Lois Kimbrough's garden was a riot of blossoms and blooms. "Well *someone* gave Jasper Davis a lethal injection," she said finally.

"And then someone took a shot at you," said Drayton. "And a little while later tried to terrify you with that nasty note."

"I'll be okay," said Theodosia, taking another quick sip of champagne. "But I think Burt Tidwell believes I'm in mortal danger of being assassinated."

A pained expression suddenly appeared on Drayton's face and he uttered a small choking sound.

"Relax, Drayton," said Theodosia. "I was kidding. Things aren't *that* desperate."

"No," protested Drayton. "It's this tea. It's simply awful!"

As the overhead sky turned from indigo blue to inky blackness and the nearby miniature waterfall *burbled* away, Lois Kimbrough emerged from her house.

"Looks like your friend is about done in," said Drayton, nudging Theodosia.

Theodosia followed his gaze toward the bar, where Lois was gratefully accepting a cup of tea from the bartender. Lois did look a tad bedraggled and almost, but not quite, pooped. But when she caught sight of Theodosia and Drayton watching her, she strolled over to their table.

"Whew," she exclaimed. "I had no idea how exhausting this was going to be. Meeting and greeting the public, doing endless recitations on the history of the house."

Drayton, whose own tiny Civil War-era home had once been a stop on a garden tour, nodded in agreement. "It's beyond comprehension," he said. "You end up answering the wildest questions. And then people always ask to use your bathroom."

"Yes, they do," said Lois. She downed her tea in a succession of gulps, then set her empty cup down on their table. "Hope that tea was chock-full of caffeine," she told them brightly. "I've got another half hour to go." Then she turned and dashed back inside.

"Caffeine yes, flavor no," said Drayton, looking slightly amused. "We really should find out who the caterer is and send the poor soul a tin of *real* tea, not the pitiful dregs and dust they must have used to brew this swill. Maybe we'll make a convert and gain a new customer to boot."

But Theodosia's mind was suddenly humming and firing on all eight cylinders. She was barely listening to Drayton.

"Is anyone looking?" she asked him abruptly.

"What do you mean?" said Drayton, frowning slightly.

"I want to slip Lois's cup into my handbag and I'd rather nobody see me do it."

"You're not serious," said Drayton.

"Come on Drayton," said Theodosia. "Be a sport. Somebody's got to be my lookout."

"I *suppose* no one is watching," said Drayton, with some hesitation. "But why exactly do you want to pinch Lois Kimbrough's tacky little styrofoam cup?"

"Because she handled it," said Theodosia.

"Ohhhh," said Drayton, suddenly catching on. "Fingerprints. And you intend to . . ."

"Anybody looking?" Theodosia asked. She grabbed a tissue from the depths of her handbag, secreted it in her hand, and grabbed for the cup.

"I think Mavis Beaumont over there might have . . ." Drayton was mumbling.

"Got it," Theodosia whispered.

Drayton shook his grizzled head. "I can't say I've ever been part of a heist quite this strange before," he said. "A plastic cup."

"Sure you have," said Theodosia, gently patting her handbag. "Remember that time we *borrowed* those cut glass plates from the Heritage Society?"

"Please," said Drayton, suddenly looking sour. "Don't remind me."

15

***

Charleston's oldest church, St. Michael's Episcopal, at the corner of Meeting Street and Broad Street, was a stunning example of Colonial construction. Soaring steeple contributing to the skyline of the Holy City, elegant columns gracing its stately front. George Washington had worshipped here, as had the Marquis de Lafayette and General Robert E. Lee.

The church's distinguished interior boasted mahogany and South Carolina cedar woodwork, a wrought iron communion rail imported from England, and an octagonal pulpit with a heroic, canopied sounding board.

It was this very pulpit that held Theodosia's rapt attention as she listened to the minister, Dr. Jeremiah C. Russell, eulogize Dr. Jasper Davis. Dr. Russell seemed like a sincere man, but he hadn't really *known* Jasper Davis. Which made his words seem just a trifle generic. Theodosia listened, of course, but she was really staring at the crisscrossed scars at the pulpit's wood base which marked the spot where a Union shell had struck the church one fateful, long-ago day in 1863.

Looking sober and dignified in one of the dark three-piece power suits he normally wore in the courtroom, Jory sat next to her, clutching her hand in a vise-like grip. Theodosia knew this final service was terribly difficult for him. Was probably difficult for the entire Davis clan. Relatives had literally come out of the woodwork to be in attendance at Jasper Davis's funeral. Uncles, aunts, nephews, nieces, and cousins from cities and towns all around Charleston such as Walterboro and Beaufort and Moncks Corner, had shown up. Two second cousins had even flown down from Calabash, North Carolina in their private plane.

She was also pleased to see that her Aunt Libby and Margaret Rose Reese, her aunt's companion, had shown up as well.

Then there were the Cardiotech and Medical Triad contingents. Rex Haggard, who was still on the docket to speak, sat perched on a black metal folding chair next to the pulpit, looking somber and thoughtful. His wife, Peaches, had accompanied him and sat amongst the rest of the congregation looking nattily turned out in a tailored navy suit and matching wide-brimmed hat. Lois Kimbrough, looking tired and wearing a dark veil, sat across the aisle to the left. Clustered near her were three dozen or so other Cardiotech executives and Medical Triad people who had undoubtedly worked with Jasper Davis over the years.

Ben Atherton, accompanied by Emily Guthro, occupied the seats directly behind Theodosia and Jory. And across the wide aisle, sitting front and center, was Star Duncan. Attired in a stylish black silk sheath, she clutched the arm of Vance Tuttle and had spent most of the service whispering in his ear.

The usual suspects, thought Theodosia. *All gathered together in one convenient place. Now if I could just fit the pieces together . . .*

She snuck another glance at Jory. Gazing straight ahead, he looked tight-lipped and grim. The rest of his relatives had the same somber, funereal look.

I wish I could figure this out. For his sake. For their sakes.

Which suddenly made her wonder if Burt Tidwell was somewhere in the church.

Theodosia craned her neck around, gave a quick glance. She saw the faces of many people she knew, but didn't see Detective Tidwell tucked in among the congregation. Hard to miss a big fellow like that.

Was Tidwell perhaps hiding in the sacristy? Lurking outside behind one of the columns? Parked down the street in his Crown Victoria, waiting to get a good look at everyone? Or, better yet, waiting to pounce?

No. No sign of him. And, chances are, he's still just as puzzled as I am.

Theodosia put her mind back on autopilot. She listened as Dr. Russell finished up, then watched as Rex Haggard walked heavily to the podium and began his eulogy. His speech wasn't a whole lot different from the one he'd delivered this past Friday at Cardiotech, except he seemed to throw in a little more showmanship and punch up his delivery.

She listened absently as Rex Haggard talked about the brilliance of Jasper Davis's scientific mind, his skill as a surgeon, his fortitude even in the face of certain adversities. As before, Rex Haggard assured everyone that Cardiotech would "boldly push ahead."

Boldly push ahead. That's what Ben Atherton keeps saying, too. Like before the company wasn't going to? Could Ben have taken matters into his own hands? Or had Peaches?"

Theodosia sank deeper into thought until she felt a sudden nudge from Jory. She looked around. Much to her surprise, everyone was standing and reaching for their printed programs. Then, responding to some unseen cue, the congregation collectively raised their voices in song.

They're singing "Amazing Grace." The service must be over.

Embarrassed that she'd allowed her mind to drift so much, Theodosia grabbed for her program and turned to the back page where the verses to "Amazing Grace" were printed. Mustering her enthusiasm, she joined in with the soprano section. Behind her, Ben Atherton's voice rang out in a strong baritone. She turned her head slightly, saw him drop his program on the seat behind him and then, eyes closed, sing the verses from memory.

As the final notes echoed and died, Jory reached over and grasped Theodosia's hand again. Then they were filing out of the church surrounded by a pod of Davis relatives, with the rest of the mourners falling in behind them.

Out on the sidewalk, Theodosia found herself being introduced to even more of Jory's relatives. With the funeral concluded and the initial grief beginning to subside, the event was starting to evolve into a sort of family reunion, as is typical with many funerals when dozens of family factions are suddenly pulled together.

Theodosia was introduced to Jory's Aunt Polly, a school teacher from Bonneau, a little city tucked between Lake Moultrie and Francis Marion National Forest. And his uncle Otto, who was a banker up in Sumter. And his cousin Jimmy Joe from Spartanburg, whose life's ambition was to become a NASCAR driver.

Out of the corner of her eye, Theodosia saw Delaine pushing her way through the crowd.

"Theodosia!" she called. "Oh, Theo!"

"Hello, Delaine," said Theodosia, giving her a quick hug. "Thanks for coming."

"Oh honey, you knew I'd show up. After all, I think the world of you and Jory." She looked about brightly. "My, such a large family. I didn't know Jory had such a large family. Nice lookin' folks, too." Delaine's parents were deceased and her sister lived up in New York. She had a few cousins living in Savannah, but that was pretty much it for her. And, of course, an ex-husband who, as she put it, had "disappeared out west."

"Thanks so much for coming," Jory said to Delaine, giving her a decorous peck on the cheek.

She responded by throwing her arms around him. "Such a sad time," she cooed. "Sad, sad, sad. You have my deepest sympathies."

"Thank you," said Jory, trying to extricate himself from Delaine's grasp.

"Goodness," exclaimed Delaine, suddenly releasing Jory and turning her attention elsewhere. "Will you look at Star Duncan! What a perfectly *delicious* dress." Her eyes narrowed. "Maybe a Giorgio Armani? Or possibly Emmanuel Ungaro? You can usually tell with that trademarked slim cut."

Theodosia looked over to see Star Duncan and Vance Tuttle advancing on them.

"How do," Delaine gushed to Star. "Nice to see you again. Love your dress. Did you get it here in Charleston?" she asked innocently.

Star gave a Cheshire cat smile. She knew she looked good, knew Delaine was impressed. "No, I picked it up in Palm Beach last year."

"They *do* have lovely shops along Worth Avenue, don't they," agreed Delaine, suitably impressed.

Star fixed Jory with a questioning gaze. "You brought the journals and things?"

He nodded and glanced at Theodosia. "Theo?" he said.

Theodosia promptly dug into her oversized Prada bag. Jory had called her earlier in the morning while she was deliberating over her black dress versus her black suit, and asked her to bring Jasper Davis's journal and Palm Pilot along. He told her that Star had called and asked if she could have them as mementos. Since Theodosia hadn't found anything earth-shattering contained within them,

Jory had figured it was the least he could do for the woman who had been Uncle Jasper's wife. Except, of course, for the little camera phone. Jory had emphasized to Theodosia that the phone was still hers to keep.

"Here you go," said Theodosia. She handed the journal and Palm Pilot over to Star, who promptly passed them to Vance Tuttle.

"You two have gotten awfully cozy," remarked Delaine, still all smiles.

There was a pregnant pause, as though no one wanted to acknowledge Delaine's somewhat forward remark, then Vance Tuttle answered in an icy tone: "Ms. Duncan has graciously become my organization's financial angel."

"You're supporting the Charleston Repertory Company?" babbled Delaine, suddenly aware that her earlier remark might have been a bit of a faux pas. "That's so *admirable*."

Without bothering to answer, Vance Tuttle clasped the journal and Palm Pilot tightly, while giving Star a gentle tug. "Shall we?" he asked.

"Oops," said Delaine after they had moved on. "Sorry about that." She gave a sheepish grin.

"Don't worry about it," Jory told her. "Because you can be sure Star won't."

"Star certainly has a good deal of . . . ah . . . poise," stammered Delaine. She managed a big smile, but now it seemed forced. "Excuse me a moment, will you? I have to say howdy to a couple familiar faces over there." Her high heels clacking, Delaine engineered a quick getaway.

Tucking her bag under her arm, Theodosia put a hand on Jory's shoulder. "Are you sure you don't mind me taking off for a few hours?" she asked him. She was edgy about leaving Drayton and Haley alone at the tea shop, plus she hadn't been able to reschedule the taping with Constance Brucato over at Channel Eight.

Jory smiled and shook his head. "Not in the least," he

told her. I think you'd probably be bored out of your skull at the family luncheon anyway."

"I doubt it," said Theodosia. "But I promise I'll make it to your Uncle John's house by three o'clock. Three-thirty at the latest."

"Go," urged Jory. "You've given so much of your time already. Good lord, if you hadn't helped me out, I wouldn't have known where to hold this luncheon or even what flowers to order!"

"See you later, then," she said, giving him a quick peck and then slipping away.

As Theodosia pushed her way through the crowd that still milled about in front of St. Michael's, her gaze happened to land on Ben Atherton. He was talking loudly into his cell phone, and seemed to be royally chewing someone out. Poor Emily Guthro stood a few feet from him, eyes casting about nervously, looking embarrassed.

Poor girl probably wishes she could bug out on her own, thought Theodosia. *That Ben certainly is a strange duck. Nice one minute, super cranky the next. Very strange, indeed.*

Theodosia pushed to the edge of the crowd.

Strange enough to commit murder? I wonder.

She stared at the open doors of the church, thinking. Then, with no more than a moment's hesitation, Theodosia ducked back inside St. Michael's.

Footsteps echoing in the vast openness of the church, Theodosia made her way back to where she'd been sitting just a few minutes ago. But stopped one row short. Stopped at the pew where Ben had been sitting.

Slowly, she side-stepped her way into the pew, easing herself toward the center. She sat down, bowed her head, tossing a wild idea around.

Should I? a voice inside asked.

"You're here, aren't you? came the response.

Slowly, Theodosia snaked her hand down and, using the very tip of her long silk scarf, grabbed the program Ben Atherton had left behind.

Taking a gulp, Theodosia slipped it into her bag, then glanced quickly up toward the altar, fervently hoping she wasn't committing some sort of sin. Praying the Lord would overlook this tiny infraction in the hopes of finding justice.

16

❦

"*I didn't think* you'd be back," called Haley, as Theodosia dashed in the back door, plucked her hat from her head, and laid it atop the perpetual clutter of her desk.

"I was worried about you guys," Theodosia told her as she eased into the kitchen and draped a long white apron around her neck. "I knew we were completely booked for lunch and that Drayton had scheduled a couple of tea tastings for one-thirty."

"We could've managed," said Haley. "We always do."

Tying her apron behind her, Theodosia shrugged. "It was preying on my mind."

"Our plight? Or Jory's?" asked Haley, lifting one eyebrow.

"Good question," replied Theodosia. "Both, I guess."

"So how was the funeral?" asked Haley.

"Sad," said Theodosia. "And crowded. Jory certainly has lots of relatives."

"That can be very comforting," said Haley. "In times of

duress you *want* to have your family around you. When all is said and done, family's what matters most." She pulled open the refrigerator and grabbed a round package wrapped in tin foil. "I feel kind of guilty that Drayton and I didn't go with you," she said as she peeled the tinfoil back, inspecting her sandwich rolls. Haley had sliced a large loaf of bread horizontally, spread those super thin slices with smoked salmon and cream cheese, then rolled everything back up tightly.

"Don't feel bad," said Theodosia as Haley hefted a long, sharp knife, then began cutting thin slices. Because of the way Haley had rolled her bread, each slice she cut now resembled a pink and white pinwheel. Pink where the smoked salmon had been spread, white where the cream cheese was. "Jory knows how much you care," continued Theodosia. "That's what counts. Anyway, you know how Drayton *hates* to close the tea shop. For any reason."

Together, Theodosia and Haley gently placed pinwheel sandwiches on small plates, garnished them with a dollop of chutney and slice of cucumber, then added a scoop of Haley's freshly made crab salad.

"You're going to be tied up with that taping this afternoon, aren't you," said Haley.

"I'm afraid so," replied Theodosia. "I tried to change it, but Constance Brucato said no way."

"She seems like an awfully tough cookie," said Haley. "Then again, she's a TV producer. Maybe she has to be that way. Oh well, I'm sure Jory understood that it was now or never."

"I explained about the taping to Jory and he told me to please not worry," said Theodosia. "He thought the family luncheon at the Lady Goodwood Inn would probably run late and said I should just catch up with him later at his uncle's house."

"Then don't worry about it," said Haley. She paused.

* * *

Out in the tearoom, Drayton was embroiled in his own little tizzy of choosing teas. Which made Theodosia relieved she'd decided to come back.

After quizzing her extensively about Jasper Davis's funeral, Drayton posed the real question to her: Keemun or Yunnan?

"For your tea tastings?" she asked.

"Of course, for the tea tastings," he said.

Theodosia thought for a moment. Keemun was a black tea from Anhui Province in central China. Its tiny leaves yielded a deep, full-bodied flavor. Yunnan teas were from southwest China and were known for their rich, complex flavor. If Keemun was the Burgundy of teas, then Yunnan was the Bordeaux of teas.

"And you're going to serve . . . what?" asked Theodosia.

"Haley made homemade biscotti," answered Drayton. "Vanilla almond, I believe."

"I'd go with a selection of Yunnan teas then," said Theodosia. "Play the aroma and spiciness of the tea against the sweetness of the cookie."

Drayton gave a brisk nod. "Exactly my thought. Maybe serve the Panyong Golden Needles . . . some Tippy Yunnan . . . and a Golden Monkey Yunnan for sure."

"Drayton," said Theodosia, putting her hands on her hips. "You know your teas backwards and forwards. You're a professional tea taster and tea blender, for goodness sake. Why are you asking *me?*"

Drayton beamed at her words. "Because I adore a consensus," he told her. "Even if it is just the two of us."

The tea shop was filled to capacity, the serving pace for Theodosia and Drayton slightly hectic as always. But the real surprise came when Burt Tidwell strolled in at one o'clock. Drayton bustled over to greet him and show him to the one table that had emptied just two minutes earlier.

"Kindly hand it over," said Tidwell to Theodosia as she

brought him a steaming pot of Russian Caravan tea, one of his favorites.

"What?" she said, surprised.

"You know exactly what I'm talking about," Tidwell said. He gazed at Drayton, who had circled back with cream and sugar.

"You saw me?" asked Theodosia. "You were there?"

"Half the congregation probably saw you," drawled Tidwell.

"They did not," said Theodosia, setting the pot down. "The church was empty and I was very discrete."

"Is someone going to enlighten me as to the subject of this rather cryptic conversation?" asked Drayton, wrinkling his nose. "I mean, what *are* you two talking about?"

"One of the programs from Jasper Davis's funeral service found its way into Miss Browning's oversized handbag earlier this morning."

Drayton stared at Theodosia in horror. "You pinched something from a church?"

"Not just any church," said Tidwell, obviously enjoying this enormously. "From St. Michael's."

"Good heavens!" exclaimed Drayton. "Do you know how old that church is? It's on the national historic register. George Washington . . ."

"You're acting like I stole the plaque commemorating his visit," interrupted Theodosia. "When all I took was the measly program. The janitor would have probably tossed it out when he came by to clean."

"First a styrofoam cup, now the program," sighed Drayton. "We're talking wrongful appropriations."

"Styrofoam cup?" asked Tidwell. His eyes bulged as he regarded Theodosia with a mixture of mirth and reproach.

"Last night during the Lamplighter Tour Theodosia stole a cup from Lois Kimbrough's home," whispered Drayton, pleased with his revelation. "If you ask me, I think our dear girl is turning into a regular kleptomaniac." This last part was muttered to himself as he headed off toward the kitchen.

"You're quite convinced fingerprint identification is the key to Jasper Davis's murder, aren't you?" said Tidwell. He obviously took a dim view of her investigatory techniques.

"Aren't you?" asked Theodosia.

Tidwell placed his forearms on the table and steepled his pudgy fingers together. "Fingerprints are merely evidence. They in no way constitute proof. For example, *your* sticky little fingerprints could be all over those poached items."

"But they're not," said Theodosia. "I was careful. I took precautions."

"No," said Tidwell. "You continue to take chances. Something you've been specifically warned about."

Theodosia sat back in her chair and crossed her arms. "Are you finished searching Jasper Davis's house?"

"Almost," replied Tidwell, meeting her gaze.

"You found something," said Theodosia. "I can see it in your eyes."

"You see nothing in my eyes," replied an exasperated Tidwell.

Theodosia continued to stare at him.

"A note," said Tidwell finally. "Notes."

"Threats?" asked Theodosia.

"More like sick rants," said Tidwell. "All unsigned. And no, I shall not divulge the wording. I've revealed far too much already."

"It's no use," said Drayton, returning with a plate of muffins. "She's not going to back down."

"I can see that," said Tidwell, settling his chin on his chest and peering owlishly at Theodosia.

Drayton tipped the plate for Tidwell to see. "Can I offer you a raspberry chocolate chip muffin?" he asked.

Tidwell's sour mood seemed to evaporate instantly. "I see no reason why not," he replied.

"Jam?" offered Drayton. "Devonshire cream?"

"Both. Please," said Tidwell, tucking a linen napkin across his ample front and happily settling in for a nosh.

"And what is that other lovely tea you were just pouring at the next table? With the heavenly aroma?"

"A very special Yunnan," Drayton told him, tickled that Burt Tidwell had inquired about a tea that was one of his abiding passions. "I'll pour you a cup. It's amazingly smooth. Like drinking liquid velvet."

"Excellent," proclaimed Tidwell once he'd tasted it. "Very appealing to the palate."

Theodosia sat there staring glumly at Tidwell. He seemed to have completely lost interest in their conversation. "You'll tell me nothing about the notes?"

"No," he said, in between bites.

"But you'll take the cup and program back to the lab with you?" she pressed.

Tidwell slathered Devonshire cream atop his muffin. "Perhaps."

"And what about the fentanyl?" she asked. "Have you done any checking on that whatsoever?"

Tidwell lifted his eyes to meet hers and Theodosia noted the spattering of crumbs that now adorned his shirt collar.

"Anyone can procure a vial of fentanyl these days," snorted Tidwell. "With the proliferation of offshore pharmacies, especially those in Southeast Asia, all you need are an Internet connection and a Paypal account!"

Later, just as Theodosia was about to dash out the door to her video taping, Brooke Carter Crockett popped in to grab a quick take-out cup of tea and show Theodosia one of the moon and star pendants she'd designed for Delaine using an oxidized gold technique.

"Pretty," said Theodosia, holding the piece of jewelry up to the light and watching it dance and glimmer. "Delaine's going to be selling these?"

Brooke nodded as Haley came charging up with a handful of bills. "Make change for this will you?" she asked Theodosia. "Oooh, great looking pendant!"

"Thank you, Haley. And if you ever want to create a butterfly design for me, let me know, okay?"

"Hey, I will," said Haley, grabbing the change from Theodosia. "And thanks!"

"Have you talked to Delaine lately?" Brooke asked Theodosia.

Theodosia bumped the drawer of the brass cash register closed with her hip. "She was at the funeral this morning."

"Of course," exclaimed Brooke. "The service was this morning. Sorry."

Theodosia smiled at Brooke across the cash register. The woman looked preoccupied and seemed to be tossing something around in her mind. "Something wrong?" Theodosia asked.

Brooke chewed on her lower lip for a moment. "I got the distinct impression that Delaine was definitely ga-ga over that young designer, Marcus Matteo. She even dragged him by my store the other day to meet me." She hesitated. "But then I spotted him having lunch yesterday with someone else."

"Pretty girl? Kind of young?" asked Theodosia.

Brooke nodded. "You know her?"

"Emily Guthro," said Theodosia. "Works for Vantage PR."

"Does Delaine know her king of cling may be courting someone else?" asked Brooke.

"Heavens no," said Theodosia.

"And let me guess," said Brooke. "You're not going to be the one to break the bad news to her, either."

"Would you?" asked Theodosia. "The day before Delaine's big trunk show?"

"I think it would break her heart," said Brooke, snapping a lid on her cup of tea. "For a few days, anyway."

17

~❧~

The Channel Eight studios were located across town in North Charleston. Constructed of chrome and glass, they looked very efficient, very modern, and very boring. A dozen different satellite dishes sprouted from the roof like giant mushrooms and a tall tower that looked like it had been built with an erector set was home to some type of super Doppler radar gizmo.

When Theodosia came barreling into the lobby, a good fifteen minutes late, the first person she ran into, literally, was Vance Tuttle.

"Mr. Tuttle?" she said, stunned. She'd effectively dodged a pair of leather and chrome Eames chairs, but not the effete-looking theater director.

"Hello, Miss Browning," said Vance Tuttle. "I certainly didn't think I'd run into *you* again so soon." They stared at each other, an uncomfortable silence hanging between them.

Finally, Theodosia decided she had to say *something*. "I'm

here for a taping," she said, giving him a pleasant smile. "They asked me to do a tea segment for the *Windows on Charleston* show."

Vance Tuttle nodded and seemed to slowly warm up to her. "I just taped a short segment myself for the arts feature on the five o'clock news. We have a new play opening Friday. *Carolina Heartstrings.* Perhaps you've heard of it?"

"No," said Theodosia, "but it sounds interesting."

"Listen," said Vance Tuttle, lowering his voice. "I'd like to talk to you."

"Okaaay," said Theodosia slowly. "But I was supposed to be on the set fifteen . . . no twenty . . . minutes ago."

"How long will your thing take?" he asked.

Theodosia thought for a minute. "Maybe an hour and a half? Two hours?"

"I have errands to run," said Vance Tuttle. "But I can come back. Will you wait for me?"

"Sure," said Theodosia, wondering what was so important that Vance Tuttle wanted to come back and talk to her. *Is he going to proclaim his innocence once again? Or does he want to talk to me about Star Duncan? Or Jasper Davis?* "No problem," said Theodosia, suddenly burning with curiosity.

Constance Brucato, the producer of *Windows on Charleston,* wasn't merely grumpy, she seemed to have wound herself into a full-blown snit. Stalking the floor of Studio B, shaking her head, Constance looked stressed and overworked. And from the way the floor director, lighting guy, and camera man collectively rolled their eyes when she wasn't looking, Theodosia had the feeling Constance was in a *perpetual* grumpy mood.

"Now The-o-do-sia," said the somewhat stout Constance, pronouncing every syllable of her name, "I need you to stand behind this table and look right into the camera. Hopefully the crew has everything set to go since we're running seriously late!"

Theodosia moved obediently behind the butcher block table that was on the set. The crew had been fooling with lighting and camera angles for the past hour and hadn't yet rolled a second of tape. But that was pretty much how all shoots went, Theodosia decided, whether they were shooting film, tape, or doing still photography. The technicians fussed and fidgeted to get the shot set up perfectly, then once they rolled tape or clicked the shutter the whole she-bang was over.

"I'm still picking up a shadow," announced Raleigh, the camera man.

Constance pushed a button from inside the glass-walled control booth and her voice boomed across the studio. "Then have Harvey throw up a scrim," she screamed. "He's supposed to be the lighting expert!" There was a click and a high-pitched hum then everyone on the studio floor heard Constance mutter: "He's the one who's always talking about what this station can or can't do pursuant to *union* regulations."

"Problems?" Theodosia asked Raleigh.

He gave a grimace as he coiled a length of black cord. "Nothing we can't handle."

Then as Constance came barreling across the floor of the studio, her heels making staccato sounds, dark hair flying, and her face beet red, Raleigh slid away discreetly on crepe-soled shoes.

"Now Theodosia," she began, "we need you to do a very quick introduction . . . and I mean like forty seconds at best . . . on the tea accessories we've laid out." Constance blinked rapidly and Theodosia could see she was shedding eye makeup like crazy. "Can you do that?" Constance asked.

"I'll give it my best shot," said Theodosia. "You want me looking straight into the camera, right?"

"Correct," said Constance. "Just pretend we're all idiots and we know absolutely nothing about teapots and tea cozies and things like that. Just touch lightly on each of the tea accoutrements."

Pretend you're all idiots, thought Theodosia. *Okay. I can do that.*

After a few false starts, Theodosia made it through a credible introduction to the world of tea. She popped the cozy off the Brown Betty teapot, poured a nice steady stream of tea through an antique silver strainer and into a pretty Limoges cup, all the while trying to keep her voice light-hearted and her delivery interesting.

When Constance yelled "Cut! We got it," Theodosia was thrilled.

Until, of course, they had to move on to the next setup. Which was supposed to be a quick two minute lesson about various kinds of tea.

Now, anyone who knows *anything* about tea understands that the varieties of tea are infinite. But Constance wanted just the basics. Tea drinking 101. So Theodosia held her tongue and gave her what she wanted. A quick, superficial lesson.

Theodosia decided it might be helpful to beginners if she presented a few teas that were popular for breakfast, a couple of teas that paired nicely with food, and a couple of teas that were suited for an afternoon pick-me-up.

Sending a silent thank-you to Drayton for putting together a huge bundle of teas for her to bring along, Theodosia pulled out several small tins of tea. Teas she hoped would be intriguing to Channel Eight's viewers.

For breakfast, she was going to recommend a nice malty Kettala Estate Assam that went well with milk and sugar. And a terrific Castleton Estate Darjeeling that was full-bodied with a slightly nutty aftertaste.

A spiced plum herbal seemed like a natural for lunch, even though it really wasn't a tea at all but an infusion. As well as Hyson, a fragrant and mellow Chinese green tea.

And for afternoon sipping, Theodosia decided to feature a nice Ceylonese silver tips that had a pale pink color and slightly sweet taste. And a smoky Lapsang Souchong, an ancient Chinese tea whose large leaves were traditionally dried over pine fires.

Her presentation would be superficial at best, touching only on a few tea basics. Yet she hoped her presentation would give viewers a tiny peek into the fascinating world of the *Camellia sinensis* plant. The plant whose precious leaves had been transported across the central Asian desert on the backs of camels, been bartered for goods and gold in the markets of Europe, and become the flash point that ignited the American Revolution.

Ninety minutes later it was all over. The footage taped, viewed, and scrutinized.

Theodosia was free to go.

"Thanks, Theodosia," Constance called to her from across the studio. "Good work!" She held up a thumb, flashed a wide grin. If the session hadn't been such a scream-fest, Theodosia would've believed her. Then again, maybe her tea segments *had* turned out well. And the snarling and gnashing of teeth between producer and crew was a daily occurrence.

"Excuse me," Theodosia said to the receptionist as she made her way out of the Channel Eight studios. "I'm Theodosia Browning. I just came from Studio B with Constance Brucato . . ."

The receptionist, a woman with an amazing pouf of big blond hair, gave her a disinterested glance from behind a behemoth black desk.

"Has anyone stopped by looking for me?" Theodosia asked.

The receptionist glanced back down at the papers spread in front of her. "No," she replied.

"You're sure?" Vance Tuttle had seemed pretty emphatic about coming back her to talk to her.

"Positive," said the receptionist. She touched the top of

her pen to her lips as if to indicate their conversation, however one-sided it had been, was concluded.

"Okay," said Theodosia, giving a dubious glance. "Thanks."

She strolled out the double doors of the Channel Eight studios and looked around. No cars were parked and waiting in the large, impressive circular drive in front of the building. Not much going on at all, in fact. Just the whistle of traffic over on the Mark Clark Expressway.

Figuring Vance had probably got hung up, or maybe even decided against meeting with her, Theodosia headed around the side of the building to the parking lot.

Feeling tired and more than a little wrung out, she decided she'd head back to Timothy's house and take the very patient Earl Grey out for a well-deserved walk. Then she'd take a quick shower, get dressed, and go over to Jory's Uncle John's house.

Theodosia climbed into her Jeep, stuck her key in the ignition, and cranked the engine over. She took a quick peek into the rear view mirror to make sure no cars were behind her, then started to back out of her parking spot. Glancing to her left, she caught sight of a Mercedes-Benz. An older model, maybe a 190e.

Isn't that Vance Tuttle's car?

And on the heels of that thought . . .

Is that him sitting in it?

Halfway out of her parking space, Theodosia stomped on the brake. Something wasn't right. But since her Jeep sat so much higher than the Benz, she really couldn't tell *what* was going on.

Did Vance fall asleep waiting for me? Or is he just engrossed in something? Pouring over a script or making a few quick scratches on a note pad?

Theodosia put her Jeep into "park" and climbed out. Walking around the back of the Benz to the driver's side, she was about to tap on the window.

But the window was already rolled down.

And Vance Tuttle wasn't busily absorbed in some little activity, he was dead. Slumped in his seat, eyes open, head lolled back on the headrest. With a small black hole directly in the center of his forehead.

Theodosia inhaled sharply, put a hand to her mouth.

Oh my lord, she breathed. *Somebody shot him!*

Both hands still clutching the steering wheel, Vance Tuttle stared straight ahead into nothingness.

Inadvertently taking a step back, Theodosia tried to collect herself. She didn't panic, didn't scream, or turn and run. She was made of much sterner stuff than that. Rather, Theodosia tried to force herself to think.

Who did this? Star Duncan?

It could have been, but it didn't feel right.

Good lord. Tidwell told me to be careful. He was right. I could have been sitting next to Vance, talking with him.

This time a bolt of fear shot through her and she felt her knees begin to shake.

"Miss, are you okay?" called a voice behind her.

Startled, Theodosia whirled around to find Raleigh the cameraman staring at her. He'd been about to climb into a brown minivan.

"I'm . . . yes, I'm okay," she told him in a halting voice. "But I'm afraid there's been a terrible accident."

Not sure *what* was going on, Raleigh took a few tentative steps toward her. When he saw Vance Tuttle, his eyes widened in surprise. "Mother of pearl!" he exclaimed. "That's no accident!"

Theodosia gave a tight nod. "You're right. He's been shot."

"You say he's *dead?*" Raleigh had gone from surprised to stunned; Theodosia was already there.

"Yes," said Theodosia, "I'm afraid the poor man is gone."

Raleigh yanked his cell phone off his belt and looked around in amazement. "Right here in our parking lot. Jeez!"

* * *

When Tidwell showed up some twenty minutes later he was maddeningly efficient and unapproachable. Standing just inside the flapping boundaries of the yellow and black tape that had been hastily strung up, he consulted with the crime scene technicians, made his own notes as they took their photos, dusted the car, and methodically searched the area surrounding the Mercedes-Benz.

Once the news spread inside the Channel Eight studios, everyone had coming pouring out of the building to gawk, shoot film, pester the police and, presumably, get the TV scoop of the day.

When Tidwell finally ducked under the tape and sauntered over to Theodosia, the Channel Eight crew pointed their cameras at her.

"His wallet is missing," were the first words out of Tidwell's mouth. He had been talking on his cell phone and Theodosia saw that he, too, used one of the newer camera phones. Probably to send quick images back to the precinct house.

Theodosia nodded. "Of course it is. That's because it's supposed to *look* like a robbery." Now that she'd had sufficient time to recover from her initial shock and mull the situation over, she'd decided that Vance Tuttle *must* have known or suspected something about Jasper Davis's murder. He must have possessed some kind of information that had made the killer extremely uneasy. The question was—what information?

Tidwell rocked back on his heels. "Made to *look* like a robbery, you say. So you subscribe to a conspiracy theory."

"Not conspiracy," Theodosia said. "One person. One cold, calculating, dangerous person."

"The same perpetrator who so rudely dispatched with Dr. Davis?"

"Yes. Of course," she said.

"The same person who took a potshot at you?" Tidwell's furry eyebrows pulled themselves into fierce arches as he stared at her.

He had her there.

"Maybe," Theodosia said slowly. She pushed her mass of auburn hair off her face, thinking. "Probably."

Shaking his head, Tidwell's jowls did a slow dance. "You were the one who was fairly positive the investigation would lead to someone at Cardiotech. Now we have this poor dead actor who struts his stuff upon the stage and then is no more," he said, breaking into a bit of Shakespeare. Tidwell shrugged. "But this poor dead actor had a fragmentary connection at best."

"Not so," said Theodosia. "The Charleston Repertory Company used to be funded by Cardiotech and Vance Tuttle had been escorting Star Duncan around town. And Star was Jasper Davis's estranged wife. So I'd say there's a big-time connection."

Tidwell let loose an audible sigh. "And the conclusion you draw is . . . what?"

"Well," Theodosia said, "I don't have one. Yet."

"You don't have one," said Tidwell in his most magnanimous manner. "Could it be," Tidwell continued, "that you feel you have to, shall we say, pull something out of the hat for the sake of your gentleman friend?"

"You mean for Jory?" Theodosia asked.

"Quite correct," said Tidwell. "And because of certain warm, fuzzy feelings you harbor for this young man, you feel compelled to try to wrap everything up oh-so-nice and neatly."

Theodosia thought about this for a moment. Tidwell had scored a point there. Maybe she *was* chasing after shadows in an effort to help Jory. But she wasn't about to give Tidwell the sublime satisfaction of agreeing with him.

"Listen," she said. "I have to go home." A faint sun was sliding down over the horizon and the early evening was suddenly cool. The crime scene technicians were setting up lights and the coroner had just arrived in his large, black station wagon. "Do you need me for anything else?" she asked.

"Not at the moment," said Tidwell. "I believe the Charleston Police Department is reasonably capable of taking it from here."

Theodosia turned to leave.

"Miss Browning?" Tidwell called.

She glanced back toward him. "Yes?"

He held a business card in his outstretched hand. It was the duplicate of the one Drayton had passed on to her. "My various e-mails, t-mails, and such are listed on that card. Just in case."

"Okay, thanks," Theodosia said, reaching for it.

But he held onto the card as she tried to take it. "A couple more words of advice."

"Yes?" she said.

"Let the pros do the investigating."

"I believe you mentioned that before," she said. "What else?"

"Lock your doors."

18

❧

Still feeling shaky and discombobulated, Theodosia drove to Timothy Neville's home in the historic district. As if on autopilot, she changed her clothes, fed Earl Grey his ration of kibbles, then clipped a leash to his collar and led the anxious hound outside for his evening constitutional.

Truth be known, Theodosia was hoping the walk would be beneficial for her, as well. Help relieve some of the stress she was feeling, clear her head, and help her focus. Allow her to puzzle out some of the terrible goings-on and maybe, just maybe . . . see something she hadn't seen before.

White Point Gardens, the spectacular park and greenbelt that stretched around the tip of the Battery, was just what she needed tonight. As Theodosia jogged and Earl Grey loped easily beside her, she reveled in the fact that the crashing sea was just to her left, lovely, landscaped gardens on her right. Beyond the gardens, enormous homes sat shoulder to shoulder, glowing like glorious lanterns as light spilled out from their windows and front verandahs.

Up ahead were the war memorials, bandstand, and clusters of old cannons that made White Point Gardens such a popular spot.

Wind whipped at Theodosia, bringing tears to her eyes and unfurling her hair like a banner. The smell of the sea, salty and slightly metallic, only served to drive her on and Theodosia gulped air as she quickened her pace.

Just before she'd come out for her run she had phoned Jory, who was still at his Uncle John's house. Giving him what felt like a halting and somewhat rambling explanation, she'd brought him up-to-date on what had happened to Vance.

Jory had been shocked beyond belief. Had told her to stay put, to please not bother coming over to his uncle's tonight. He argued that she'd been through enough for one day. And, for once, Theodosia had to agree. It *was* enough. Too much, in fact.

But even as her body seemed to shed its stress, her mind remained filled with runaway thoughts. And so, when she finished her run and walked through the door of Timothy's house, she consulted the card Tidwell had handed her and called him on his cell phone.

Tidwell answered on the first ring.

"Has Star Duncan been informed of Vance Tuttle's death yet?" she asked. Theodosia was sitting at Timothy's desk with Earl Grey stretched out beneath. Still panting a little. She could feel his hot doggy breath on her ankles. But it felt good. Reassuring.

"We've run into a slight problem in that regard," replied Tidwell.

"What?" asked Theodosia, instantly alert. "Tell me."

"We can't seem to *find* Star Duncan."

Theodosia let Tidwell's statement sink in. "You can't find her?"

"Let me put it this way. She's not at her home over on the Isle of Palms and she's not answering her cell phone."

Could Star be with Jory and the rest of the family? "Did you check with Jory. At his uncle's house?"

"First place I checked," said Tidwell. "They say they haven't seen her since the funeral this morning."

"How about putting out an APB on her car?" suggested Theodosia. "Star drives that sporty little Porsche 911."

"We're not certain the woman has actually *done* anything," answered Tidwell. "Certain libertarian lawyers frown on law enforcement personnel apprehending people before they've been accused of a crime. Or crimes," he added.

"I hate to keep hammering away at this," said Theodosia, "but have you tested the program with Ben Atherton's prints on it and the cup with Lois Kimbrough's prints? You know, compared them to anything found on Vance Tuttle's Mercedes?"

"Rest assured, those items will be at the lab tomorrow," said Tidwell. "I can't imagine we're going to find any sort of match, but there's no harm in ruling those two out."

Theodosia held the phone away from herself for the moment and smiled. Tidwell was suddenly treating her like a colleague rather than a ditzy snoop.

"But if you find something . . .?" asked Theodosia.

"It would be a first step," allowed Tidwell.

"There's something I didn't tell you," said Theodosia.

"What's that?" asked Tidwell.

"I think my house might have been broken into this past Saturday night."

"*Your* house?"

"Timothy's house. You know what I mean."

"Were any doors jimmied?" asked Tidwell. "Is something missing?"

"Not that I can tell," said Theodosia as the chime from the front door echoed down the hall. "I don't know, I could be wrong, but it was just a feeling I had. That and I heard a noise."

Someone's at the front door. Jory?

"Listen, I have to hang up," Theodosia told Tidwell.

"Exercise a modicum of caution, will you Miss Browning?" said an exasperated Tidwell. "And lock those doors!"

Theodosia was cautious. Peering through the wavery glass of the double doors before she pulled them open, she saw that Ben Atherton had come to pay her a visit.

Ben. I wonder what he wants.

"Ben," she said, opening one of the doors. "What can I do for you?"

He gave a perfunctory smile. "I didn't want to disturb Jory, but I found a couple of things at my office that belonged to his Uncle Jasper." He held up a large manila envelope. "I was going to mail them, but that seemed so impersonal. Then I thought of you . . ."

"That's very considerate," said Theodosia. "Come in." She opened the door, allowing him to step into the entryway.

Ben looked around at the vast expanse and whistled. "Say now, this is quite a place." His eyes came back and landed on her. "Aren't you afraid to stay here alone?"

"No, not really," said Theodosia. *Yeah, I am. Especially when rocks come whistling through windows. Or men I don't really know all that well ask strange questions like that.*

"How did you know I was staying here, Ben?" she asked.

Ben furrowed his brow. "I think your friend, Delaine, mentioned it."

Thanks a lot, Delaine.

Ben turned dark eyes on her as he handed over the envelope. She noted that the envelope was sealed.

"Did you hear about Vance Tuttle?" he asked.

"Yes, I did," said Theodosia. She decided there was no reason to tell him she was the one who found the body. He'd probably find that out soon enough.

Ben Atherton frowned and shook his head. "I just heard it on the news. Driving over here, as a matter of fact. This whole thing is very weird. First Jasper Davis then Vance Tuttle." He stuck his hands in his pockets and jingled his change. "It feels like the two deaths are related, but . . ." he paused. "I don't quite see any connection. Do you?" he asked, staring at her intently.

Click click click

They both turned to watch Earl Grey saunter down the hallway. His motions were casual, but his eyes were bright and his head was held high as he carefully scoped out this new visitor.

"Oh jeez!" exclaimed Ben. "You've got a dog. A big guy at that."

"You like dogs?" asked Theodosia. Earl Grey sidled up next to her then extended his neck to give Ben a perfunctory sniff.

Ben stiffened. "Cleo and I are really cat people."

Earl Grey shifted his body around so he was now standing between the two of them.

"Cats are terrific," said Theodosia. "Timothy has a cat prowling around here somewhere. Big Manx by the name of Dreadnought. We don't see the old fellow much. Just put out a can of Fancy Feast at night and find it empty in the morning."

But Ben was edging toward the doorway. "Let me know if you hear anything, okay?"

"Sure," said Theodosia. "Will do." *Yeah, right.*

She stood on the verandah with Earl Grey and watched Ben Atherton walk to his car. He paused, gave her a nod and a big friendly wave, then jumped into his Volvo and roared off.

It was only when Ben's car turned the corner that Theodosia heaved a sigh of relief.

19

❧

Drayton clinked his spoon against the side of his teacup as he stared wide-eyed at Theodosia. Haley sat sprawled in a chair, a look of utter amazement on her youthful face. The minute they'd shown up at the Indigo Tea Shop this morning, Theodosia had sat them down and quickly related the bizarre events of late yesterday afternoon. They'd been visibly stunned and shaken by her news. And caught by surprise, too, since this was the first either of them had heard of Vance Tuttle's death.

"You really didn't see *anything* on the news last night?" Theodosia asked them, searching their faces. It had been on every channel.

"Didn't watch the news," said Drayton, his lined countenance looking stricken. "I was plowing through a new book about the Battle of Gettysburg and never bothered to turn the idiot box on. Not even for the ten o'clock news."

"I was at class," Haley told them. "Marketing Methodology in the New Millennium." After several fitful starts and stops at a college major, Haley had finally settled upon Business Administration. Now she was diligently taking college classes two nights a week.

"Vance Tuttle dead," said Drayton, shaking his head. "How utterly bizarre." He pulled out a white hanky, unfurled it, and blew his nose loudly. "I didn't really know the man, but still . . . you hate to see . . ." His voice trailed off.

Haley shuddered, eyeing Theodosia with something akin to morbid curiosity. "Does it frighten you, Theo, that once again *you* were in close proximity to someone when they died? Or rather, when they were killed?"

"Please," said Theodosia. "Burt Tidwell has drilled that thought into my head to such an extent that I was nervous as a cat staying at Timothy's house again last night."

"Doesn't Timothy have a security system?" asked Drayton. "I was sure he did."

"He does," said Theodosia, looking sober. "And you can be sure I used it. But, think about this . . . whatever sick, malevolent person committed those murders, they must also be extremely clever. They've obviously been able to get very close to their victims without arousing suspicion."

"You're right," murmured Drayton. "I hadn't thought of that."

"That kind of behavior indicates a very cunning mind," said Theodosia. "Someone who's highly organized. And, I hate to say it, probably someone who might be able to circumvent a security system, too, don't you think?"

"Good lord, Theodosia," said Drayton, taking a sip of tea. "Then I suggest you err on the side of conservatism and move back home immediately!"

"Drayton's right," agreed Haley.

Theodosia took a sip of Lung Ching tea, Dragon Well. Drayton had brewed a pot some ten minutes earlier and it was just what they needed. One of China's prized green teas, it was both bracing and slightly sweet.

"When I talked to Jory this morning," Theodosia told them, "he thought I should move out immediately."

"I'm with Jory," said Drayton, thumping his hand on the wooden table for added emphasis.

"I'll bet Jory is plenty flipped out, huh?" asked Haley. "Vance Tuttle getting shot the afternoon of his uncle's funeral. It certainly doesn't seem like any mere coincidence."

"Jory's stunned that the police still haven't located Star Duncan," said Theodosia.

"The police really suspect Star?" asked Drayton.

Theodosia offered a shrug.

"That is so strange," said Haley. "Star was married to Jasper Davis, who got killed. Then she was chumming it up with Vance Tuttle . . . and now *he's* dead, too!"

"One might call it the black widow spider syndrome," said Drayton ominously.

"I saw a movie about that exact same thing!" exclaimed Haley. "There was this woman who was married to *three* different men. And they all died—bim, bam, boom—under very suspicious circumstances. One of the main characters in the movie, a police woman, decided the wife *had* to be the killer."

"And was she?" asked Drayton.

Haley frowned. "I don't remember. I *think* so."

Drayton switched his attention back to Theodosia. "Have you talked with Detective Tidwell yet today?"

"Not since last night when he give me a stern warning about exercising caution and staying as close as possible to the home fires."

"You're supposed to go to Delaine's today," said Haley. "Today's her big trunk show."

"*We're* supposed to go," said Drayton, correcting Haley. "Do you know that woman phoned me *three times* yesterday afternoon. She's in an absolute tizzy that the tea and treats we're supplying won't be absolutely perfect." He paused.

"Now I ask you, when has the Indigo Tea Shop *ever* dropped the ball."

"Never!" cried Haley.

"I can't believe either of us will be in mortal danger serving tea at Delaine's shop," said Theodosia. "So I suggest we try to carry on as usual."

"Agreed," said Drayton. "Even with these strange goings on we can't allow ourselves to be held hostage." He stood up, doing his utmost to appear his typical jaunty self. "What's on tap for lunch today, Haley?" he asked.

"Asparagus and Gruyère cheese tarts," she told him. "Plus I was planning to bake a super-sized batch of profiteroles. We'll keep a few dozen here for our afternoon tea service and you can take the lion's share along to Delaine's shindig. Maybe we'll even fill some with lavender egg salad. That woman is absolutely *batty* over lavender."

"Tell me about it," said Drayton as he moved behind the counter, quickly pulling various tins of tea down from the shelves. "Remember this past summer when Delaine demanded lavender iced tea for the Fashion Bash fund-raiser?"

"Do I ever!" said Haley. "And you know how *that* turned out!"

While Drayton and Haley took care of their morning customers, Theodosia set about getting everything ready for Delaine's trunk show this afternoon. Since Cotton Duck was a relatively small shop, they obviously couldn't go overboard on refreshments. Plus, Delaine was always a little nervous about serving food and beverages in her store. Paranoid, in fact, about customers spilling on her expensive silks and velvets.

Theodosia thought she might have worked out that little problem. The Indigo Tea Shop had a rather extensive collection of small Chinese teacups. Pretty ceramic teacups without handles that were decorated with elegant glazes of autumn gold and oxblood red. They would hold just the right amount of tea, but were certainly deep enough to curtail any sloshing.

As for the goodies, Haley was planning to send them off with baskets of cashew meringues, miniature maraschino cherry scones, and profiteroles. All foods that were delicious yet virtually bite-sized. Very quick and easy to eat. Plus, Drayton was going to prepare some sort of tea sparkler and Haley had alluded earlier about coming up with a very special treat.

If Drayton handled the serving and she circulated with a silver tray, Theodosia mused, then she could collect the tea cups, small plates, and whatever else as soon as people finished with them. Again, that would keep the spillage factor down to a bare minimum. Something that was sure to please Delaine.

So she was going to need the cups, silver trays, lots of their indigo blue cocktail napkins and . . . what else?

The hum of activity and buzz of conversation in the tea shop soon lulled Theodosia into a state of relaxation and relative calm. Which made her wonder . . . was that how Jasper Davis felt before someone jabbed him with a hypodermic needle?

Had Vance Tuttle let his guard down before someone lifted a gun and blew a little black hole in the center of *his* forehead?

Had this very cunning killer, whoever he or she might be, lulled these poor victims into a false sense of security? Maybe the killer had been chatting them up, friendly as all get out, and then, when they'd least expected it, ka-pow!

But who? Who could have insinuated his or her way into the lives of Jasper Davis and Vance Tuttle?

Theodosia sat at the table near the kitchen, deep in thought.

Hmm. Who indeed.

She glanced out across the tearoom where Haley was flitting about, serving almond scones and looking exceedingly efficient. Drayton was charming their guests with his dry wit, dispensing his usual treasure trove of tea lore.

Theodosia decided that the two of them were soldiering on as gamely as possible. Trying their best to look composed and not appear rattled by the events of the past few days. *Trying.*

But the reality of the situation suddenly made Theodosia uneasy and she reached for her phone, thinking she'd phone Burt Tidwell.

Then she hesitated.

Yes, she wanted to stay right here, with an eye on the front door and an ear to the conversation in the tearoom. But she also didn't want to carry on a conversation with Tidwell that might get Drayton and Haley any more nervous than they already were. Because even though they appeared to be carrying on with an air of quiet confidence, she felt sure it was all just a very good act.

And, she didn't want any other ears to overhear, either.

So, Theodosia decided to do the next best thing. Send Detective Tidwell a text message.

It took her just a few seconds to tip tap the telephone buttons and send the following text message: "Whr did Lois K go aftr funrl?"

Barely a minute later, Tidwell text messaged her back: "Still chkng."

She thought about this for a moment, then sent: "Rex Haggard?"

His words came back: "Back off pls."

Okay, she thought, have it your way Tidwell. Considering his request or order or whatever it was, Theodosia tapped out two more text messages: "Find Star Duncan yet? Anything re finger prints?"

But nothing came back to her. The tiny screen on her phone remained blank.

"Those baskets give me an idea," said Haley.

Theodosia straightened up and smiled at Haley. She'd

packed all the Chinese teacups she'd been able to scrounge up into a couple of good-sized Carolina sweetgrass baskets. "What's that, Haley?"

"You and Drayton are always so wildly creative with your tea blends. And then, of course, *you* designed the tea shirts, of which we sell a ton. And your T-Bath products . . ."

Theodosia nodded. Haley was obviously leading up to *something*.

"But I have a new product idea, too," said Haley, finally getting to the crux of the matter.

"What's that, Haley?"

"Well . . . I guess if I had to *name* it, I'd probably call it Tea Party in a Basket."

Theodosia had to smile. It was a cute name. "Tell me more, Haley."

"You know how we already do gift baskets?"

Theodosia nodded. They sold *tons* of gift baskets. Usually filled with tea, cookies, chocolates, and their own green tea body lotion.

"Well this would be arranged in a sweetgrass basket, too, but instead of a *random* selection of gifts like we have now, we'd include absolutely everything you need for a tea party." Haley pushed a hank of long hair behind one ear, then continued. "You know, three different tins of tea, a package of scone mix, small jars of jam and lemon curd, those little gold spoons people love so much, maybe a tea towel, and, of course, a couple sets of teacups and saucers."

But Theodosia was already swept up by Haley's enthusiasm and liked the idea very much. "We do seem to have an abundance of teacups and saucers around here," Theodosia admitted. Early on, when she first launched the Indigo Tea Shop, they'd all gone out to the countryside, attending auctions, yard sales, and tag sales. They'd picked up as many small plates and sets of cups and saucers as `they could find, stumbling upon a surprising number of antique teacups by Limoges and Barbotine as well as lots of more contemporary teacups by Staffordshire, Royal Winton, Rosenthal, and Charles Sadek. And now their collection of teacups probably numbered close to five hundred.

"So you like the idea?" prompted Haley. She was gazing at Theodosia with a sparkle in her eyes and a crooked grin across her face.

"I think it's absolutely marvelous," said Theodosia. "And you're right, we've done gift baskets before but never with a full complement of tea and tea accoutrements."

Drayton came zipping by, a teapot in each hand. "Did Haley finally tell you about her Tea Party in a Basket?"

Theodosia nodded. "Yup."

"Did she also tell your about our little surprise?"

"No," Haley said to Drayton, "I was waiting for you."

Theodosia looked up at them expectantly. She waggled a couple fingers as if to say *come on*.

Haley jumped right in. "Remember when Delaine said she wanted to serve something with even more pizzazz than Drayton's tea sangria?"

"Oh yes, I do," said Theodosia.

Haley was fairly beaming now. "Well, Drayton came up with the *perfect* drink."

"I call it a Green Tea Tippler," said Drayton, stepping in to explain. "My own splendid concoction of vodka, green tea, lemon juice, and fresh ginger. Shaken, not stirred, and served in tall glasses."

"Delaine will adore it," said Theodosia. She was starting to work up a little more enthusiasm for Delaine's trunk show this afternoon.

"And to accompany Drayton's exquisite drink . . . caviar!" exclaimed Haley.

Theodosia narrowed her eyes. "That sounds a trifle extravagant."

"Not to worry," Haley assured her. "We're not talking beluga or sevruga or anything really upscale like that. This is more like domestic caviar. Affordable but still very tasty."

Drayton pushed his tortoiseshell glasses up on the bridge of his nose and blinked. "Good heavens, Haley, where did you learn so much about caviar?"

She lifted one shoulder and grinned. "I once dated a Russian exchange student. His father was a big muckety-muck in the party."

"The *Communist* Party?" asked Drayton. Theodosia wasn't sure whether he was aghast or impressed.

"Of course, the Communist Party," said Haley. "But last time I heard from Serge, his father's cushy position was pretty much a thing of the past."

"The party's over," quipped Theodosia.

"Exactly," said Haley. "Now Serge and his dad run a Starbucks in St. Petersburg."

"Good heavens," declared Drayton. "Is nothing sacred?"

20

❧

"Honey," cooed *Delaine* to Angie Congdon, "that dress is positively *adorable* on you."

Angie Congdon, one of the proprietors of the Featherbed House B&B, surveyed herself in a three-way mirror while, around her, dozens of women "oohed" and "ahhed" over Delaine's array of clingy knit dresses, stiletto-heeled pumps, crocodile bags, and elegant gold pendants.

An ordinary man walking in off the street might have thought the scene bedlam. But every fashion-forward woman who'd come to Cotton Duck today knew she was participating in a fabulous seasonal ritual: the trunk show.

Marcus Matteo stood in the midst of Delaine's store, reveling in his orchestrated chaos and savoring his role as savvy designer, clever stylist, fashion guru, and sales dynamo. Pulling lush, vibrant-hued knits from rolling racks, Marcus color-matched his dresses and gowns to each customer's hair and skin tones. And, like a ballet master sending his troupe on stage for a command performance, he sent each woman into her dressing room with whispered words of encouragement.

"Does he really think every woman should wiggle into one of those clingy costumes?" Drayton asked Theodosia. He'd been serving Green Tea Tipplers for almost an hour now and was flabbergasted at the number of women who continued to pour into Delaine's store. And pour themselves into Marcus Matteo's form-fitting dresses.

Fanning out a handful of cocktail napkins, Theodosia gave Drayton a sideways glance. "That's the secret to haute couture," she told him. "If you create a piece that's fabulous, frothy, and not everyone can wear, then everyone will want to wear it."

"And price it sky high," said Drayton, beginning to get her drift.

"Ridiculously high," agreed Theodosia.

"But *you* certainly don't fall for that nonsense," Drayton said, watching two women warily approach Marcus Matteo. The king of cling was reverently holding a lipstick-red, floor-length gown and it was quite apparent that *each* woman thought the gown would be perfect for her.

"Actually," said Theodosia, "Delaine has a cream-colored knit put away for me."

"You got first crack at the collection?" asked Drayton, looking bemused.

"You don't think we're doing this just for fun, do you?" asked Theodosia as she popped the lid on another jar of caviar and slid the shiny, black fish eggs into a silver bowl.

"Uh oh," said Drayton. Delaine, looking slightly frazzled yet smashingly turned out in a candy apple-pink clingy dress, was chugging determinedly toward their table. "Here comes our genial hostess."

"How's it going, Delaine?" asked Theodosia.

Delaine sighed heavily and rolled her eyes heavenward. "Sales are fantabulous. And can you believe the buzz we generated? Everyone who's *anybody* is here today!"

"Seems to me they're also buzzing over poor Vance Tuttle," said Drayton.

Delaine put a finger to her mouth and frowned. "Shhh! We certainly don't need to bring *that* up."

"Heaven forbid we have a moment of silence for the dead," intoned Drayton.

"I suppose you two will be snooping around that *accident,* too," said Delaine, looking unhappy.

"It wasn't an accident," Theodosia told her. "Someone deliberately shot Vance Tuttle."

"Theodosia was *there,* Delaine," said Drayton. "She could just as easily have been hit."

But Delaine was still pouting. "I just hope you don't go poking around Cardiotech anymore, Theo. If Rex Haggard gets ticked at you, he could take it out on me! One word to his wife, Peaches, and she could expand her clothing line and crush me like a bug."

"That's not going to happen," said Theodosia.

"Still," said Delaine, "its would be better if you just leave this whole thing alone."

"Have a Green Tea Tippler," said Theodosia, handing Delaine a tall, frosty glass filled with the enticing drink. "It'll calm you down."

But, at that moment, Jeanine, Delaine's overworked and perpetually frazzled-looking assistant, was heading their way. And Jeanine had "problem" written all over her face.

"Where did you stash the beaded evening bags?" Jeanine gasped to Delaine.

Delaine took a sip of her drink, considering. "The sequined butterflies or the embroidered chinoiserie?" she asked.

"Butterflies," gasped Jeanine, eyeing Delaine's drink.

"I believe those are in the red Chinese cabinet," Delaine told her. "Along with the scarves. Just pull the double doors open and let everything flutter out. Purses, scarves, bustiers, those ruffled tank tops." She waved a hand theatrically. "It's that kind of crazy, topsy-turvy day."

Delaine uttered a long sigh as Jeanine dashed off in search

of the elusive beaded bags. "Wouldn't you know it," she told them, "my feet are absolutely *killing* me!"

Drayton glanced down at Delaine's matching pink pumps. "Good heavens, woman, the heels on those things must be three inches high!"

"Four," said Delaine, looking pleased.

"And they're *teensy*," said Drayton, frowning. "Why don't you wear something *sensible* instead of tottering around with just straps on your feet?"

Delaine uttered a short laugh. "Listen to him. This from a man who puts on a bow tie, starched white shirt, and tweed jacket when he goes to the grocery store."

"I find my mode of dress *extremely* practical," huffed Drayton. "Good looking, comfortable, ever so appropriate. Besides, what if I should encounter a potential donor to the Heritage Society?"

"That's right," said Theodosia, "you'd want to impress them with your strict decorum."

But Delaine had turned her focus to Marcus Matteo, who was vigorously nodding his approval as Emily Guthro suddenly emerged from one of the dressing rooms. Wearing a clingy two-piece outfit in pale peach that showed off her petite figure to perfection, Marcus Matteo fussed over Emily, gently pulling the boat neck top off one shoulder, then another.

"Humph," said Delaine, narrowing her eyes. "He's certainly making a fool of himself over *her*."

"Isn't that the point?" asked Drayton. "Give the illusion of exacting attention and sell like crazy?"

"That's the problem," snarled Delaine. "I'm not sure it is an illusion."

Drayton cast a sideways glance at Theodosia. A glance that clearly said *Now what?*

Clearly upset that Marcus Matteo was fussing over Emily, Delaine continued on. "That silly little girl has set aside three of his pieces. Can you believe it?" she asked in a frosty tone.

"Three?" exclaimed Drayton. "I thought those clingy little things were prohibitively expensive."

"Oh, she's got money," said Delaine. "From some sort of inheritance. And she's not afraid to spend it."

"Then Marcus is doing his job," murmured Theodosia. "This is, after all, a retail venture."

"Well, I'm impressed," said Drayton, trying his best to lighten the mood. "Even though it feels like I'm stuck in the first level of Dante's Inferno, there isn't a woman here who hasn't been charmed by your designer friend. He mumbles in their ear and they hang on every word."

As if on cue, Emily bent over with laughter at some whispered remark from Marcus Matteo. Then, when she caught sight of Theodosia, Emily gave her a wink and a big wave.

Delaine's eyes glittered as she continued to stare at Marcus and Emily. "Isn't it just too sad when some little girls doesn't know they're being handed a line," she said, her voice dripping with contempt.

An hour later Theodosia and Drayton were ready to pack it in. No one had ventured near the refreshment table in the last twenty minutes. Rather, the late-comers were wriggling into the samples that were left, preening before the mirrors, and hastily placing orders.

"The caviar and Green Tea Tipplers were a major hit, the maraschino cherry scones were not," declared Drayton. "What are we going to tell Haley?"

"We'll tell her that butter, flour, eggs, and candied cherries are not high on the list of women who are attempting to squeeze their bodies into clingy knits," laughed Theodosia. "Haley won't be upset. She's knows she's a star when it comes to baked goods. People drive from all over the low-country just for a taste of her scones and muffins."

"Hmm," said Drayton thoughtfully. "And here I've been deluding myself that they came for the tea. Silly me."

"You know what I'm saying," said Theodosia, giving him a nudge with her elbow. "Stop being so darned thin-skinned."

They met Peaches Haggard on the way out.

"Tell me I'm not too late," she said, gazing mournfully at Theodosia. "I'll slit my wrists if I don't get a shot at one of those knits."

"They're still writing up orders," said Drayton, sounding like an old hand on the trunk show circuit. "I'm sure Delaine will be delighted to add your name to her list."

"We just received a huge shipment at Petite Provence," groaned Peaches, "and it took us forever to unpack." She put her hand to her head and ruffled her hair. "Tons of stuff I bought at a Marseilles flea market last season. You should drop by and take a look," she told Theodosia. "You, too," she added, shifting her gaze to Drayton. "I hear you're a lover of all things historical. I've got a brass desk set that's a fantastic replica of one used by Napoleon. Archaistic, they call it. A copy, to be sure, but still quite old. And handsome."

The ring of a cell phone punctuated her sentence.

"That must be mine," said Peaches, fumbling in her leather bag.

"No," said Drayton, "that musical ring strangely reminiscent of the *Macarena* means it's Theo's new handy-dandy phone."

"Get it, will you Drayton?" said Theodosia, her arms encumbered by baskets and bags. "It's tucked in the basket there."

Fumbling at the buttons, Drayton pursed his lips and held the little phone to his ear. "Yes?" he said. He listened for a few moments, his expression suddenly going from passive to instantly alert. His eyes widened as he turned his grizzled head to stare at Theodosia.

"What?" she said, setting her parcels down.

"It's for you," said Drayton. "Tidwell."

Theodosia grabbed the phone. "This is Theodosia."

"We have a match on the prints," he told her without preamble.

"Who is it?" she asked, keenly aware of Peaches Haggard lingering beside them.

"Ben Atherton," said Tidwell.

"No!" Theodosia was stunned. She dropped the phone to her chest and smiled tentatively at Peaches Haggard. "Excuse me, will you?"

Still curious, Peaches Haggard pulled herself away and continued into Delaine's store.

"What about Star Duncan?" Theodosia stammered into the phone, now that she had some privacy. After Vance's murder she'd been nervous that Star might be the common denominator.

"No," said Tidwell. "In fact we finally located her at a resort over on Hilton Head. She's hosting some sort of special seminar for condo buyers."

"But Ben's prints matched," marveled Theodosia, shifting her thoughts back to Ben Atherton. *The very person who paid me a visit last night! Had he been fishing for information? Or had he intended to do me harm?* Theodosia shuddered. She supposed she'd never really know.

"Not a complete match," Tidwell cautioned, "but enough to stand up in court. Enough to get us *into* court."

"But how . . .?" fumbled Theodosia. This was great news. Phenomenal news! She couldn't wait to tell Jory. *Where is he right now?* she wondered. *Driving one of his uncles to the airport?*

"That funeral program you swiped," Tidwell told her. "We got confirmation from the lab a little while ago. The prints on the program matched those on the syringe. Then, when we went to the offices of Vantage PR, we found another rather incriminating item."

"What?" said Theodosia, fascinated. And feeling greatly relieved.

Tidwell was rolling now, greatly enjoying this. "We didn't

have a search warrant yet, of course, since this all bubbled to a conclusion rather swiftly. And the office was closed. But a very enterprising young officer located a janitor who let us rummage through Vantage PR's trash."

"Dumpster diving," said Theodosia.

"Something like that," said Tidwell. "It seems the building's owners are in the process of having the parking lot resurfaced. So with all the construction work going on, trash hadn't been picked up this past Monday." Tidwell hesitated.

"And you found . . ." prompted Theodosia.

"A curiously empty vial."

"Fentanyl?" said Theodosia.

"It will require chemical analysis," said Tidwell, "but I'm fairly sure we'll have another match."

"You've picked him up?" asked Theodosia.

"Two cruisers should be at Mr. Atherton's house even as we speak."

"So it's all over," said Theodosia.

"For all practical purposes, I suppose it is," replied Tidwell.

21

"*You're the one* who really broke the case!" exclaimed Jory.

Theodosia was back at Timothy's and had wasted no time in phoning Jory with the good news.

"It was good police work that broke the case," replied Theodosia.

"But you were the one with the suspicious nature who had enough sense to steal that program and plastic cup."

"Well, I wouldn't exactly call it a theft," said Theodosia. Reclining on Timothy's leather couch, with Earl Grey stretched out at her feet, she was feeling very accomplished. And safe. The double homicide would hopefully begin to fade in everyone's battered psyches.

"Whatever," said Jory, still in jubilant mode. "Listen, kiddo, my entire extended family is going to want to throw a victory celebration. With you as honored guest. Maybe we can talk Haley into baking one of her special cakes and decorate it with a blindfolded lady justice and her scales."

"Oh gosh," said Theodosia, suddenly thinking about Jory's family, "I never did call your Uncle John and apologize for not making it to his house yesterday."

"You were out fighting crime," exclaimed Jory. He sounded positively euphoric after being down for so many days. "Listen, I'm going to be burning up the phone lines tonight, spreading the good news. But how about a celebratory dinner tomorrow night? Wine, candlelight, and some highly amusing conversation at Le Papillon?"

"You're on," said Theodosia. "I even have the perfect new dress to wear."

"Would this be one of those clingy outfits?" Jory asked.

Theodosia grinned. She could picture him wiggling his eyebrows in a Groucho Marx parody. "Have to wait and see," she told him.

Earl Grey was pushing his food dish around the floor, either having a fast game of kitchen floor hockey or trying to glean every morsel of food, when the doorbell rang, echoing throughout Timothy's vast house. Padding down the long hallway in her stocking feet, Theodosia peered through the wavy glass windows only to find Delaine Dish standing on the front verandah.

She unlatched the dead bolt and threw the door open in a gesture of exuberance. Which came to an abrupt halt once she caught sight of Delaine's pained expression. Tears sparkled in Delaine's eyes and deep furrows creased her normally placid brow. Pale and anxious, she looked like her emotions were bouncing wildly between anger and despair.

"Delaine!" exclaimed Theodosia. "What's wrong?"

"Everything!" said Delaine as she thrust one of her shiny copper-colored shopping bags into Theodosia's hands.

"What's this?" asked Theodosia, momentarily put off by the package that had been shoved at her.

"May I *please* come in?" sniffled Delaine. "Can we *talk*?"

"Yes, of course," said Theodosia, wondering if Delaine's

tears might be crocodile tears from some self-imposed snit. She was good at that. Renowned for over-reaction, in fact. On the other hand, Delaine did appear genuinely upset.

Leading Delaine down the hallway into Timothy's office, Theodosia settled herself back on the sofa with the un-opened shopping bag next to her. Delaine plunked herself down in a leather club chair directly opposite Theodosia and posed demurely.

"I have a *huge* favor to ask," Delaine said finally, gazing at Theodosia with great intensity.

"Okaaay," said Theodosia. When Delaine told you she had a huge favor, you never knew *what* it could be. She might be requesting a small tin of tea, or she could be put-ting you on the spot to cater a black tie party for two thou-sand symphony patrons. In Delaine's world there wasn't a lot of differentiation as to what was huge. To her everything was huge.

Delaine jerked her head at the shopping bag. "Deliver that for me."

Theodosia looked blank for a moment. Then she reached for the shopping bag and peered cautiously inside.

Nestled beneath layers of white tissue paper lay a froth of peach-colored knit.

Peach knit. I saw someone modeling this earlier today, didn't I? Theodosia thought for a minute. *Oh, rats, now I remember who it was. Emily Guthro.*

Delaine's "huge problem" suddenly became clear to Theodosia. Crystal clear. "You want me to deliver this," said Theodosia. Her flat tone indicated she wasn't exactly thrilled.

Delaine twisted her hands and gave a tight nod. "Please."

"To . . .?"

Delaine's face bore a pained expression as she whispered the name: "Emily Guthro."

"You could send it by messenger . . ." began Theodosia. Truly, the last thing she wanted to do tonight was run over to Emily Guthro's house.

Delaine was blinking rapidly now, trying to stem the flow of tears. "I certainly could," she said in a strangled voice. "But then I wouldn't know if the young lady is . . . uh . . . um . . . home alone tonight."

"Delaine," said Theodosia in what she hoped was a kinder tone. "Does Emily have a date or something with Marcus Matteo tonight?"

Anguish washed across Delaine's heart-shaped face. "No," she said, looking horribly embarrassed, "I do."

Theodosia had no intention of causing Delaine any further pain, but she wanted to make sure she was absolutely clear in understanding Delaine's request. "You want me to deliver Emily's dress and check to make sure she's alone?"

"Please," implored Delaine, clasping her hands together in a gesture of supplication. "Would you do that for me? You've just *got* to do that for me!" Delaine pulled a hanky from her suede bag and daubed at her eyes. "I simply couldn't meet Marcus in public for a farewell dinner knowing he'd been canoodling with another woman." She blew her nose discreetly. "And if I went over to Emily's and he was there . . ." Her chin quivered wildly. "I'd just *die*," she whispered.

Theodosia stared at Delaine. That's what this whole scene was about. Marcus Matteo's purported canoodling.

Okay, I suppose I understand. I guess I understand. I wouldn't be thrilled either if Jory was wining and dining me on the second shift.

When Theodosia's cell phone rang, her mind was still processing Delaine's request, and so she answered with an almost casual air. But her caller's greeting was abrupt and deeply intense.

"Miss Browning . . ." It was the anxious voice of Burt Tidwell.

"Detective Tidwell?" said Theodosia.

Strange that he would call again. Has there been another break in the case? Or cases?

"We didn't get him!" Tidwell exclaimed.

"What?" responded Theodosia, her heart suddenly skipping a beat.

"He was gone when the officers arrived."

"Gone?" repeated Theodosia, stunned.

"Missing, vanished, flew the coop." Tidwell's delivery was harsh and clipped, his anger and frustration obviously beginning to boil up.

"Was Ben's wife there?" *What was the woman's name again?* "Was Cleo there?" asked Theodosia.

"Of course she was there," barked Tidwell. "But the woman clammed up completely. Wouldn't tell us a thing. Says she wants an attorney. That it's her right."

"Well it is," said Theodosia.

Tidwell made a guttural sound somewhere between a snort and a grunt. "Stay in," he advised. "Stay home." And then he was gone, the phone line humming in Theodosia's ear.

Theodosia stared into the inquisitive eyes of Delaine Dish across from her. And a new thought suddenly bubbled up in her very active brain . . .

What if Emily actually knows something? Maybe not about the murders per se, but about Ben Atherton. About his personal life. Like does he have a second home to run to? Or close friends who might help him?

"I'll do it," Theodosia announced to Delaine. "I'll take that dress over to Emily Guthro. You have her address?"

Delaine dug in her pocket and produced a piece of paper on which was scrawled Emily Guthro's name, street address, and phone number.

"She lives over on Chalmers Street," said Theodosia, squinting at Delaine's pinched writing.

"Yes," said Delaine. "So you'll call me?" Delaine was still blinking back tears but looked decidedly heartened. And more than a little surprised that Theodosia has so readily agreed. "The minute it's been delivered?"

"Count on it," Theodosia promised.

* * *

Zipping across town in her Jeep, halfway to Emily's house, a very scary thought popped into Theodosia's head. One that gave her great pause.

What if Ben is also on his way to Emily's?

What if Ben's on the run, feeling angry, desperate, and cornered? He's a big man, a powerful man. What if he tries to force Emily to help him? What if he threatens her or puts her in danger?

That terrifying thought ran through Theodosia's brain like neon chase lights on a theater marquee. Scaring the daylights out of her. And so, when Theodosia stopped at the next red light, she pawed in her handbag for her cell phone and the crumpled piece of paper Delaine had given her.

Emily Guthro answered on the first ring.

"Hi," said Theodosia, trying to sound casual and low key. "It's Theodosia. I'm running a few errands for Delaine and I was wondering if I could drop your dress by." She paused. "What with the big trunk show today, she's been awfully swamped." *Come on, Emily, say yes.*

"Sure," said Emily. "Come on over. You probably won't believe this, but I just put a batch of scones in the oven."

Theodosia smiled to herself in spite of being tired and edgy. "Sounds heavenly," she said. "Good thing I've got a couple tins of tea stashed in the back of my Jeep." *Doesn't sound like Emily is entertaining the oh-so-amorous Marcus Matteo this evening. Or being held hostage by a crazed Ben Atherton, either. Good.*

"Aren't you a dear," murmured Emily. "You have my address?"

"Sure do," Theodosia told her.

22

Emily Guthro lived near the French Quarter in a Charleston single house. Tall and deep, but just a single room wide, these unique Charleston homes were greatly prized as residences. Emily's single house was constructed of dun-colored brick, featured tall, shuttered windows, and fronted directly on Chalmers Street. The main entrance, situated on the side of the house, was accessed via a narrow walkway lit with tiny wrought iron lanterns.

"Come in," said Emily as she greeted Theodosia at the door. Elegantly attired in gray wool slacks and a camel-colored cashmere sweater, she looked, strangely enough, like a younger version of Delaine. Dressed to kill even when she was just lounging around at home.

"Great house," said Theodosia, doing a quick perusal and taking in the oil paintings that graced the walls and the lush Oriental carpet that lay on the wood floor of the small entryway.

Emily smiled down at the carpet. "This rug is *tea* washed," she exclaimed. "Isn't that a kick?"

Emily's intricately patterned Oriental carpet had been loomed in shades of muted Chinese red and gold. The plushness of the fibers meant the rug was obviously fairly new, yet the tea wash imparted a rich, aged quality and gave the rug a slightly patinated appearance. Theodosia thought the look highly effective and instantly decided to scout for a rug just like it to put in the Indigo Tea Shop. If anything, a tea washed rug would be a great conversation piece.

"That really *is* a great rug," said Theodosia, finally turning her gaze to Emily. "And you look great, too."

"Thanks," said Emily, leading her down a narrow hallway into a living room where a cozy fire crackled, "but I feel like a wreck. After I left Delaine's trunk show I had to deliver some press proofs to a client in Mount Pleasant. Tobago Software, do you know them?"

"Not really," said Theodosia as she surveyed Emily's living room with its small but tasty white marble fireplace and gleaming brass candlesticks resting atop the mantel. She also noted that Marcus Matteo did not seem to be lurking about anywhere. Maybe Delaine had overestimated the extent of Emily's and Marcus's relationship—if there ever really was one to begin with. It wouldn't be the first time an imagined problem had clouded Delaine's judgment.

"Anyway," responded Emily, "I haven't had a moment to change." She nodded at the shopping bag Theodosia still carried. "Is that my dress?"

She doesn't know about Ben Atherton, thought Theodosia. *She's been out and about and doesn't know a thing. Hasn't heard the news that he's a wanted man, nor that his wife, Cleo, is down at the police station right now making like a clam.*

"Your Marcus Matteo original," said Theodosia, handing the shopping bag over to Emily. "Direct from the designer to you." *Should I tell her about Ben? Or let her learn about him tomorrow when she shows up for work? Or a better question might be—should I warn her? Would Ben really have the audacity to show up here?*

"I can't believe Jeanine did the alterations already," said Emily.

"She's a real pro," replied Theodosia.

"Do you know Marcus Matteo is up for a FIT Award this year?" asked Emily as she poked in the bag, smiling. FIT was the Fashion Institute of Technology in New York, an organization that routinely handed out awards for "best new designer" as well as "most influential designer."

"Wonderful," cooed Theodosia, still wondering how much she should tell Emily.

"I'd be amazed if Marcus didn't win *some* sort of honor," said Emily. "He's an absolute genius with fabric."

But this time Theodosia found herself smiling and pushing away thoughts of Ben Atherton breaking into Emily's house like a crazed maniac. Emily sounded so happy, chattering away, filled with over-the-top enthusiasm.

Rummaging in her oversized handbag, Theodosia pulled out a tin of tea. "The promised tea," she told Emily, handing the small package to her.

We'll sip some tea and then I'll break the news about Ben, Theodosia decided. *The poor girl deserves to know, especially since she works . . . or worked . . . for Ben. This is the kind of thing that could severely impact her career.*

Emily studied the gold label wrapped around the blue tin. "Jasmine Moon." She nodded her approval. "I take it this is one of Drayton's special blends?"

"One of many," said Theodosia. She glanced past Emily down the long hallway where she supposed the kitchen was located. "Do you need help in the kitchen?"

"Not at all," replied Emily. "Please make yourself at home. I'll be just a second."

While Emily rattled cupboard doors in the kitchen, Theodosia wandered around Emily's small but elegantly furnished living room.

It's funny, she thought. *When I was twenty-five I lived in a tiny one bedroom rental that was nothing compared to this. Emily may claim to be just starting out, but she must be doing something right. Or, as Delaine was quick to point out, she has some money.*

"You want sugar . . . lemon?" Emily called to her.

"No thanks," Theodosia called back.

Emily had filled the living room with quality pieces of furniture. Brocade love seat, walnut cocktail table, pretty Tiffany-inspired lamps. A small spinet desk of bird's eye maple set in front of a curtained window also caught Theodosia's eye and she wandered over to it. Tracing the pattern of burls with her fingertips, Theodosia noted Emily's collection of antique glass paper weights as well as an impressive collection of photographs, all lovingly displayed in silver frames.

Theodosia smiled at a photo of a little girl, undoubtedly Emily, with her arms thrown around the shoulders of a huge black and white dog. Next to Emily's girlhood photo rested a photo album. A lovely green leather album with gold embossing. Theodosia gazed at it, lost in thought.

She'd been thinking about putting together a genealogy scrapbook on her own family. Gathering up all the old photos of her mother and father and her long-dead grandparents and putting them into a book in some meaningful way. Emily had obviously done this already. Could probably even give her a few valuable pointers.

Theodosia stared down at the green leather album with the initials ECG embossed on the front cover.

Nice touch. Classy.

Opening the album, Theodosia glanced at the inside front cover where Emily had scrawled Emily Catherine Guthro in looping longhand, then continued to flip through a few pages. By the fourth or fifth page, Theodosia realized this wasn't really a family album at all. This album contained pictures of one single person. A thin man with a kind but lined face who had the same soft eyes as Emily.

Who is this? Emily's father?

Turning ahead, Theodosia found more pages filled with photos of the man.

Interesting. Has to be her dad. They must have been very close.

Theodosia closed the book, stared at the cover again.

ECG. Hmm.

For some strange reason, the initials pulled at her, reminded her of something she'd seen before.

What?

Theodosia pondered the album cover as a lone thought swam to the surface, then dove back down again.

Come on, she prodded her brain. *Why on earth are Emily's initials suddenly reminding me of . . . something.*

She had no idea.

Okay, forget it.

And then, like a car ignition that had been grinding away, stubbornly refusing to turn over, something *pinged* and fired inside Theodosia's brain.

Emily Catherine Guthro. ECG.

Theodosia blinked and stared at the name, astonished.

ECG? Isn't that the notation I saw in Jasper Davis's journal? Sure it is. Something like it anyway. Something to the effect of . . . what? Oh lord. I think his exact notation said "Check ECG!"

At the time, Theodosia had simply assumed Jasper had made a note regarding an electrocardiogram. He was, after all, a practicing cardiologist.

But what if he'd made a notation to check on Emily Catherine Guthro?

Now Theodosia's brain slammed into overdrive as she thought back on the strange incident with Emily the day of the memorial service at Cardiotech.

What if Emily hadn't simply been embarrassed when she overheard Star read Jasper Davis's notes aloud? What if that look on Emily's face had been one of dismay? What if, by reading that notation, Star had unwittingly revealed that Jasper had been checking up on Emily?

Theodosia stared at the gold curtains that hung behind the desk, her brain going a mile a minute.

Checking up on what? Had Jasper Davis uncovered some information about Emily Guthro before he died? Something that upset him or made him nervous?

Theodosia inhaled sharply as puzzle pieces came rushing together and clicked in place.

Ohmigod! Emily Guthro must have murdered Jasper Davis!

Theodosia dropped the album back on the desk as if it might bite her.

But Tidwell said Ben Atherton's fingerprints were a perfect match! They were on the syringe. The exact same prints as on the program. So what's going on? Did she set him up? Is Emily that wily?

A loud shriek pierced the uneasy quiet. Startled, Theodosia jumped then recovered when she recognized the shrill of a teakettle. Nervously, she glanced down the hall toward the kitchen.

Emily will be coming back soon. Now what?

Theodosia dug in her purse for her cell phone just as she heard Emily's footsteps in the hallway. There was the rattle of teacups, the distinct *clink* of silver.

Do I have time? I have to have time!

Frantically, Theodosia plopped herself down in a chair and punched the buttons on her phone. Then, carefully placing the phone on the coffee table in front of her, she leaned back just as Emily entered the room.

"You were looking at my album," said Emily, as she bent forward and set the tea tray down.

Yes, her book and pictures are disturbed. I suppose she would notice that.

"I was thinking of doing a family album of my own," said Theodosia, trying to remain calm while frantically attempting to work out her next move.

Emily twisted her mouth to one side as if carefully weighing Theodosia's response. "Were you," she replied.

Things had suddenly changed big time. The atmosphere in the room, which had seemed so serene a few minutes earlier, now crackled with tension. Where Emily's smile had appeared warm and genuine before, she now wore a determined cat-that-swallowed-the-canary smirk.

She knows, thought Theodosia. *She knows that I know.*

"You like to snoop, don't you?" said Emily, her voice suddenly dripping with sarcasm. "And you're *good* at it. So good."

"Not really," said Theodosia, as Emily stared down at her.

"Pour the tea, will you?" said Emily. She smiled, but it was mirthless. The smile of a barracuda appraising a potential morsel of food.

Are we going to sit here like civilized people and talk this out? wondered Theodosia. *Nah. Not a chance.*

Theodosia picked up the teapot and slowly poured a cup of tea for Emily. Trying to stall. Trying desperately to think. But when she looked up, her breath caught in her throat. There was a gun pointed at her head. A nasty looking, dull gray snub-nosed revolver.

Oh lord.

"You don't need that," said Theodosia, fighting to retain her composure.

"Oh, I think I do," said Emily, waggling the gun back and forth. Her lips curled in disdain, her eyes had narrowed to slits. The girl suddenly looked unhinged.

As Theodosia poured tea into the second cup, she gazed up at Emily with what she hoped was a commiserating look, then deliberately over-poured the tea, sloshing tea in the saucer and onto the tea tray. "Clumsy," Theodosia muttered to herself as she grabbed an embroidered towel from the tray, then deftly wiped the lip of the teapot, blotted the saucer, and managed to push the camera button at the end of her elaborate maneuver.

And I'll try to hang on to this teapot, too. Wield it as a weapon if I have to.

"Put the teapot down!" barked Emily. As the gun waggled again, Emily's normally clear skin was suddenly covered with red blotches.

From anger? Stress? Homicidal rage?

Theodosia very deliberately put the teapot down.

"You think you're smart, don't you?" challenged Emily. "You think you've got it all figured out."

"The only thing I know is that you're in a great deal of pain," said Theodosia, trying to remain calm, trying to telegraph a certain reasonability.

"You think I'm responsible for those deaths," said Emily in a monotone now. She shook her head. "But you don't understand."

"Try me," said Theodosia. "I want to understand, I really do."

"Jasper Davis was the *real* killer," said Emily.

"What are you talking about?" asked Theodosia. "Explain it to me."

"He killed my father!" Emily screamed suddenly.

"Jasper . . ." began Theodosia, but Emily suddenly jabbed her gun in close to Theodosia's face. Theodosia choked on her words and could almost swear she felt the tip of the barrel touch up against her hair, figured her mass of auburn hair had to be functioning like some kind of super-sensitive antennae. Like a cat's whiskers.

"Retribution," Emily said in a low, hoarse whisper. "Feels good."

"Let me get this straight," said Theodosia. She tried to keep her voice even and reassuring. *Isn't that how you're supposed to deal with crazy people? Sure it is. I think it is.* "You're saying Jasper Davis killed your father?"

"Oh yes he did," hissed Emily.

"And Jasper Davis had an inkling that you were going to come after him?" It was a wild guess, but Theodosia hoped it would keep Emily talking.

"Let's just say he had a crazy hunch!" Emily's outburst, followed by a giggle, had a maniacal ring to it. "Then again, he was a smart man. Too smart for his own good!"

Oh Lord, thought Theodosia. *I'll bet it was Emily who came tiptoeing into Timothy's house early last Sunday morning and scared me half to death. She must have been looking for Jasper's journal. Only she didn't find it. And because Delaine blabbed about how I was looking into things, Emily tried to scare me off. She took a shot at me when I was out riding, then tossed a rock through the window later that night.*

Theodosia knew Emily must have been frantic to retrieve that journal. To destroy all evidence that Jasper Davis had been suspicious of Emily, had been nervous about her.

Then, when Emily spotted the journal at Uncle Jasper's funeral yesterday, she must have been really crazed. She saw Vance take the journal from Star and pocket it, so she followed him. When she couldn't get it back for whatever reason, she shot him.

Theodosia blinked and took a deep breath as the reality of Emily Guthro's actions washed over her.

Emily Guthro killed Jasper Davis. And then Vance Tuttle! And now she's going to try to kill me!

Theodosia turned her full attention to Emily, ready to launch a passionate appeal, but Emily was staring down at the steaming cups of tea that sat on the tray untouched. As she stared, Emily suddenly noticed Theodosia's phone. "What's that?" she shrilled, her face twisting with anger.

"Uh . . . my telephone?" stammered Theodosia.

That's right, play dumb. It's a tried-and-true technique that sometimes works.

"Turn it off!" shrieked Emily. "Now!"

"Sure," said Theodosia amicably. "No problem." She slowly reached for her phone. "See? I'm turning it off." Sending a quick prayer up to heaven that the little phone was canted in the right direction, Theodosia gently depressed the button a second time before she closed it, fervently hoping she'd taken and transmitted yet another photo. But, of course, everything hinged on the fact that the person on the receiving end actually *looked* at the photo. And *understood* what was going on.

Emily continued to gaze suspiciously at the little phone.

"The light's still on," she said, her voice like ice. "Why is the light still on?"

Theodosia, who'd pulled her hand away, reached back for it. "Sticks sometimes," she explained. "Sorry." *Better to let her think she's in control, right? And with that gun pointed directly at my head, I'd have to say she's definitely in control.*

Theodosia drew a deep breath, willing herself to assume a compassionate look on her face. "I'm so sorry about your father," she told Emily.

"No, you're not," snapped Emily. "You're just saying that because you're afraid."

"How did he die?" asked Theodosia.

"Jasper Davis *murdered* him," shrilled Emily. "With that ridiculous machine of his."

"Had your father been ill a long time?" asked Theodosia.

"Shut up!" yelled Emily.

"Sometimes the Lord calls people early," said Theodosia. "*We* may not be ready for their passing, but it's still their time."

"Not like that!" screamed Emily.

"My mother died when I was eight," said Theodosia. "My dad when I was twenty."

"You don't know anything!" screamed Emily at the top of her lungs. She waved the gun about wildly, but always managed to keep it aimed in the vicinity of Theodosia's face.

Theodosia, who could still hear the *pop* from last Sunday afternoon echoing in her head, could also picture in her mind's eye the tiny black hole in Vance Tuttle's forehead. And she was afraid. Very afraid.

"You must have loved your father very much," said Theodosia. She glanced over at the desk where the photo album sat. "Could I look at the rest of the pictures?"

Emily's eyes narrowed, fearing it might be a trick, then she motioned with the gun. It was okay. She *wanted* Theodosia to see the photos.

Getting up from the chair, Theodosia moved swiftly to

the desk and grasped the album. She hesitated a moment, trying to peer through the space where the heavy curtains came together.

Is that a Crown Victoria that just slid up to the front curb?

"Get back here and sit down!" thundered Emily.

"Sure," said Theodosia, obliging her. "Whatever you say."

Emily reached across and tapped the cover of the green leather album. "Open it," she ordered.

Theodosia looked up with an inquiring look on her face. "Are those scones ready yet?" she asked.

"What?" exclaimed Emily, completely taken aback.

"When I phoned earlier you said you had some scones in the oven," Theodosia explained, giving Emily what she hoped was a loopy grin.

"Are you completely *nuts?*" snorted Emily, her derisive laugh a sharp bark that echoed off the walls. "I was just *saying* that. I knew you were really coming over to snoop. What do you think I am? A little homemaker?" She tipped her head back and let go a condescending laugh just as her front door exploded.

"What!" screamed Emily as wood crunched and shards of glass crashed in. Thunder echoed in the hallway as Emily began to turn. Then, like a pair of trained ninja, two police officers in black jumpsuits and kevlar vests suddenly materialized in perfect combat stance.

"She's got a gun!" yelled Theodosia, ducking her head, trying to protect herself with her hands.

"Drop it," one of the officers shouted at Emily. He was young and lithe with piercing blue eyes. "Do it NOW!" he ordered.

Emily had whirled instinctively and was struggling to bring her pistol up level to take aim against the officers. But she was slow. A split-second slower than the determined blue-eyed officer.

Wham!

Emily gave a spastic jerk and her pistol erupted. The

ceiling burst open and giant chinks of plaster crashed to the floor. Then, as if all the air had suddenly been let out of her, the pistol flew from Emily's hands and she collapsed in a heap. Blood spattering everywhere, her face in a rictus of pain, she clutched at her leg.

"Noooo!" came Emily's blood curdling scream. "Noooo!"

23

Detective Burt Tidwell had not been far behind. In fact, he seemed to materialize even as Emily thrashed on the floor, pleading for help as blood spurted crazily from her wounded leg.

Tidwell had most definitely received the menacing photo Theodosia had transmitted to him. A face-front shot of a determined-looking Emily clutching a pistol. Tidwell had recognized Emily instantly and immediately dispatched a special team to her house.

When he'd arrived, his gallant officers had already pulled Emily to a seated position and handcuffed her hands behind her back. Only when she was fully restrained did the blue-eyed officer kneel down to apply a tourniquet.

A second police cruiser arrived seemingly on Tidwell's heels, ready to throw up a cobweb of black and yellow tape, take photos, and do whatever was necessary. An ambulance came screeching to the scene as well, siren blattering,

lights whirling, white-coated attendants looking very offi-
cious.

And so a shaky Theodosia and a much-relieved Tidwell
retreated to the quiet of the Indigo Tea Shop where they
could converse privately.

But it wasn't long before Haley, who occupied the garden
apartment directly across the back alley, sprinted over to see
what was going on. Especially when she spied cars pulling
in and lights flashing on.

And a shaken Haley, much to Tidwell's consternation
and Theodosia's amusement, quickly summoned Drayton,
who came huffing into the tea shop some five minutes later.

"Lucky me, the gang's all here," said Tidwell with a sar-
donic gaze at his impromptu audience. Perched at one of the
large wooden tables, he looked like an unhappy bullfrog in
a lily pond.

Haley, who had bustled about brewing tea and warming
up scones, was in no mood for his caustic humor. "Listen,
Tidwell," she began, "we have a perfect right to know what's
going on, too. After all, Theodosia was almost killed!"

Tidwell fixed Haley with a fierce stare and she retreated a
safe distance from his table.

"Oh, please let's be civilized, shall we?" pleaded Drayton.
"Let's not resort to blustering and silly intimidation." He
stared pointedly at Tidwell who gave no visible sign of
backing down.

But when Haley plunked a plate of raisin scones and a
bowl of Devonshire cream directly in front of Tidwell, his
ferocity seemed to waver. And eventually crack. Slowly, he
stretched an arm out for the plate of scones, hooked the edge
with one chubby finger, then reeled it in.

Drayton gave Haley a knowing wink. The old "there's
more than one way to skin a cat" look. Haley poured cups of
nice strong Hyson tea for everyone, then settled into a nearby
chair to listen spellbound as the story of Emily Guthro unfolded.

"From what our people have been able to glean so far from her protests and babbling, Emily's father died seven months ago," Tidwell told them. "Of complications during a cardiac procedure."

"Did Dr. Jasper Davis do it?" asked Drayton.

"No," said Tidwell, "that's the strange thing. It was done at University Hospital by one of their own cardiac teams."

"Let me guess," said Theodosia, "this team was using the experimental Novalaser."

Tidwell nodded. "Afraid so."

"I take it Emily was quite convinced her father died as a result of the Novalaser," said Drayton.

"Yes, and she obviously held Jasper Davis responsible," replied Tidwell. "What we know so far from our ongoing investigation at Cardiotech is that their president, Rex Haggard, had pushed for early release in using it experimentally at a few area teaching hospitals. Interestingly enough, Jasper Davis had taken a more cautionary approach. He didn't feel it was perfected yet."

"So it wasn't FDA approved?" asked Drayton.

"Approved for Phase II clinical trials," said Tidwell. "Which is a kind of pre-market approval. Final approval in the category of Class III medical devices was still pending."

"So Cardiotech's in trouble?" asked Theodosia.

Tidwell shrugged, then reached for his cell phone as it twittered loudly. "Not my area of expertise," he told her. "But I doubt it. From what I understand the Novalaser was only being used in cases where all else had failed."

"In other words," said Theodosia, "it was a last ditch effort to *save* lives."

"Something like that," replied Tidwell. "But you'd have to take that up with the FDA's regulatory people. Tidwell here," he said into his phone, turning his bulk away from the table.

"I always thought Emily was a little weird," said Haley from her nearby perch.

"Are you serious?" responded Drayton. "I thought you said you *liked* her. That she seemed so successful, a good role model."

"Duh," said Haley. "Role model for fruitcakes maybe." She gazed about suddenly. "*Now* whose phone is going off? It's like Grand Central Station in this joint."

"Mine," said Theodosia, digging in her handbag. She flipped the phone open, punched it on. *Great little phone. Saved my life tonight.*

"Did you give Emily the dress?" came Delaine's inquisitive voice.

"Yes, Delaine," said Theodosia. *Except where she's going, she won't be needing it.*

"Guess where I am, Theo," came Delaine's coy whisper.

"Why don't you just tell me," said Theodosia. "I'm not exactly in the mood for guessing games."

"Snugged in a back booth at Solstice," purred Delaine. "You know . . . that wonderful new restaurant with the tapas menu and the wine list to *die* for?"

"I've been to Solstice, Delaine," sighed Theodosia.

"And Marcus . . . oh, he's just coming back," whispered Delaine. "Gotta go! Ta ta!" And she was gone. Happily, dizzily, just like that.

"What was *that* all about?" quizzed Drayton.

"I hope the final chapter in the Delaine saga," said Theodosia.

"Which is . . .?" Drayton prompted.

"She always gets her man," replied Theodosia.

"Which reminds me," said Haley. "I want you guys to see something." She jumped up, scurried to the counter, returned with an oversized book.

"What's this?" asked Theodosia, yawning.

"My sister's yearbook," said Haley, paging through it. "Remember when I told you guys that Marcus Matteo looked familiar to me?"

"Mm hm," replied Theodosia as Haley found the page

she was looking for, then passed the yearbook over to her.

"Does this guy look familiar?" Haley asked, pointing to a grainy, black and white yearbook photo.

Theodosia studied the picture of a good-looking, dark complected young man who *did* look strikingly similar to Marcus Matteo. Only the fellow in the photo was a good ten years younger. She glanced at the caption. "Mark Mattingly."

"Same guy?" asked Haley.

Drayton peered over Theodosia's shoulder. "Good grief, I think that is Marcus Matteo!" he cried. "In a younger incarnation anyway."

"From right here in Goose Creek," chortled Haley. "*Not* Milan. He's a charlatan. All the guy did was adopt a phony accent and change his name."

"And his address," said Drayton in a kinder tone.

The two women looked at him.

"Well, he *did* become a designer," Drayton offered. "And a rather successful one judging by sales today. And he's apparently taken up residence in Milan *now*."

"I can't wait to tell Delaine," chortled Haley.

"Let's hold up on that little revelation, shall we?" said Theodosia, as Tidwell turned to them with a self-satisfied grin on his broad face.

"Looks like proof positive just turned up with a very unusual piece of evidence," he announced.

"What do you mean?" asked Theodosia.

"Ben Atherton's fingerprints on the syringe had been puzzling me," said Tidwell, reaching for a second scone. He broke the scone in two, generously slathered on a layer of jam, then added a froth of Devonshire cream. "That was one of our crime scene techs on the phone," he explained, eyeing his scone hungrily. "Seems they found a key piece of the puzzle." Tidwell paused for effect, then took a large bite. "Emily Guthro *created* the fingerprints," he said with his mouth full.

"You mean she *faked* them?" said Theodosia, incredulous. "To throw the blame on Ben?"

"Nonsense," added Drayton. "I've always heard that was impossible."

"Ah," said Tidwell, "I'd have thought a man as erudite as you, Mr. Conneley, would also be a reader of the *Atlantic Monthly*. A while back they published a most illustrative article about a scientist who actually took a clay model of prints, melted down gummy bears, then poured said liquid candy into the mold and let it harden again."

"Gummy bears!" snorted Drayton.

"Clay mold?" asked Haley. "How would Emily get that?"

"Ohmygosh!" exclaimed Theodosia, looking at Tidwell. "The Ceramics Guild! Ben and his wife, Cleo, were not only on the board of directors, they were amateur potters. And Emily was always there, helping with PR on various events and promotions. She could have easily gotten Ben's prints!" said Theodosia, recalling the black and white photo Emily had shown her of Ben posing with his hands stuck in a giant gob of wet clay.

"Our Emily was a very clever girl," said Tidwell. "She obviously wormed her way into Vantage PR so she could get access to Cardiotech."

"So you think she set Ben Atherton up from the start?" asked Theodosia.

"Maybe not right away," said Tidwell. "But I'd say fairly early on she decided he'd make a dandy patsy."

"Wow," said Haley. "It's scary how people's minds work."

"When we didn't go after Ben fast enough to suit her, Emily planted the empty vial of fentanyl," continued Tidwell, looking strangely pleased. "That vial was obviously meant to be the nail in Ben's coffin." He paused. "Emily possesses an ingenious criminal mind. Dangerous, in fact, to the point of being psychopathic."

"Psychopathic," repeated Haley. "Sounds serious. Can she be treated?"

"My dear girl," laughed Tidwell. "We don't treat psychopaths, we incarcerate them."

"Excellent idea," said Theodosia, as her eyelids began to

slowly droop. It was all catching up to her. The stress, the sadness over two senseless deaths, her own harrowing experience an hour earlier. "And now it's time to . . ."

Wham wham wham.

"What's that?" asked Haley, startled.

"Front door," said Drayton. He was already on his feet and heading for it.

Wham wham wham.

"Hold your horses," instructed Drayton. "I'm . . ." He twisted the dead bolt latch and threw the door open.

"Theodosia?" Jory stood silhouetted in the doorway, looking wild-eyed and worried. "Theodosia? Are you okay?"

All eyes went to Theodosia, but she'd already jumped up and was sprinting across the tearoom floor. Then she launched herself into Jory's outstretched arms. "I'm *wonderful!*" she sang out. "Now that you're here!"

Jory clutched her to his chest and whirled her around, her feet flying out from under her.

"Good heavens," exclaimed Tidwell. "This kind of exuberance from a woman who was dead on her feet barely ten seconds ago?"

Drayton nodded sagely. "Classic teakettle syndrome."

"What?" squawked Tidwell as Haley broke into giggles.

Drayton assumed a deadpan expression. "Once in a while our Theo has to let off a little steam."

The Indigo Tea Shop

Ham and Apricot Preserve Tea Sandwiches

4 slices raisin bread, sliced very thin
2 tbsp. apricot preserves
1 tbsp. Dijon mustard
¼ lb. ham, sliced very thin

SPREAD two bread slices with apricot preserves. Spread the remaining two slices with mustard, then layer on the ham and top with the bread spread with preserves. Carefully trim crusts and cut each whole sandwich into 4 finger-sized sandwiches.

Disappearing Buttermilk Scones

1¾ cups flour
1 tbsp. sugar
¼ tsp. salt
½ tsp. baking soda
2 tsp. baking powder
6 tbsp. chilled butter
¾ cup buttermilk

BLEND dry ingredients together. Cut in butter. Blend in buttermilk to form loose ball. Divide dough in half and press on floured board to ½" thick. Cut into 6 pie-shaped pieces. Brush with buttermilk and bake at 400 degrees for 10–12 minutes.

Tea-Smoked Chicken

3 cloves garlic, chopped
1 tbsp. freshly peeled ginger, grated
1 tbsp. honey
¾ cup soy sauce (low sodium)
½ cup cream sherry
12 chicken thighs
¾ cup brown sugar
1 cup Lapsang Souchong tea leaves
Sesame seeds for garnish

PUT garlic, ginger, honey, soy sauce, and sherry in a blender and process for 30 seconds. Pour this marinade into a 9" × 13" baking pan, then put chicken thighs in pan, coating well. Cover and refrigerate two hours, rotating thighs

once. Line a cast iron skillet with aluminum foil and sprinkle the brown sugar and tea atop the foil. Place a wire rack
in the skillet and put the chicken on top. Cover with lid and
cook chicken on medium-high for 30 minutes—without
lifting the lid! Sprinkle chicken with sesame seeds and serve
with peanut or hot mustard sauce.

Chocolate Sour Cream Muffins

> 5 oz. semi-sweet chocolate
> 2 squares of baking chocolate
> 1/3 cup butter
> 3/4 cup sour cream
> 2/3 cup brown sugar, packed
> 1/4 cup corn syrup
> 1 egg
> 2 tsp. vanilla extract
> 1 1/2 cups all-purpose flour
> 1 tsp. baking soda
> 1/4 tsp. salt
> 1/2 cup chocolate chips

MELT semi-sweet chocolate, baking chocolate, and butter
together in microwave or over double boiler. Cool to luke-
warm, then mix in sour cream, brown sugar, corn syrup,
egg, and vanilla. Blend flour, soda, and salt together in large
bowl, then add the chocolate mixture and blend well again.
Add the chocolate chips. Pour batter into greased or paper-
lined muffin tins (makes about 12) and bake in preheated
400 degree oven for 20 minutes. Remove from muffin tin
and cool on wire racks.

Haley's Chocolate Zucchini Tea Bread

    3 cups all-purpose flour
    3 eggs
    2 cups sugar
    1 cup oil
    1 tsp. vanilla extract
    1 tsp. cinnamon
    1 tsp. baking soda
    1 tsp. baking powder
    ½ cup buttermilk
    2 cups shredded zucchini
    1 cup semi-sweet chocolate bits

COMBINE flour, eggs, sugar, oil, vanilla, cinnamon, baking soda, baking powder, and buttermilk in a mixing bowl. Beat at medium speed for two minutes. Stir in zucchini and chocolate bits. Pour batter into two well-greased loaf pans and bake at 350 degrees for one hour and 15 minutes. Cool, slice, and serve with cream cheese and orange marmalade.

Poached Pears with Chocolate

    2 large, firm pears
    6 tbsp. apple juice
    ½ tsp. vanilla extract
    ¼ tsp. ground cinnamon
    1 dash allspice
    1 dash nutmeg
    1 tsp. corn starch
    ½ cup semi-sweet chocolate chips
    1 tsp. water

CORE pears and cut each pear into 8 sections lengthwise. Combine apple juice, vanilla, and spices in a saucepan. Add pears to saucepan and bring to a simmer. Cover and simmer over low heat until fruit is fork-tender. Combine cornstarch with just enough water to dissolve it, then add to the saucepan liquid until mixture thickens. Remove from heat and cool slightly.

COMBINE chocolate chips and water in the top of a double boiler until mixture is smooth. Arrange pear slices in two dessert bowls and artfully drizzle chocolate sauce over them. Serve immediately.

Jasmine Tea Truffles

8 oz. high quality bittersweet or semi-sweet chocolate
½ cup whipping cream (32% milk fat)
¼ cup unsalted butter
4 tsp. jasmine tea

CHOP chocolate into coarse pieces and melt with whipping cream in a heavy sauce pan over low heat. Stir occasionally until chocolate melts. Add butter and continue stirring until completely melted in. Remove from heat and let cool to room temperature, then mix in jasmine tea. Chill in refrigerator until hard (about 8 hours). To form truffles, scoop out mixture using a melon baller and form into balls. Roll balls in finely chopped walnuts or almonds, cocoa, or coconut. Serves 2. (Just kidding! This recipes actually makes 36–48 pieces. And you can substitute Earl Grey, spiced chai, or your favorite tea if you want to experiment.)

Jory's Favorite Chicken Bog

6 cups water
Large onion, chopped
1 tbsp. salt
1 3–4 lb. chicken
2 carrots, quartered
2 ribs celery, sliced
1 cup long-grain rice
½ lb. smoked sausage
2 tbsp. butter
1 tbsp. poultry seasoning
1 tbsp. dried parsley flakes

PLACE water, onion, salt, chicken, carrots, and celery in a large pot and bring to boil. Cover and reduce heat until chicken is tender (about 1 hour). Remove chicken and let cool, reserving cooking liquid with vegetables. Remove skin and bones from chicken and chop meat into bite-sized pieces. Skim fat from cooking liquid and measure 3½ cups of this liquid into a large saucepan. Add chicken pieces, cooked vegetables, rice, sausage, butter, poultry seasoning, and parsley flakes. Bring to a boil, cover, then reduce heat and cook for 30 minutes. Yields 6 servings.

Haley's Heartwarming Carrot Bisque

3 tbsp. unsalted butter
1 lb. carrots, peeled and thinly sliced
1 onion, chopped
1 tbsp. fresh ginger
2 tsp. grated orange peel
¼ tsp. ground coriander

2½ cups chicken stock
½ cup cream (or half and half)

MELT butter in a saucepan over medium heat, then add carrots and onions. Cover pan and cook until vegetables begin to soften, stirring occasionally (about 15 minutes). Stir in ginger, orange peel, coriander, and half the chicken stock. Reduce heat to medium-low. Cover and simmer for 30 minutes. Puree soup in batches using food processor or blender. Return soup to saucepan and add remaining stock and cream. Season with salt and pepper, cook over medium heat until hot. Note: Haley likes to top this with toasted pumpkin seeds.

Drayton's Crabby Apple Salad

1 can (7-8 oz.) crab meat
1 cup Granny Smith apples (diced)
½ cup mayonnaise
1 tsp. fresh lemon zest

COMBINE all ingredients in a bowl, then add salt and pepper to taste. Divide salad into four scoops and arrange atop nests of baby field greens. (Can also be used as a filling for mini-croissants.)

Sweet Potato Comfort Pie

3 tbsp. butter
¾ cup sugar
3 cups mashed sweet potatoes (canned or fresh cooked)

4 eggs, separated
1 cup milk
1 tsp. vanilla
1/2 tsp. nutmeg
1/2 tsp. cinnamon
1/4 tsp. cloves
Dash of salt

CREAM butter and sugar, then beat in sweet potatoes, egg yolks, milk, vanilla, and all seasonings. In a separate bowl, beat egg whites until stiff. Fold egg whites into sweet potato mixture, then pour into pastry shell. Bake for 50 minutes at 350 degrees or until knife inserted near center comes out clean.

Drayton's Green Tea Tippler

8 oz. vodka
1 cup strong green tea (cooled)
1/2 cup fresh lemon juice
1 tsp. grated fresh ginger
1 tbsp. sugar syrup
lemon for garnish

TO make sugar syrup, mix 1/2 cup sugar and 1/2 cup water in saucepan over low heat and stir until sugar dissolves (about 5 minutes).

FOR drink, combine all ingredients in a large shaker, then shake and strain into 4 tall glasses with ice and garnish with a slice of lemon.

TEA TIME TIPS
from Laura Childs

Inviting friends into your home for tea? There are so many wonderful things you can do to make this a memorable event.

Invitations

Think outside the box! A handwritten invitation on the back of a flower seed packet is perfect for a garden tea. Or include a tiny tin of pastilles or a pressed flower in your envelope. You could even roll up an invitation and put it in a tiny vase.

Enhancing Your Tea Table

Handwritten menu cards make great souvenirs. Go to your favorite craft or scrapbook store and select something luscious. Maybe floral card stock or pastel vellum?

Fill a crystal vase with flowers or go rustic—tie raffia or ribbon around faux-finished clay flower pots.

Net-winged dragonflies or pipe cleaner bees from craft stores are inexpensive and look adorable when perched on place cards.

Pretty napkin rings can be made from real flowers! Wrap flower stems in flexible wire then follow with a layer of green floral tape. Then simply wind your handiwork around folded or fanned-out napkins.

Staging the Event

Remember, your tea doesn't have to be a sit-down tea. If you have a good-sized group coming, you can do a bountiful buffet on a second table or sideboard. Create a spectacular backdrop with flowers and candles and pull out all the stops by using silver trays, treasured serving pieces, or cake stands. Pick two key colors and try to coordinate everything—flowers, candles, ribbons, etc.

Try your hand at cake decorating. A cake in the shape of a hat or teapot is adorable.

Edible flowers always enhance trays of tea sandwiches.

When it comes to background music, keep it light and airy—strings, flutes, harp.

Did you ever think of having a teacup exchange? So many women are fast becoming teacup collectors. Why not have all your guests bring a gift bag containing a teacup and saucer, then orchestrate an exchange?

Tiny boxes of chocolate, homemade biscotti, or Tea Shop Mysteries make great favors or parting gifts!

TEA BAG TRIVIA

While Theodosia and her friends at the Indigo Tea Shop favor the use of loose leaf tea, they understand that time is often at a premium and, these days, we often have to fix our "cuppa" fast. That said, you'll be amazed by how much life your old tea bags have left in them!

* * *

Tea bags make marvelous scent sachets. Used for travel, they can greatly improve musty hotel closets and dresser drawers. Of course you can always pop your tea bag into hot water if you need that emergency cup of tea!

* * *

Instead of using a fake pine cone air freshener in your car, hang a tea bag near the heat vent or AC. Revel in the enticing scent of your favorite brew.

* * *

Create an aromatic Christmas tree (or all-season topiary) by decorating a small tree with an assortment of colorful tea packets.

* * *

Since tannic acid in tea is a natural anti-inflammatory, a moist tea bag can soothe tired eyes, relieve sunburn, and take the pain out of bee stings.

* * *

Toss your old tea bags into the kitty litter box to cut down on odor or put one in the refrigerator to absorb pesky smells.

* * *

To patch small bare spots on your lawn, put down a used tea bag, then sprinkle grass seed on top of it. The tea bag will provide much-needed moisture as it gradually breaks down.

DON'T MISS THE NEXT
INDIGO TEA SHOP MYSTERY

Chamomile Mourning

Spoleto Festival ushers in a two-week explosion of music, art, theatre, and dance for Charleston. But during the Heritage Society's first-ever Poet's Tea, Roger Crispin, the head of Charleston's staid auction house Crispin & Weller, ends up a hapless performance art victim!

Find out more about the author,
her Tea Shop Mystery series,
and her Scrapbook Mystery series
at www.laurachilds.com.